FORE PLAY

Linda Sheehan

Black Rose Writing | Texas

The author grants the final approval for this literary material.

First printing

This is a work of fiction. Names, characters, businesses, places, events, and incidents are either the products of the author's imagination or used in a fictitious manner. Any resemblance to actual persons, living or dead, or actual events is purely coincidental.

ISBN: 978-1-68433-916-7
PUBLISHED BY BLACK ROSE WRITING
www.blackrosewriting.com

Printed in the United States of America
Suggested Retail Price (SRP) $19.95

Fore Play is printed in Georgia

*As a planet-friendly publisher, Black Rose Writing does its best to eliminate unnecessary waste to reduce paper usage and energy costs, while never compromising the reading experience. As a result, the final word count vs. page count may not meet common expectations.

Praise for
FORE PLAY

"A company of spineless, scheming men try to gouge a California country club for every penny it's worth in Sheehan's seamy, steamy comedy of errors."

—Kirkus Reviews

"Sheehan's plot is witty and droll, and very easy to get caught up in. I had a grand time reading *Fore Play*. It's highly recommended."

—Readers' Favorite

"For a rollicking read, *Fore Play* delivers a hole in one in this engaging and funny novel from the rousing story to the high-voltage characters."

—Sublime Book Reviews

"Sinfully delicious!"

—David Noonan, author of *Memoirs of a Caddy*

"You won't find a more twisted tale of human nature and egos clashing. You won't find one that is more fun, ridiculous, and yet rings of the possibility of truth."

—Julia Walker, Julia Picks 1 Review Blog

FORE PLAY

Prologue

Thursday, April 28th 2011

After days in the air interrupted only by brief stops for refueling, the travelers began the descent to their destination. Entire families spanning generations; young adults, parents, grandparents, and great-grandparents were anxious to arrive at their homeland. They were exhausted and hungry, but on schedule as they banked in formation with the sun reflecting off white wings against the blue skies over Los Angeles. They flew high above the film lots of Century City, and through Hollywood over Paramount Studios with its iconic water tower and arched entrance, then up the hill past Gower Street 'til they reached the famous Hollywood sign partially concealed by the famous Los Angeles smog. Heading west over Universal City, they saw King Kong and the Jurassic Park dinosaurs giving tourists a thrill ride, before soaring over the Santa Monica Mountains, still green from the winter rains. In the distance, the 101 Freeway traffic was moving well before rush hour would bring commuters to a crawl. Moments later, the fliers entered the airspace above Tarzana, California, a town that took its name from the legendary man of the jungle. Catching sight of their destination, all systems were readied for touchdown at the place their ancestors had raised their young for centuries. The birds bobbed their heads forward, arched their breasts back and held their wings still and wide to allow the winds to maintain lift and decelerate before their feet hit the surface of the lake. The white trumpet cranes had returned to Bellstone.

One

Friday, May 5th 2011
Two months before the Bellstone 2011 Women's Club Championship

"It's all up to you, pal," a trembling Bradley Watchtower whispered to his playing partner, the country club president, Newt Sizemore, who was all too aware of how much his putt could cost the pair if he missed it. That day's competition had left him and Bradley down $5,000 to their opponents, Joe Pesci and Shorty Columbo. Now, the two men had one last chance for redemption. Before they'd teed off on the 18th and last hole, Joe and Shorty made them the offer of an aloha bet. Win the final hole and clear the deck. Tie the hole, the loss remains. Lose the hole, double the loss. After the other three had putted out, it was Newt's turn. If he sank his very makeable six-foot putt, his birdie would win the hole and he and Bradley would owe nothing. A two-putt would keep their loss at $5,000. A dreaded three-putt would cost them a whopping ten grand.

"Thraight in the back of the cup, Mr. Thizemore," Bones, the old caddy lisped to his player as the president eyed his line.

"You can do it, big guy, you can do it," Bradley assured Newt, who could feel his heart banging back and forth in his chest.

Newt's ruddy complexion had darkened to a shade of purple after four hours in the L.A. sun, and the added stress of the putt only deepened his unhealthy color. A string of costly defeats over the past few months had taken a toll on his financial stability. Now, the threat of another big loss sent his legs twitching as he stood over the ball. He took a deep breath as his partner, his opponents, the caddies, and all golfers within sight of the 18th green stood like statues while the president of the club focused on the putt.

C'mon Sizemore, you've sunk this one a thousand times, Newt assured himself as he visualized the subtle curve the ball would follow before dropping into the cup. With head still, he drew the putter back with a smooth stroke. But as the club moved toward the ball, the ground under his feet began to vibrate, and the sound of a revving 12-cylinder Ferrari exploded through the silence while the car's owner gunned the engine as she entered the club parking lot to alert the valet of her arrival. The ear-splitting noise caused Newt's hands to jerk and blast the ball eight feet past the hole.

"Fucking bitch!" he roared as he turned toward the parking lot. "I'm gonna smash that car's roof with a hammer!"

"Just don't dent that driver's beautiful headlights. She paid big bucks for those cans!" Shorty cried out, as Joe fist bumped his partner in agreement.

Now, the furious president's only chance to minimize a huge loss would be to make the comeback putt. He struggled to control his anger by shutting his eyes and taking a deep breath as he tugged at his shirt collar to make room for the pulsating veins that ran through his neck. Aware that the chances of making an eight-foot putt for the best players were only fifty percent, he said a quick prayer before executing his stroke. All within eyesight held their breath as the ball rolled straight towards the hole—and checked up one blade of grass short of falling in. Joe and Shorty high-fived each other in celebration of their $10,000 win, while Newt smashed his putter into the into the perfectly manicured surface of the green.

•   •   •

Out in the parking lot, Bernardo the valet snapped to attention as the red Ferrari screamed to a stop at the porte-cochere of the club house. When the driver's door opened, a pair of shapely legs glistening with tanning oil slid out that belonged to Mandy Manville. She was dressed in a royal blue skort, a combination of skirt and shorts popular with lady golfers and a white and blue nylon polo shirt that hugged her ample breasts. Her blonde hair was crowned with a visor accented by a row of faux diamonds that glittered in the LA sun. Oblivious to what her dramatic arrival had cost Newt and Bradley, she handed her keys and a ten-dollar bill to Bernardo as she cell-yelled instructions into her phone with a playful Southern accent.

"Scotland gets cold by Octobah, so I'll need warmth, Rick. Ask your sales reps if they've seen any cute little kilt-style woolen skorts. You know, plaid with the two buckles on the side? They're bound to give a rise to those Cialis-poppin' geezer viewers. Gotta run. That lesbo from *Golfing Magazine* is waitin' for me at the range. She wants a few quotes from you too, so meet us out thah in twenty. *Ciao.*"

With that, Mandy marched toward the lady's locker room to change from her spike heeled sandals into golf shoes as the valet revved the Ferrari's engine and guided it into a parking spot.

• • •

In the back office of the Bellstone pro shop, Rick Lightfoot slammed down the receiver of the phone on his desk. He leaned forward and applied pressure to his forehead with his thumb and index finger to fend off another throbbing tension headache.

"Ya want me to do a national search to find a sexy kilt-style skort for you ta wear ta Scotland, Mrs. Manville?" he said as the headache took hold. "How 'bout picking up your dry cleaning like ya had me doing last week? Maybe ya want me to make you an appointment at your gynecologist. Sure! I'm only the head golf pro around here. Must be in my job description to see ya get your pap smear on time."

"I thought you weren't gonna let that lassie get your Irish up, Ricky," Maggie O'Grady called out from the front of the otherwise empty shop as she opened a shipment of red, white, and turquoise golf shirts from their cellophane wrappings and placed them in perfect piles on the mahogany shelves of the store. Embroidered over the pocket of each shirt was a Bellstone Country Club logo with the design of a white trumpet crane in flight. "Remember," Maggie called out. "Rick Lightfoot is to Mandy Manville as Bela Karolyi is to Nadia Comaneci, as Butch Harmon is to Tiger Woods, and Phil Jackson is to Kobe Bryant. If she wins, you win. And that's no blarney!"

Maggie was right. For the previous nine years, Amanda "Mandy" Everett Manville had won the Bellstone Women's Club Championship. In the fourth week of April, the big news at Bellstone was that when Mandy captured her 10th consecutive club championship win that July, Bellstone would win too. Because any member of the Women's Southern California Golfers of America Association who was able to secure a ten-year reign as the club champion of a private golf course would receive an invitation to play in that year's Cialis Invitational Pro-Am, to be held at Scotland's legendary Saint Andrews Golf Course. The tournament would be televised on NBC, and it was expected that Tiger Woods would be among the professionals competing.

Though still ranked as one of the finest golf courses in the country, Bellstone had not hosted a major tournament in decades, and the club that once had a waiting list of those happy to hand over the $150,000 initiation fee had lost its luster. Now, the publicity surrounding a Bellstone player teeing it up with Tiger in the Scottish Pro-Am was sure to attract waves of potential new members.

Not that long ago, Rick had loved being the head pro at one of the finest and most historic golf clubs in the nation. But having grown tired of the traffic, crime, and high cost of living in Los Angeles, he and his wife were talking about a move to Arizona if he could secure a Head Pro position at a top-ranked golf club in that state. And thanks to Mandy Manville, that dream could become a reality. Sources at *Golf Pro Magazine* had assured Rick that his star student's tenth club championship win and her appearance in the Scottish Pro-Am would land him a prime spot on the magazine's yearly list of *The Top 50 Teaching Pros in Nation* and make him a hot hire at any golf club in the country. Now, with his entire future depending on Mandy winning again, he would mop the woman's kitchen floor and scrub out her toilet if it would keep her happy.

•　　•　　•

"What can I do you for, Mr. Sizemore?" Mario the bartender asked the club president who had just sat down at his usual stool at the clubhouse bar. Not waiting for an answer, Mario grabbed the bottle of bourbon from the line of bottles behind the bar and poured a heavy dose of the liquid into a cocktail glass. "Double Daniels, straight up? You got it, sir!" One look at Newt's face told Mario within fifty bucks, how much money the president had won or lost on any given morning. The larger and the darker the veins pulsating through the man's neck, the steeper the loss. It was almost like glancing at *Fox Business News* on the bar's TV. The more red numbers running across the screen, the harder the stock market had fallen.

"Thanks for the meds, Mario," Newt said as he grabbed the glass of the dark-colored liquid from the gleaming mahogany bar with hands trembling. He raised the glass to his thick lips, poured the contents into his mouth, and closed his eyes while he savored the spicy liquid as it rolled down his throat. When his eyes opened, the look of ecstasy on his face vanished as he spotted Shorty Columbo strutting up to the bar.

"Hey Newtie! Knew I'd find you at the watering hole," Shorty said in a high-pitched voice that matched his diminutive stature. Standing less than five and a half feet tall, Shorty's double wide shoulders and springy step made him look like he was always ready for a fight.

"Hey, tough break on the putting green *senor presidente*! Believe it or not, a part of me was hopin' for ya ta knock that first ball in!"

"Like hell you were," the six-foot-three Texan snarled, looking down at the man. "You've been gunning for me since I beat your ass in the election. We all know you'd have handed off your hot little trophy wife to the pimps on Hollywood Boulevard in a nanosecond if it would'a helped you win."

"Not true, chief! I'll admit that it broke my heart to lose, and not have the chance to serve the place I call home." He held his hand over his chest to signify his pain. "But with my business taking off like a pistol, I'm happy to let you do the heavy lifting." He turned to the bartender. "Hey, Dr. M . . . I'll take a glass of that Cabernet I was sippin' last night."

"Saved the rest of the bottle just for you, Mr. Columbo," Mario said as he set a wine glass down on the bar and filled it with the deep purple liquid.

Shorty took a sip of the wine and turned to Newt. "I know we've butted heads over the years, Newtie. But who's not a fan of the man behind the 20,000 bottle, state-of-the-art wine cellar that's gonna turn this joint into a world class watering hole?" He pointed to the mammoth wine cellar that was being constructed next to the clubhouse bar and lounge area.

"Just a minute here, little man," Newt shot back. "During the election, you called the new cellar an obscene waste of money. Said you'd kill the project on your first day in office."

"Times change, people change. These days, Destiny and I can't wait to have our hotshot guests from the boxing world watchin' their 300 dollar French merlots arrive at the bar in style. All thanks to your hard work and foresight, I might add."

Newt puffed out his chest and held his chin high. "Hmmm . . . well, I'm glad you're finally seeing things my way, Shorty."

"Thing is," Shorty said pointing out the window that had a stunning view of the golf course and the Santa Monica mountains in the distance. "I can't ignore those folks out on the course who're sayin' you're in deep doo-doo 'cause of the job's overruns. Some are sayin' it'll be double what you said it would cost. I've heard numbers as high as half a million. And you've only got 200 thou in the member's treasury to pay for the thing. That could spell a big assessment for us members, Newt ole buddy."

"All lies my little man, all lies!" Newt roared as he slammed his empty glass down on the bar. "The rumors have been vicious since I got the vote. What people don't seem to understand is that—"

"No excuses necessary, Mr. President," Shorty said, raising his hands in the air. "I'm on your side. And to show my appreciation for what you're doin' here, as well as my respect for the new board of directors, I'll tell you how you can pay for that cellar in a heartbeat."

"I don't know why I'd trust you on that one, Shorty."

"Here's exactly why you can trust me, Newtie." Shorty looked toward the window and took a moment to savor the rolling green fairways, the majestic oak trees, and the sparking lake in the distance. "'Cause Bellstone is like a second home to me. And if you think I'd risk my membership here by giving you a bum tip, that bourbon has boiled too many of your brain cells."

"Well, that's true," Newt agreed. "You do make more from my missed putts than anyone else around here."

"So, here's the deal . . . I've got the skinny on Saturday night's Louie Lopez, Manny Guillermo fight. And you *know* my sources are golden. With just a call, you can triple whatever you've got in that Bellstone bank account."

The president moved closer to Shorty with narrowed eyes. "A tip from Rocket? King's inside guy?"

"The one and only Rocket man. And he's never yanked my joystick." Shorty wedged himself even closer to Newt, stood on tiptoes, and whispered in the taller man's ear. "Lopez is taking a dive in the third. And you can take that to the bank, Mr. President. Let's just call it 'my payback' for all you're doin'."

·　　·　　·

"Come on through, folks— it's a beautiful day at Bellstone! I'll let the fellas up front know you've arrived." Bob at the guardhouse ushered the silver BMW640i convertible through the majestic wrought iron entrance to the club as Derrick and Jody Benson gave him a wave of thanks. The couple in the car made a pretty picture. The young woman's face was unadorned by any hint of make-up. No eye shadow or mascara was needed to enhance the sparkle of her light green eyes. Her mane of black hair was loosely knotted in a chunky braid and looped through the back of a baseball cap. One glance at her strong square shoulders and the long, toned muscles of her legs and arms spoke volumes about her athletic abilities.

Jody looked over at her boyishly handsome husband. She loved how a few renegade locks of his shiny brown hair always managed to rebel against his meticulous styling and curl onto his forehead. She wondered how any woman could resist that mischievous smile or his twinkling brown eyes. Her gaze settled on that sexy cleft in his chin that had sent her heart pounding the moment she set eyes on him. Not for the first time, she told herself how blessed she was to be married to Derrick. Besides being drop dead gorgeous, he'd come to her rescue during the darkest chapter of her life. For that alone, she'd love him forever. And now Derrick needed her support.

He took her hand and gave it a squeeze. "Thanks for being a trooper about this, hon. I know coming back here isn't easy for you."

"It'll never be the same place that I loved so much. And I can't promise that I'll ever be anywhere close to the kind of golfer I was." She wiped a tear away from her eye. "You get that, right? But I'm willing to start with some baby steps."

"Yup, baby steps. That's all I'm asking for," Derrick said as he stroked his wife's thigh and looked toward the sprawling clubhouse up the road. "Having a membership here takes me to a whole new level of coolness. Instead of being just another boring insurance salesman, I'll be someone who can offer my clients a slice of Hollywood glamor. They can warm up at the range next to stars like Trevor Studley and Chandler Dane. Practice their putting next to Larry David and Ray Romano. And no pressure, Jo, but getting you back in the game could be a great asset for the company. We can invite clients with golfing spouses to those couples tournaments they have here. You'll knock their socks off with your killer—"

"Derrick? Derrick!"

"I know, I know. Baby steps."

They pulled up in front of the clubhouse, where the passenger door was opened by a tall Hispanic man in uniform.

"*Buenos dias*, Bernardo!" Jody called out, as she jumped out of the car and gave the man a hug.

"*Buenos dias, senorita!* Or I should say, *senora!*" Bernardo turned to Derrick.

"Welcome to Bellstone, Mr. Benson! And I wish you and your wife many happy years at our fine club, sir." He pulled the couple's golf bags from the trunk and set them on the valet station's bag rack. "Jorge will be out in a moment to take these to the bag room."

"Thanks *amigo!*" Derrick said as he handed the valet a crisp twenty-dollar bill.

"*Gracias senor.*" He glanced at Derrick's spanking new set of clubs, and Jody's well-worn bag, with its Princeton University logo and tiger mascot head covers. "Will you both be going down to the driving range today?"

"We will," Derrick said as he looked at his wife with concern. "That is, I think I've convinced Mrs. Benson to hit a few balls too."

"Hey Bernardo, is Eddie here today?" Jody asked the valet.

"He sure is. And he can't wait to see you!"

Jody turned to her husband. "Hey Der, I think I'll run and try to catch Eddie now. Meet you in the clubhouse in a few."

"Cool babe, no rush."

•   •   •

In a tall booth with windows overlooking the golf course, sat an eighty-eight-year-old Bellstone icon. When the club opened in 1948, the young Eddie McDermott was brought in as the best caddy at any private course anywhere. He served as Bellstone's best caddy for years before graduating to caddy master and starter—the traffic cop who controlled the caddies and the tee times on the course. The inside of the booth he'd sat at for over sixty years was lined with pictures of the young Eddie toting bags and shaking hands with some of the most famous amateur golfers of the last century; Amelia Earhart, Harry Truman, Ronald Regan, Jackie Gleason, Diana Shore, Perry Como, and a beaming Jack Kennedy.

But during his years at Bellstone, those that touched Eddie's heart the most were the kids he watched grow up at the club— toddling across the practice green one day and, it seemed, teeing off with their parents the next. And of all those progenies, none meant more to him than the granddaughter of his friend Forrest Wheeler, the founder of Bellstone Country Club.

"Well, here she is, the top bird doc for the U.S. Department of Fish and Wildlife!" Eddie stepped out of his booth. "And my favorite lady golfer of all time!"

Jody gave the spry little man a big hug. "Can I take some of your DNA into the lab, Eddie? I haven't seen you since Grandpa's memorial. What was that? Seven years ago? You look like you haven't aged a day!"

"Never mind me, young lady. I just hope you're getting back in the game. You know your grandpa's greatest joy came from watching you become a champion golfer. He'd be heartsick to know you gave it up because of what happened to him."

"I haven't given it up. But like I told my husband, I'm just not ready to play anytime soon. I've agreed to try hitting some balls on the range, but that's it."

"Well, that's a start, hon! We've got a lady golfer here that's got them all in a tizzy, but she can't touch you when it comes to talent. I'd love to see you give her a run for her money out there."

"Enough about me, Eddie. I want to hear about what you're up to. Is the great Eddie McDermott still getting the respect he deserves?"

The sparkle in the old man's blue eyes faded. "They treat me okay, honey. But guys like your grandpa and his pals don't exist anymore. Not around here, at least. Back in our day, golf was all about honor and the love for the game. We have a new kind of membership now. Folks who only joined this place for the contacts they can make. They're all about sucking up to whoever can help them rake in more damn money in whatever cutthroat businesses or schemes they're into."

"Oh, come on, Eddie. It can't be all that bad!"

"It is, little girl. Believe me . . . it is."

•   •   •

Derrick was waiting for Jody in the lobby of the clubhouse when his wife came in through the heavy oak doors.

"Eddie's still going strong, babe," she told her husband. "Physically at least. He seemed a bit down though. Misses the good old days."

"Doesn't every old guy miss the good old days? But I'm sure he got a boost from seeing you."

"Well, I sure loved seeing him," Jody said as she took in the aroma of the oak paneled walls that she remembered so well from her childhood. Her eyes fell on the heavy gold trophies on the shelves with the names of famous golfers that played in the major tournaments once held at the club. On the walls were photos of Bobby Jones, Ben Hogan, Sam Snead, Arnold Palmer, Jack Nicklaus, and other golf legends who competed there during the club's heyday. She froze when she came face to face with a life-sized portrait in the center of the photos.

Seeing her reaction, Derrick put his arm around his wife. The subject of the painting was a smiling man who looked to be in his late thirties, with a strong chin, light green eyes, and dark hair. Holding a wooden golf club that would now be considered an antique, he was dressed in woolen golf knickers, a button-down shirt, and an argyle vest bearing the Bellstone logo with a white trumpet crane in flight.

"I haven't seen this painting since I left for college," Jody said in a small voice. "He was really handsome, wasn't he?"

"He sure was. And lucky for me that his granddaughter got his good-look gene." Derrick kissed his wife on the cheek and took her hand. "C'mon sweetheart, let's get our golf shoes on." The couple entered a hallway leading to the men and ladies locker rooms. "Hey Jo, look at these cool old photos! There's Stan Laurel and Oliver Hardy on the course!" he said in an effort to distract his wife. "Oh wow . . . Bob Hope and Bing Crosby! Dean Martin and Frank Sinatra! I love the history of this place." Further on down the hall, the walls displayed portraits of the winners of the yearly club championship that determined the club's best man and best woman golfer. On the men's side of the hall, a different name and face appeared for each of the past ten years. But on the women's side, though the hairdo kept changing, the smiling face on every portrait belonged to one woman.

"Hey, Der! Check this out." Jody looked at the name on the plaques below the paintings. "This Mandy Manville must be the hot lady player Eddie was telling me about. Seems she's got this Woman's Club Championship thing locked up."

"You mean, *had it locked up*, don't you? Mrs. Manville won't know what hit her when she's facing Hurricane Jody in this year's championship."

"Whoa! Down boy! Baby steps, remember?"

• • •

"Beautiful strike!" Michelle Tambour exclaimed, as Mandy sent another ball whistling into the distance. "Anything special you're working on with your swing to tell our readers about?" Michelle was doing a cover story for *Woman Golfer* magazine about Mandy that would hit the newsstands right after her club championship win and just before her appearance in the Scottish Pro-Am.

"It's all about fundamentals, as our wondahful head pro Rick Lightfoot keeps reminding me," Mandy replied in her most cheerful drawl. "I'm just tryin' to stay balanced and finish my swing."

"It must be incredibly exciting for an amateur to be taking such a huge leap into the professional golf arena." Michelle held up her iPad to record Mandy's response.

"Let's not jump the gun heah," Mandy told the writer. "To have won nine championships in a row is a thrill for any golfah, but I really like what I see happenin' with the other ladies in our group. And any numbah of them could win this yeah. For me, it's not just all about winnin'. It's about the love and respect for the game, abidin' by the rules, and encouragin' one's opponents to play their best."

"Okay, got that!" Michelle stopped her recording. "Now, how about if I get some pictures of you hitting the driver? You go ahead and swing when you're ready."

The photo session attracted a small crowd of onlookers who "oohed" and "aahed" each time Mandy hit the ball. Farther on down the range, another woman was attracting some attention of her own. It was Jody, trying to find her swing. And though the balls were flying every which way; hitting a ball shack out yonder and a truck on a distant path, they were easily traveling fifty yards farther than Mandy's balls. The contrast between the two women was striking. Mandy, in her perfect golf attire, with a swing as smooth as silk, displayed what years of lessons can buy. Jody, in her white polo shirt and khaki-colored capris, had the natural power and ease of the born athlete with her tremendous body rotation, and a release move that caused the ball to snap off the face of the club.

"Who's that wild child, Rick?" Mandy asked the head pro as he walked up to join the interview session. "Not one of ah ladies. Is she a guest?"

"That's Mrs. Benson . . . Jody Benson," Rick said. "She and her husband, Derrick . . . the guy next to her . . . are the new Junior Members. Word has it that she played here as a girl and was a ranked college golfer. All before my time. Her parents are members, but they don't seem to play much golf. Just use the club for the social, mostly."

"Well, I've just *got* to meet her. We do need some new blood in ah ladies group, now *don't* we? But not until ah darling Michelle is through with us." Mandy put an arm around the writer's thick waist and gave it a squeeze.

In the stall past Jody and Derrick, a middle-aged man with a penguin-shaped physique and a clerical collar fastened to the top of his golf shirt was hitting balls. He took a break from finessing his perfectly timed golf swing to meet the new couple.

"Excuse me, but you folks must be the new junior members I've been hearing so much about," he said to Jody. "I'm Father Norm O'Malley of the All Saints Church over in Encino."

"Pleased to meet you, Father," Jody said, offering her hand for a shake. "I'm Jody Benson and this is my husband, Derrick." She pointed to her husband as he hit a booming drive.

"Wow!" Father Norm exclaimed, before he turned back to Jody. "You surely inherited your grandpa's green eyes, young lady. I had the privilege of playing with Forrest Wheeler a few times when I was a new member way back when. What a delightful man! Great golfer too, of course!"

Father Norman O'Malley was the beneficiary of what golf clubs call a Courtesy Membership that's offered to certain local public leaders such as police officers, fire chiefs, and church officials. In exchange for getting full access to the club's facilities, these chosen few assist the club by providing counseling to members, assisting them with legal issues, and using their positions to benefit the club. The fact that Father Norm was at Bellstone 24/7, and it was a rare event that he could be found at the church, was the subject of much whispering among Bellstone members and those in the congregation of All Saints.

When Father Norm resumed his practice, he seemed visibly irritated by the sound of a voice with a Southern drawl behind him. "I just have to meet this excitin' new couple!" Mandy exclaimed as she and Rick approached.

"Jody and Derrick . . . meet Mandy Manville, our woman club champion," Rick said.

"Pleased to meet you, Mandy," Jody said as the two women shook hands. "And congrats on all of those championship wins! Nine in a row—wow!"

"Well I'm sure you know how the game goes," Mandy told her. "The golf gods give, and the golf gods take away."

"They do indeed," Jody said, sounding a bit melancholy.

"Hey, I can't begin to tell you how *thrilled* I am to have another golfing lady here at ole Bellstone. The moah the merriah, as I always say."

"Well, thanks," Jody started to say. "I'm afraid I won't be what you'd call a golf—"

"Are y'all coming to the dinner-dance tomorra night?" Mandy interrupted. "If so, please sit with us! We've got seats at the president's table. And I undastand your parents are membas heah too, Jody. How 'bout if you ask them to join us?"

"Thanks, but I think we'll have to pass," Jody said. "I've got a report to finish this weekend that I have to—"

"Report? What report?" Derrick asked his wife.

"I told you about that, babe. For the Senate subcommittee? About the effect of global warming on California waterfowl?"

"Well, that's perfect!" Mandy exclaimed. "The white birds in that lake over thah are the theme of the party! What betta inspiration could you get for that report you're doin'!"

"I don't know about that," Jody said. "But I guess I can find time for some fun."

"That's my girl," Derrick chimed in, giving his wife a kiss.

"Super!" Mandy clapped her hands together. "See y'all tomorrow night then. Wear some comfy dancing shoes, now Jody, ya heah?"

When Jody and Derrick walked off, Father Norm turned to Mandy. "Mrs. Manville must be tickled pink to have a lady who can hit the ball a mile join the club just two months before her big championship," he snickered. "Something tells me you'll make sure that girl will not be playing this year."

"You've got some nerve, Norman. Mooching off those of us who pay good money to play at this club, and then you insult us," Mandy hissed at the priest. "Don't you have some altar boys to fondle?"

"As you're well-aware, that's *far* from being my style." He gave her a satisfied smile, then teed up a ball and banged it to the far end of the range with his driver.

Two

Saturday, May 6th 2011

"Those of you old enough to remember this little ditty of ours are definitely... old! A one, a two, a one, two, three: *I thought love was only true in fairy tales. Meant for someone else but not for me. Love was out to get me. That's the way it seems. Disappointment haunted all my dreams.*"

On the second Saturday in May, the Bellstone dining room was decked out for the gala named in honor of the birds whose annual migration to the Wheeler Garden Lake signaled the beginning of spring for the club. Beneath the bandstand's "White Trumpet Crane Spring Fling" banner, the members were dancing to the tunes of the 1960s band called The Monkees.

"Comfy dancing shoes? Who was she kidding?" Jody asked Derrick while the two were dancing. Jody had spotted Mandy standing and chatting at the bar wearing pointed peep toed sandals with five-inch-high-heels. Every man in the room seemed to be eyeing her robust cleavage that burst forth from a form-fitting Versace dress.

Mandy's husband Monty was sipping his second margarita as he sat at the president's table with Jody's parents along with the members of the Bellstone board of directors and their spouses. Servers in crisp white uniforms were pouring the pricy wine from the club's cellar into crystal glasses.

"Well, yes, I am old, and I do remember The Monkees and their songs," Jody's mom, Stacy Stafford told those at the table. "And those fellows are not The Monkees. Davy Jones was the head of the band, and he's dead."

"My talented and dear wife, Hope, can fill you in on that one," board member Bradley Watchtower told Stacy. "She's the one who organized this shindig and hired the band."

"These fellows aren't the real Monkees," explained Hope. "The surviving members of the original group have franchised the rights to their name and songs to other performers. Lots of those old groups have done that."

"Don't say that word *'old'!*" Mandy warned, as she sat down and pointed to Derrick and Jody who were walking to the table from the dance floor. "You're remindin' our new baby membas here that they're sittin' with a bunch of old fogies. These twenty-somethin's must think I'm ready for Sunset Hills at thirty-five." She consumed the rest of her wine and held out her glass to a server for a refill.

"Feel free to argue that point with my wife," Monty told the others. "You'll make her night by telling her she's wrong."

"Oh shush, Monty," Mandy said, as she thrust an elbow in her husband's ribs. "Can't remember the last time I argued with anyone at this club. Plus, everyone knows I'm about the most agreeable person out on that golf course. Thanks to my southern upbringin'. But enough about li'l ole me." She stood up and began to tap her water glass with a spoon. "Heah, heah y'all! I'd like to make a toast to our brand new, adorable arrivals, Derrick and Jody! Welcome to Bellstone, you two!"

"Welcome Derrick and Jody!" the others at the table called out, holding their glasses toward the couple.

"Thanks so much everyone," Derrick said as goblets of red and white wine met and emitted a series of clinks.

Mandy sat down and took a long sip of her Cabernet. "And girls . . ." she looked at Hope and Newt Sizemore's wife Noreen. "We just have to convince little Jody to become a membah of our women's golfing group."

"Of course!" the two women said in unison as they nodded their heads in approval. "Hey Jody, how about joining us this Tuesday for a little game and lunch?" asked Noreen.

"Thanks for the invite," Jody said as she grabbed and stroked the long ponytail hanging on one side of her shoulder. "But I'm a working girl. Besides, I haven't been out on a golf course in years. If you were saddled with me out there, your lunch might become a dinner."

"C'mon hon," Derrick said, giving her ponytail a playful pull. "Playing golf is like riding a bicycle. Once you learn, you never forget. Anyway, you've got a slew of vacation days coming to you. Go out there and have some fun with these ladies. Do it for me . . . *please?*"

"All right, just for you, Der," Jody said. "I'll play with the girls on Tuesday. But you're on your own tomorrow. I'd like to spend some time down at the lake here so I can see how those trumpet cranes are faring. Some crazy things are going on with those poor birds. Plus, I've gotta get my preliminary draft out to Senator Feinstein on Monday."

"Deal!" Derrick put out his hand for her to shake.

"Are you against making a little wager on the course, Benson?" Newt asked Derrick.

"I've been known to roll the dice now and again," Derrick replied with a grin that produced a pair of impish dimples.

"We need a fourth for tomorrow's game. Tee off at eight-thirty."

"Count me in!" the younger man told the president.

Stacy turned to Noreen and spoke in a low voice. "Thanks for inviting Jody out with you ladies. Ya know, my dad started bringing her here as a little girl. The golf gene must have skipped a generation because I stunk at the game. But my daughter took to it like a duck to water. It brought her grandfather such joy to teach her. I only wish she'd stop blaming herself for what happened and get back on the course. Forrest would want that."

Ray Stafford nudged his daughter. "Hey Jody, honey . . . when can you lasso that husband of yours away from his office and get him out to the beach house for a weekend? We'd love to get him aboard The Mulligan."

"I'll try my best, Dad," Jody said. "But I can't promise anything soon. That boss of his has been on the warpath lately so there hasn't been much time for fun."

Two servers arrived at the table to present each guest with a large plate holding filet mignon, roasted potatoes, and asparagus topped with hollandaise sauce. Newt signaled for one of the waiters to fill the glasses of those at the table from a magnum of 2006 Opus One

Cabernet that he'd ordered from the club's expansive leather-bound wine list.

Jody nudged her husband and spoke in a low voice. "This wine's gotta be costing a fortune! Who's paying the tab on these bottles?"

"The prez probably gets a great deal on the booze here," Derrick whispered back. "So, just enjoy yourself, hon."

"Why not?" She picked up her newly filled glass and tapped it against her husband's glass. "Here's looking at you kid!" she said with a wink.

"Hmmm . . . Patrick Swayze to Jennifer Grey in *Flashdance*?" he asked as he tapped his glass against hers before taking a sip of the wine.

"Nope. You're almost fifty years off. It was Humphrey Bogart to Ingrid Bergman in *Casablanca*."

Newt turned to the orange-haired and freckled-faced Monty Manville. "So, tell me Red, how're your Guard Rite guys doing with the installs?"

Monty drained his glass of the remaining margarita before speaking. "As of tonight, the cameras are live in the pro shop and the bag room. The ladies locker room is next on the list."

"Great! And be sure to tell those fellas that if the cameras catch any hot broads showering in the ladies locker room, the club president needs to review the footage!" Newt followed his remark with a guffaw that sent remnants of the roasted potatoes flying toward Stacy Stafford before he rose from the table. "Would you all excuse me if I made a visit to the little boy's room? And I need to borrow my partners in crime for a moment."

Having consumed far more than his usual two glasses of wine, Monty was unsteady on his feet as he and Bradley followed the president into the men's room. Once inside, Newt checked under the doors of the stalls to make sure they were alone. "What's up Newt?" asked Bradley.

"Our money woes are about to become a distant memory, fellas. The wine cellar project will be fully funded after all!"

"The only way to found it . . . to fund it . . . is to access . . . is to assess the membership," Monty stammered. Even in his inebriated state, he could smell one of Newt's get-rich-quick schemes a mile away.

"No need, Red," Newt said. "Got the lowdown on tonight's fight from Shorty Columbo. Lopez is taking a dive in the third. And Shorty's sources are golden. We take the 200 grand sitting in that no interest-bearing account, and *bingo!* We'll triple our bet and put a nice chunk of the profits in our own pockets. All with a quick phone call to my man, Pete."

"No, nope, don't like it. Don't like it at all." Monty shook his head while he grabbed the lavatory counter to steady himself. "Gotta be illegal to gamble with a club's treasury. And I don't wanna be writing a check for 200 grand to your bookie on Monday morning. And why would you trust Shorty? Everyone knows he's been on the warpath since you stole . . . I mean won . . . the election. Nope. I smell a rabbit . . . a raccoon . . . I mean a rat."

"But think about it, Red. *If* you're in any condition to do so," Bradley began. "The only guy who logs more hours on this golf course than Father O'Malley is Shorty Columbo. Ya think he's gonna risk his membership here by screwing with the Board? Plus, I'll bet he's already been bragging to his hotshot Vegas gang about that new wine cellar. I say place the bet. We'll find a creative way to fund the treasury when the cash comes in."

"And what if Shorty's wrong, and we're out the money?" Monty cried. "What are ya two gonna do then?"

"Not gonna happen, Red. No way," Newt assured the treasurer. A sober Monty would have squashed the plan then and there. But his drunken state had killed all resolve to butt heads with Newt.

The men returned to the dinner table during a break in the music. Newt rose from his chair, tugged at the collar of his dress shirt to allow more room for his ever-expanding neck, trotted up to the stage, and took the microphone.

"Good evening my fellow members! I hope you're all enjoying the tasty food at this always wonderful event at our beautiful club. Now, I'd like to make a special toast to the lady who'll be playing her little heart out in just a few short months at that Cialis Pro-Am Tournament in Scotland, right after she wins our ladies club championship here at old Bellstone. And I want to remind all of you who plan to cheer Mandy on at Saint Andrews Golf Course to book your flights and hotel rooms

ASAP, 'cause you don't wanna miss all the fun we'll be havin' over there. Now, please raise your glasses to the golfer soon to be crowned our Bellstone Woman Club Champion for the tenth year in a row, Mandy Manville!"

The crowd broke out in applause and whistles as Mandy stood and raised her glass of wine in the air. She wiped a tear from her eye and downed what remained in the glass. The room erupted with chants of "speech, speech, speech, speech," while she made her way to the stage where Newt handed her the microphone. She looked around the now silent room.

"Fa fa fa friends . . . my deah, deah fellah membas . . ." Mandy uttered, before pausing to wipe a tear from her eye. She sniffled, blew her nose with her cocktail napkin, and spoke again. "My deah friends and fella membas. Havin' had the honah of being your club champion these past nine yeahs has been the most rewardin' chapta of my life. And with the golf gods willin', I shall proudly represent each one of you come Octobah. But I must warn y'all that my game is a bit rusty right now. And I've got my work cut out for me to get it, as they say, 'match ready'. So please wish me luck on that. Now, do enjoy the rest of this wondahful evening."

The audience chanted "Mandy! Mandy! Mandy!" as their club champion paraded back to her table with breasts thrust forward.

"My heart is thumpin' right out of my chest," she told her dining companions when she took her seat. She then placed a hand between her partially exposed bosoms that were still heaving from the rush of excitement and took a moment to catch her breath. "And y'all can trust me, my game *is* rusty. This yeah's championship *could* go to any one of our golfin' gals."

"Well, you don't have to worry about us stealing your title," Noreen assured Mandy as Hope nodded in agreement.

"Stop puttin' yourself down and start pickin' yourself up, Reeny," Mandy told her friend. "And you know just as well as anyone heah how fickle those golf gods can be. One day they give, the next they take it all away." After finishing another glass of wine, Mandy checked her diamond encrusted Tiffany watch. "Now if y'all can excuse me for a moment, I have to grab something from the bag room." She gave her inebriated husband a peck on the cheek and made her way from the table.

Hope kept her eyes on Mandy as she exited the dining room. "You must thank the good Lord every day, Mr. President, for blessing our club with a golfer as talented as that lady," she told Newt with an almost religious reverence.

Ignoring the woman, Newt craned his head toward the oversized TV in the bar. From where he sat, he could see color commentator Jim Lampley doing pre-fight analysis at the MGM Grand Arena in Las Vegas. Men were gathering near the screen to watch the Lopez versus Guillermo fight that would begin in the next twenty minutes. Newt glanced over at another table where Shorty Columbo gave him a thumbs up sign and mouthed the word "payback" to the president.

"Newtie," Noreen Sizemore said in a lowered voice, "Don't tell me you bet our money on another fight, baby boy."

"No, Nor," Newt told his wife as he took one look back at the giant screen that showed the fighters warming up. He then rose from his seat and muttered, "not *our* money", while he headed for the door to the parking lot with a cell phone to his ear.

"What are the odds tonight, Pete?" the president asked his bookmaker.

"Five to three, Mr. Sizemore. Lopez is still the crowd's golden boy. He was looking like a killing machine in the training ring. More than ever these past few days."

"Put 200G on Guillermo for me."

"Guillermo? He's a rookie! You *sure* about that? Unless you know somethin' I don't."

"Just place the bet please, Pete."

"You got it, sir. You're a valued customer, so if things go sour, I'll give you 'til noon Monday to pay up. Just lettin' ya know, Mr. Sizemore."

Newt returned to the clubhouse, confident that in just a few minutes, his headaches over that wine cellar project would be a distant memory. He made his way toward the bar that was now filling up with members anxious to watch the most anticipated heavyweight match of the past five years. At nine o'clock sharp, ring announcer Jim Lampley introduced the fight.

"Ladies and gentlemen . . . from the MGM Grand Arena in Las Vegas . . . the 2011 World Heavyweight Championship! In the red corner, weighing 180 pounds . . . he hails from Atlanta, Georgia and was rated by many as the best pound for pound boxer of the last decade. With 35 wins, 25 of them coming by the way of knockout, and only 3 defeats, he is, the former middleweight champion, former super middle weight champion, former light heavyweight champion, and defending HEAVYWEIGHT CHAMPION OF THE WORLD, Louie Lopez.

From the blue corner, weighing 200 pounds, a relative newcomer making headlines here in a fight to claim his title. He's been battling his way into the boxing world over the last 15 months with 6 wins and no defeats – 'The Avenger from Denver' Manny Guillermo!"

"Yeah, *'The Avenger from Denver'!* That's my Manny!" Newt roared in triumph as the referee barked instruction and made the fighters touch gloves before beginning their face-off. For the first two rounds, Lopez displayed the definite advantage by assaulting his opponent with lightning-fast jabs. The rookie appeared to be no match for the furious fists and springy steps of his opponent, causing Newt to fear that he'd made a terrible mistake. Mario the bartender took one look at the president's haggard face and handed him his double Daniels.

When the bell signaled round three, the crowd hooted at the action in the ring, but the president was too nervous to breathe. With eyes glued to the screen, he stood fixed as Jim Lampley resumed his commentary.

"Left hook from Lopez—on a mission to search and destroy. Guillermo on the offensive with counterpunching. Lopez is pure firepower. One more combination for Guillermo. Guillermo taking a beating down the stretch— hell of an assault. Big punch from Lopez to punctuate the

third round. But Guillermo comes alive and makes a powerful move to show he's a force."

"Here he comes!" screamed Newt. "That's what Shorty was talkin' about!"

"Down goes Lopez on a straight left hand! What a turnaround! After dominating the ring, Lopez may be down for the count in round three of this fight. Looks like a stunning win for Guillermo!"

"Yes! Yes! Yes! Sweet fuckin' A!" Newt's voice thundered through the crowd as he raised his fists toward the ceiling in triumph. Then, like a bolt of lightning, Lopez sprung to his feet, as if mocking his opponent, and blasted a furious fist to Guillermo's jaw.

"It's not over! Lopez is up and comes back with a perfect shot! Holy cow! Guillermo is down! Could be lights out for Guillermo!"

While the ref counted the seconds, a stunned and confused Newt turned to Shorty for answers. The president's longtime enemy smiled and mouthed the words *"payback"*.

"It is lights out!" screamed Lampley. "Guillermo is down for the count! Lopez has indeed proven himself to be the KILLER!"

•　　•　　•

"Who's the killer? Who's the killer? Who's the killer?" a woman's voice demanded through the rhythmic rocking of the metal shelves in the darkness of the Bellstone golf bag storage room. Though the voice belonged to Mandy Manville, her Southern drawl was replaced by a New Jersey accent.

"And who's gonna beat the bitches here and become the ten-time Bellstone club champion?" she demanded.

"*You* will Mrs. Manville! *You* will!" the panting bag room attendant told her.

"And who's gonna make those bitches back in Bayonne sorry for being so bad?"

"*You* will, Mrs. Manville! *You* will!"

"Who's the killer? Who's the killer? *Who's the killer?*"

"*You* are Mrs. Manville! *You're* going to take them all down and go on to win the tournament in Scotland with the world watching," the boy assured the woman.

"Oh yeah! Oh yeah! *Oh yeaaaaaahhhhhh!*" Mandy cried, as her screaming reached a crescendo before all was silent for a good thirty seconds.

"Mrs. Manville? Mrs. Manville? Are you okay?" But the only sound to be heard from the woman was a soft snoring. The combination of wine and sex had caused Mandy to fall into a deep sleep.

Jorge made use of the moment to get the results of the fight on the TV bolted to the bag room wall. He was a huge fan of Louie Lopez and had been looking forward all year to watching the fighter defend his title. Though Mrs. Manville had interrupted him at the worst possible moment, the always eager-to-please Latino would never disappoint a lady who handed him a crisp twenty-dollar bill on a regular basis. He looked over at the sleeping woman wedged between a row of golf bags on the shelf. Through the snores, her body twitched as she yelped like a dog in the middle of a dream.

Then the cries began. "Drop me off here, Mommy. Drop me off here. I don't want them to see me in our old beat-up Pontiac. Let me get out. Please Mommy, please!"

"Mrs. Manville! Mrs. Manville . . . are you awake?" The bag boy gently shook Mandy's shoulders. "Time to get back to the party. Mr. Manville must be wondering where you are."

Mandy startled and looked around the now-dark room. "Where am I?" she asked in a near-panic before hearing a zip as Jorge closed the fly of his jeans. "Oh, Jorge! Must'a dozed off for a minute." She twisted her body as she struggled to pull her skintight dress back down over her hips and thighs, taking no notice of the tiny infra-red light shining toward her, one of the new features of her husband's security upgrades. "And Jorge . . . be sure to have my clubs cleaned and waiting at the counter for my eight a.m. tee time on Tuesday. And don't forget to lock this place up tight. There's been some theft around here, and I don't want to lose my brand-new Lady's Big Bertha."

Three

Sunday, May 7th 2011

"Top of the morning to ya pretty lady!" Eddie called out to Jody from his booth overlooking the golf course. The old man had spotted her on the morning after the Spring Fling Dinner Dance. "Your husband looked mighty happy as he teed off first light with some of the men," he added. "But what brings *you* here so early?"

"Going to check out Grandpa's favorite place on earth, Eddie," she answered. "Got some work to do, and some demons to face."

"One of the members called and said they left a club on the practice green. I'll take a walk with ya," the old man said as he stepped out of his booth. Though he was once nearly six-feet tall, the years had compressed Eddie's spine to the point that he now looked up at Jody when standing by her. "You know you're like family to me, honey. Having you here kind'a brings back the old days. When this place was in its glory."

"Nice to be here, Eddie. Though to be honest, just the thought of coming back was giving me nightmares. I'm sure you can understand that better than anyone."

"You're a brave girl, and I love you for it."

When the two walked down a hill that led to a spot known as the Wheeler Garden, Jody looked out at a lake that bordered a practice area for chipping and putting. On the bank of the lake stood a bronze statue of her grandfather, Forrest Wheeler, with a white trumpet crane on his shoulder and a golf club in his hand.

"Oh Eddie, it's all just as beautiful as I remembered it to be," she said as she took in the pastoral scene. Willows and oak trees surrounded the lake, where egrets stalked the shallows, and mallards and wood ducks glided on the rippling water. The white trumpet cranes were busy pecking insects from the oaks and sounding their mating calls. After arriving at Bellstone each April, the cranes would remain there throughout the spring and summer months to build their nests and raise their young before returning to their winter home at a town south of Albuquerque, New Mexico. Each November the town's residents would hold their annual White Trumpet Crane Festival to greet the returning flocks.

"This is such a special place," Jody said with a sigh as she looked up at the towering oaks that had rays of sun streaming down through their heavy branches. "It's almost like time has stood still for these trees and waterfowl. You'd never guess by looking at those trumpet cranes that they're close to landing on our department's Highly Endangered list."

"Not the trumpet cranes, honey!" Eddie raised his eyebrows in surprise. "They seem to multiply around here just fine!"

"They do. And elsewhere they've been putting up a gallant fight against climate change, disappearing habitats, and pollutants. We also know that they help the environment by gobbling up those nasty gold-spotted oak borers that came in from Asia a few years back. Those pests wreak havoc on California oaks."

"Then thank God for those birds," Eddie said. "This place would be a desert without our oaks."

"Tell that to the people who are poaching the cranes," Jody said. "See if they care."

"What?" Eddie asked as he looked out at the majestic birds. "People are hunting these creatures?"

"Not hunting them. They're stealing the babies right out of their nests. Seems the beaks of the newly hatched chicks are packed with a unique form of beta keratin that helps form their trumpet-shaped beaks in the first few weeks of life. One of those South American cosmetic drug developers figured out that the substance works wonders on wrinkles."

"Ya mean it could make this eighty-eight-year-old face look twenty-five again?"

"It's no joking matter, Eddie."

"Sorry honey. I know that anything threatening these, or any birds can't be taken lightly. I'll leave ya to your business," he said, holding a hand in the air to signal 'goodbye'.

"Thanks, Eddie. Enjoy your morning," she said, waving back at the kind old man.

Jody sat on a near-by bench and pulled her iPad from her bag to work on the final draft of her report. After several hours, her eyelids became heavy, and she plopped down beneath a mighty oak tree offering glorious shade from the Los Angeles morning sun. The cool breeze coming off the lake and the sounds of golfers hitting shots that floated down from the driving range lulled her into a dreamy sleep that took her twenty years back in time. She was a little girl again, with two black pigtails, hitting one golf ball after another onto the practice green.

"I think that's enough of those chip shots, Jody. You'll be beating me any day now and embarrassing me in front of my buddies," Forrest Wheeler told his granddaughter. "Tell me . . . what's your swing thought when you chip those balls so close to the pin? I may be able to learn something from you."

"I'm not thinking about golf, Grandpa," little Jody answered. "I'm thinking about the white birds and wondering why they decided to move to a golf course."

"The birds didn't decide to move to a golf course, honey," Forrest answered with a chuckle. "They've been coming here long before Los Angeles was a city. Even before any buildings were constructed. I bet the only people that inhabited these parts when the cranes moved in were the native folks. And, if you think about it . . . a man named Mr. Bellstone, who bought this beautiful land, moved into the *crane's* home. Then, many years later, we built the golf course around *their* lake. That's why it's important for all of us to protect this special place and let the birds raise their families in peace."

When she awakened from her dream, Jody looked over at the statue of her grandfather. She realized that even after his death, Forrest Wheeler continued to serve as a guardian of those majestic birds. And if he were still alive, he would be proud of the work his granddaughter was doing at Fish and Wildlife.

Jody's thoughts turned to her husband, and it occurred to her that soon, Derrick would be finishing up his very first golf game since joining Bellstone. On her way back toward the clubhouse, she spotted some of the players coming in from their rounds. The men all looked so relaxed and upbeat as they kibitzed with each other and talked about the highlights of their game, while their caddies walked behind them with golf bags on their shoulders. Jody's heart fluttered when she saw that great looking guy with the hundred-watt smile walking and laughing with his new buddies. When he looked up and saw his wife, he walked over and gave her a hug.

"Hey, Jo! The course record is still intact, but I played pretty darn well. In fact, some of the guys invited me to join them this week in their Gamblers group. I started out a little rusty and nervous, but I guess overall they were impressed with me."

"Of course, they were impressed with you," Jody said. "Who wouldn't be, with your pretty boy face and a beautiful swing to match?" She took his face in her hands and kissed the lips that she couldn't resist.

"And hey, the boss is gonna like the fact that I've met some potential clients out here already! Newt Sizemore said he's close on getting financing to build an office tower in Glendale. Wants me to bid on the liability policy for the job. Could yield us a nice chunk of change."

"Seems like you had a great game, all around, Der!" Jody said as she ran her fingers through her husband's hair. "I had a good morning too. Got my report all polished and ready to send out to Senator Feinstein tomorrow."

"Sounds like we're both on a roll. So, what do ya think, Jo? Was I right by insisting we join this beautiful joint?"

"Hey, let's not get too crazy, Der. Baby steps, remember?"

Four

Tuesday, May 8ᵗʰ 2011

"Okay, who we got in the game? Tho far ithz Boomer, Marty, Gilly, Lumpy, and me. We could uth one more," wheezed Bones, the lisping, craggy-faced, seventy-eight-year-old caddy. Sixty-five years of smoking had left him with moderate emphysema and tinted the few bottom teeth that remained in his mouth an unsightly shade of brown.

The caddies were gathered in the caddy yard, an underground space behind the clubhouse that was connected to the front parking lot by a long, dank tunnel. The structure was a windowless shelter lined with rough wooden benches and folding chairs pulled up to a huge industrial spool that served as a table where the caddies read the racing sheets, played cards, and traded jokes. A black and white TV with a rabbit ears antenna was tuned to a golf tournament of minor importance.

On most days, thirty or so caddies gathered to wait in the yard for their chance to carry bags, rake sand traps, and read putts for the club's golfers who would pay them up to one hundred dollars for their services. The Bellstone caddies were a wild mix of characters. Some were former high school and college golfers with the expertise necessary to caddy for the club's better players. They were guys who might have ended up as members themselves if not for their problems with drugs, booze, or gambling. There were older men with long, tangled histories with ex-wives, dead wives, estranged children, or jail time. Others were young guys who couldn't get or hold down a regular job and loved the freedom that the caddy yard offered. Another group was comprised of the guys from Mexico who had learned the trade from their fathers and uncles. Between what they made caddying, and what their wives could earn, they were able to support their families. When their sons came of age, members would see them on the course being trained to follow in their father's footsteps.

The toughest part of the job was the uncertainty. Most caddies had no idea if they'd be working on any given day until Eddie called their names through the static and squawk of the intercom. They'd show up at daybreak and sign their name on Eddie's sheet before heading down through the tunnel to wait in the yard for the call. Most passed their waiting time in the daily poker game. And on that Tuesday in May, the game would be Seven Card Stud. Short of players, Bones called out to one of the newer guys, who was hunched over his laptop.

"How 'bout you, Mithter Lyons? You haven't joined our game thince ya got here. What the matter, you too good for uth?"

Jackson Lyons, the target of Bones' tirade, shook his head "no" without looking up from his computer. Considered an oddity by the other men, Jackson just seemed to show up one day. No one knew where he came from, and for that matter, no one asked him. Caddies respected each other's privacy since few of them were proud of their past lives. The only person Jackson seemed to talk to was Eddie, and the mystery surrounding the caddy gave rise to a variety of theories. Some said he had been an actor in Hollywood who had fallen on hard times. Others said he was an ex-FBI informant who was living under cover. But after taking one look at him, most people thought he was just plain crazy. The caddy had a long beard and an even longer mane of sandy blonde hair that hung down over his face and was parted in the middle, with only a small opening for him to see through. When he wasn't caddying on the course, he was glued to his laptop, sometimes laughing or talking to himself as he continued to type away. And no one dared to ask him about what his writings might contain.

"What about you, Armando?" Bones asked an impeccably groomed Latino man reading a Spanish edition of the Los Angeles Daily News. "Afraid your senora will hit you over the head wit da frying pan if you lose some *pesos*? Couldn't be any worse den what you gotta take from that Mandy Manville piece of work. You look like shit on a tostada after a carrying for that lady."

Armando was considered Mandy Manville's personal caddy, which gained him admiration from his Latino peers but aroused jealousy from some of the Caucasian guys. He looked at Bones and laughed a quick laugh. "Maybe if you got yourself some new teeth, and learned how to talk again, you'd get out with the kind of sweet lady ass I caddy for Bones."

As the other caddies hooted with delight at the put-down, Eddie's voice barked through the intercom. "Jackson and Armando to the first tee. Let's go!"

•   •   •

The lady golfers of Bellstone held their games on Tuesday mornings. The players competed in foursomes, and the results were announced during the luncheon that followed the game in the clubhouse. It was an automatic assumption each week that Mandy Manville would be the winner, as there were no other ladies in the group with her skills, her dedication to the sport, and her determination to win.

On that same Tuesday in May, Jody Benson was warming up on the driving range to play her very first round since her days on the Princeton golf team. She'd almost forgotten how great it felt to be swinging a club in the early morning sun and was surprised to feel a surge of excitement about playing her first round of golf in years. On her way to the 1st tee, she stopped at the club's iconic boulder known as Tournament Rock, that was surrounded by rose bushes and shaded by an ancient oak tree. Fixed to the rock was a heavy brass plate that was engraved with the names of golfers who had won professional tournaments at Bellstone throughout the decades. Among names like Ben Hogan, Byron Nelson, and Arnold Palmer, was the name of her grandfather and one-time golf professional Forrest Wheeler, who'd won the professional tournament held at Bellstone in 1948, 1949, and 1950. Gazing at Forrest's list of wins, Jody was hit by a rush of déjà vu. She felt as if the man himself was standing beside her, giving her the same advice that he'd given her so often. "Honey," he said with his voice ringing out loud and clear. "Like the great golfer Ben Hogan said, 'As you walk down the fairway of life you must stop and smell the roses.

For you only get to play one round.'" Hearing those words for the first time since that terrible day that changed her life, Jody knew that it was time to heed her grandfather's advice.

When she arrived at the 1st tee, she was greeted by Mandy, along with Hope Watchtower and Noreen Sizemore. Caddies Armando and Jackson were standing in wait with the ladies golf bags on their shoulders.

"Well, good mornin' Miss Jody!" Mandy sang out in a voice with a resonance that cut through the heavy morning air. "I was worried you'd changed your mind about playing with us today!"

"Well, I must admit that I was kind of hesitant——"

"Now you do remember my darlin' friends, Hope and Noreen, from the other night," Mandy interrupted. "By-the-way, did you and your honey enjoy the dinnah dance?"

"We did. A little too much, I'm afraid we—"

"Supa! Now rememba, I sure wasn't kiddin' y'all when I said my game really *is* rusty. So please do bear with me today. But first . . ." Mandy signaled for Jody to join her under a near-by tree.

"What's up Mandy?" Jody asked when the two were out of earshot of the others.

"Eddie sent that weird-looking Jackson fella out to carry your bag." Mandy pointed to her head. "Back home in Charleston, we have a sayin' for a fella like him. It goes, 'if leather were brains, he wouldn't have enough to saddle a June bug'."

"Oh, that's not a kind thing to say," Jody told her.

"Life's not always kind, now, is it? Anyhoo, you don't have to speak to him if you don't want to. I've never uttered a word to him myself."

Jody looked over at the long-haired, bearded man holding her golf bag. "Hmmm . . . he does have a bit of an odd look to him. Might have some type of mental disability, perhaps? But if Eddie sent him out with us, then he's good enough for me." Jody walked over to the caddy and extended her hand.

"Hi there. I'm Mrs. Benson."

"Pleased to meet you, Mrs. Benson. I'm Jackson."

"Well, I have to warn you, Jackson . . . I'm going to keep you busy hunting for my balls this morning. In fact, I'll probably be downright lousy out there."

"Yes, ma'am."

The scientist in Jody noted that the man seemed to have good motor development, but his communication skills were lacking.

"Okay now, we'll be playin' a two-woman match," Mandy called out to the group. "Jody and I are competin' against each other, and Hope and Noreen are opponents."

"Competing? Opponents?" Jody asked with eyebrows knit in confusion.

"Yes, we're competin' for low net. What's your handicap, Jody?"

"I don't have a handicap--not anymore. I haven't played an actual golf game in almost seven years."

"Hmmm . . ." Mandy held her index finger under her chin. "Then you and I can just play for gross. Don't worry 'bout it. It's all just for fun and giggles. The ladies group keeps a running tally of the wins. Only ever amounts to a few dollahs."

Armando handed Mandy her driver. She grabbed the club with her pink-gloved hand and slinked up to the tee box, swinging her hips in a motion that resembled a model on a catwalk. When she bent down to tee up her hot pink ball on a hot pink tee, she presented the group with a full view of her well-rounded derriere that filled out the expansive rear of her hot pink capris. Her white nylon polo shirt with hot pink piping outlined the curve and separation of each breast. She took her stance with legs spread, buttocks held tight, and elbows pushing her breasts together while she gripped the club. After a few waggles to loosen her hands, she drew the club back high in the air and swung down through the ball, sending it halfway up the hill of the first fairway.

"Beautiful shot," Hope exclaimed as Mandy held her finish pose for several seconds.

"That's our club champion!" Noreen said while Armando let out a sigh of relief that his player had started off on a good note. Noreen teed off next, followed by Hope. Both women hit their drives straight down the middle of the fairway, but far short of Mandy's ball.

"You girls are showing a lot of improvement!" Mandy told her friends. "I told y'all I'm gettin' worried about my chances in this year's Club Championship."

"I think you'll be safe," Noreen assured her. "Anyway, you'd better darn win again. We've both booked our flights to cheer you on at Saint Andrews, and the tickets are non-refundable."

"Guess I'm up," Jody said as she took her driver from Jackson. "Don't say I didn't warn you ladies!" She turned to Jackson and Armando. "And gentlemen!" But as she readied herself for impact, the impact of the moment hit her like a brick. This would be her first time on that tee box since that awful day seven years ago. A knot formed in her gut as it occurred to her that she would be playing the game her grandfather had taught her on the course he'd founded and loved. And it was her fault that he'd never be back to play there again. Forrest Wheeler's round was truly over.

Mandy noticed Jody's hesitation. "Is she okay?" she whispered to Hope and Noreen within earshot of the caddies. "Maybe Little Miss Bird Nerd is still hung ovah from the dinnah dance?" Jackson's eyes shifted toward the ladies as the three shared a giggle. But all giggling stopped when they saw Jody's swing that began with a huge shoulder turn that set up a powerful move down and through the ball, and ended with the club wrapped around her back. Holding that pose, she watched her ball soar high over the hill on the fairway before it veered off to the right and out of sight.

"FORE!" Jackson called out with his hands cupped to his mouth. He waited for any sounds from where the ball landed. "No damage done, Mrs. Benson. I think you made it all the way to the maintenance yard."

Mandy had never seen a woman hit a ball that far. But instead of praising Jody's powerful swing, her voice took on a sympathetic tone. "Don't worry, honey. It could still be in-bounds. But hit a provisional to be safe."

Over the first six holes of the match, Mandy's ball found its way to the pin with ease while Jody struggled to control her wild shots. Then, on the seventh and eighth holes, she felt a glimmer of hope that the swing she had once trusted was starting to return. But on the ninth hole, after hitting a booming drive, her second shot took a sharp detour toward the Wheeler Garden.

"Uh oh, another one gone, I'm afraid," Jody said, concerned that she might delay lunch for her foursome.

Jackson, who hadn't said more than a few words during the morning, marched off in search of the wayward ball.

"We'll see you on the green, sugah," Mandy said, as Jody followed her caddy's lead.

When she reached the Wheeler Garden, she spotted Jackson standing over the ball near the statue of her grandfather. She was surprised to notice that the man, though perhaps challenged in other ways, was blessed with long legs, a trim waist, and a wide muscular chest. And though it was crazy long, his golden hair shone as it caught the rays of the morning sun.

"Darn! You found it," she said. "Now I can hit another terrible shot."

Through the narrow part in his hair, she saw two turquoise eyes fixed on her.

"You can beat her, you know."

"What was that?" Jody asked, stunned.

"You've got what it takes to beat Mrs. Manville in that Club Championship. And from what I've seen and heard, someone needs to do it."

Jody squinted her eyes and tilted her head. "So, it seems you *can* verbalize your thoughts. Quite well, in fact."

"On occasion," he said.

"And why would you think I'd want to be that someone?"

"Because it's in your blood." He pointed to the statue of Forrest Wheeler. "You think *this* guy would have sat out a championship and let a lesser player take the trophy?" He looked at the sculpted bronze face. "You wouldn't have done that, would you, Mr. Wheeler? And I don't think your granddaughter should either. So, I'd be happy to help her sharpen up her game if she'd let me."

Enjoying the scene of this man with a theatrical voice staging a conversation with her grandfather, Jody smiled, but then seemed confused. "Hey, how did you know Forrest was my grandfather?"

"Eddie told me."

Jody nodded. "Of course, he did. I'm starting to think there's a conspiracy going on here."

"*Could be*," Jackson agreed.

"Sorry, but golf and I parted ways years ago, Jackson. We joined this club for my husband. I'm only playing here today to appease him. He's my priority now. Along with keeping our feathered friends safe and multiplying. And that includes our white trumpet cranes over there." She pointed to a flock of the birds across the lake.

"Sounds like you've got your ducks in a row if you'll pardon the pun. But it would be a hell of a show to watch you knock the evil queen off of her throne."

"I think you're underestimating Mrs. Manville's golfing skills, and the love the members have for her." She looked over at the statue and let out a long sigh. "Anyhow, the thrill of the game is long gone for me." She looked closer at the caddy and was surprised that the face she was peering at through that wall of hair looked somehow familiar. "Jackson, I feel like we've met somewhere."

"*C'mon you two!*" Mandy called out from the green. "If you can't find the ball, hit another one! And be sure to take two penalty strokes!"

"We found it!" Jackson called back. "Heads-up there!"

He turned to Jody. "I think you've got a shot here. Maybe try a six iron. The green is directly at two o'clock beyond that big oak tree."

"I know where the green is. I started playing this course when I was five years old." She took one look in the direction of the green, set her feet, and hit a shot that rose with a "whoosh" and flew over the top of the tall tree. A moment later, shouting erupted on the green.

"*Hijole! Hijole! Esta hoya! Esta hoya!*" yelled Armando.

"Holy shit! It's in the hole!" cried Hope.

"*Whooo!* Great shot, Jody!" Noreen called out.

Jackson looked at Jody, who couldn't suppress a joyful grin. "So, the thrill is long gone, huh, Mrs. Benson?" He turned to the statue. "Do you believe that Mr. Wheeler? Because I sure don't."

When the two joined the rest of their foursome, Mandy walked up to Jody. "You are one *lucky* lady to make that miraculous birdie!"

"If birdies are all about luck, then how come *I'm* never that lucky?" Noreen asked her.

"You're a Steady Betty," Mandy assured her friend. "She'll beat Ducky Lucky every time."

The birdie helped Jody narrow the gap in her match, but she still trailed Mandy by several strokes. Though the reigning club champion's swing was far less powerful than Jody's, she was accurate and consistent. Because she played golf almost every day and took regular lessons from Rick, she was able to land her ball in the center of the fairway, and score bogies and pars on most of the holes.

On the 10th hole, Jody began to look and feel like a real golfer again. She won the next four holes with two pars and two birdies, to Mandy's four bogies. By the 13th hole, the match was even. Jody's success did not sit well with Mandy, whose proud strut had slowed to a trudge, and whose welcoming country club smile had sunken into a menacing scowl. Father O'Malley's taunting words on the driving range about Jody posing a threat to her rung out in her head.

But Jody's hot streak ended on the 14th hole when texts from her office flooded her cell. "Oh boy, bad timing!" she told Jackson. "My team at work has a problem, and they need my help."

"Can't it wait?" he asked. "You've got a match to finish."

"Nope, it can't wait. But I'll be quick."

Jody continued with the game while she texted instructions to her team at the office. But the distraction caused her to hit two balls out of bounds on the next three holes. After she and Mandy tied the 17th hole, Jody was two strokes down on the match.

"Sorry for the interruptions," Jody said to the group, with obvious stress in her voice. "Hope I haven't messed up your games with my work issues, ladies."

"Oh, you poor li'l thing!" Mandy cocked her head in sympathy. "Now you see why I'm not in the workplace. I have enough issues out heah just tryin' to make pah. Your job is saving fish and birds, and mine is to shine a bright light on old Bellstone by qualifyin' for that Cialis Open in Scotland."

Now in the lead, Mandy's proud strut had returned. Any fears she had harbored about Jody beating her in the Club Championship had vanished. Besides being rusty, the girl had shown to choke when distracted or facing any type of pressure.

By the 18th and final hole, Jody had no chance of catching Mandy, but she could still finish well by sinking a long and difficult putt for birdie. Mandy was pleased to know that the chances of Jody making her putt were slim to none. She was even hoping the poor girl would end up three-putting for a bogey. All Mandy needed was one last short putt for par, and she would win big with a three stroke lead over Jody.

"Okay, Mrs. Benson, put that cell phone back in your pocket and sink this putt," Jackson said. "It's a monster. Gonna break about three feet to the right and will pick-up speed the last ten feet or so."

Jody stepped up and executed a smooth stroke that sent the ball on a long journey up and across the green and down the slope, where it slid to the right and finally dropped into the center of the cup.

"Another birdie!" Mandy said while the others cheered. "Your luck continues to amaze me, girlfriend!" She turned to Armando for a read on her three-foot breaking putt for par.

"Left edge, *senora. Es rapido!*" the caddy told her as he slid one hand along the top of the other.

"Oh, I do love it when you talk Spanish ta me, sugar," Mandy cooed.

After carefully lining up her feet and shoulders and making several slow practice strokes, she tapped the ball a bit too hard. It rolled downhill and didn't stop until it was five feet past the cup.

"You can have that one—" Jody started to say. But before she could finish her words, Mandy stooped down and snatched her ball from the green, her face twisted in anger.

"What cha tryin' ta do to me here, with that crappy read, Armando? It was a straight putt, ya moron!" she roared.

"Please don't scold Armando, Mandy," Jody said while the caddy stood with his head lowered in shame. "He told you left edge, but you hit it too far out. It's not fair to blame him for your bad putt."

"You seem to know a lot about golf etiquette for someone who doesn't play the game much, missy," the club champion scolded. Noreen glanced at Hope, who rolled her eyes at their friend's bad behavior. A few moments passed before Mandy took a deep breath to compose herself, forced a smile, and found her Southern drawl once again. "But thank you for the reminder, Miss Jody." She turned to the caddy. "And please accept mah apologies for questionin' your expertise, Armando. I'll put an extra ten on your tip today."

"Well, congratulations, Mandy," Jody said. "You played a lovely game. What kind of prize do you get for winning our match?"

"Today's win will add about two dollahs to this month's total," Mandy said before she marched off to the pro shop with head held high to turn in the scorecard.

Jody passed Tournament Rock on her way to the pro shop to pay Jackson. For the second time that day, her eyes settled on her grandfather's name. She heard Forrest's voice ring out once more, telling her, "Honey, as Arnold Palmer once told me, 'A golf course is a place where character fully reveals itself.'"

"Arnie was so right, Grandpa!" she said, nodding her head in agreement.

"Excuse me, Mrs. Benson?" Jackson asked as he walked behind her.

"Don't mind me, Jackson. Just thinking about something Arnold Palmer once told my grandpa." When the two reached the pro shop, Jody handed the caddy eighty dollars for his services. "For a job well done. You were a *big* help today. I'm sure I'd still be out there searching for my balls if it wasn't for you."

"Pleasure was all mine, Mrs. Benson."

She studied him for a moment with eyes narrowed and folded her arms across her chest. "The mysterious caddy of Bellstone Country Club. Hmmm . . . what secrets could he be hiding under all that hair?"

Jackson pulled his cap down to shadow the exposed sliver of his face. He took a card from his pocket with his cell number printed on it. "Like I said, Mrs. Benson. If you're interested in sharpening up your game, I'm happy to work with you—no charge."

"Thanks, Jackson. I *may* just take you up on that."

Jackson headed for the caddy yard and Jody walked over to visit Eddie in his booth.

"Well, here she is!" the octogenarian exclaimed. "Seeing you back on the course is the greatest gift this old man could ask for! How'd your game go? And how'd you like the caddy I sent out with you today, honey?"

"What's his story, Eddie? He looks like he lives in the woods, but there's definitely a brain under all that hair. He even carries business cards." She took a closer look at the card and put it in her pocket. "I don't get it."

"He's got a brain, all right," Eddie said. "The man has a degree from Yale University. He was captain of the golf team, and Ivy League champion."

"What? Yale? Mandy suggested that he was mentally disabled."

"Well, you learned two things today, sweetheart," Eddie said before taking a long puff of his cigar. "First, don't believe anything that lady might tell you. And second, never judge a book by its cover."

"But why in the world would anyone with a degree from Yale be working as a caddy?"

"I'd love to tell ya, hon. But you'll have to get that answer from the man himself."

Jody headed for the clubhouse to meet the women in her foursome for lunch. On her way, she returned smiles from golfers, tennis players and others enjoying the club. Her heart swelled as she realized that none of these folks would be a part of this special place had it not been for the tireless efforts of her grandfather. When she entered the dining room, she spotted Mandy, Hope, and Noreen seated with another woman at a table.

"Hey, Jody! We've got a couple of empty seats heah. C'mon ovah and sit yourself down!" Mandy called out. "Hey, Whitney . . . this is our new membah, Jody," Mandy told the other woman. "She hits a nice ball. Even caused me to worry a few times during the match."

"Caused *you* to worry, Mandy?" asked Whitney. "That's hard to be—"

"I'm *sure* she did," another woman interrupted as she took an empty seat at the table.

"Well, I do declah," Mandy said while she looked up from her cobb salad. "That *is* Diane Sharp! Why I barely recognized you out thah today, seeing that you can't squeeze into any of those cute skorts and tops that you used to look so trim in. Tell me, did you finally break a hundred today?"

"No, I did not," snapped the other woman. "Because some of us have to work for a living, instead of having the luxury of spending every day on this golf course." Sensing the looming cat fight, Jody stood up from the table and checked her watch.

"Whoa! It's after one! I'll just grab a bite on the way to the office. Nice playing with you ladies," she said as she turned and left the lunchroom.

•   •   •

Before Jody reached her car, she spotted Diane coming out of the front door of the clubhouse.

"Hey Jody, wait up!" the other woman called out. "Hope we didn't make you *too* uncomfortable in there," she said as she came close while fighting to catch her breath.

"If you want to know the truth, I've felt more comfortable lying on my GYN's table than I did sitting at that table," Jody said.

"I totally get that. But that's why we need you."

"You need *me*? Seems like your group needs a shrink, not a bird doctor."

"No, we need *you*. Because from what I've seen on that driving range, you could be our new Woman Club Champion in a heartbeat."

"Sorry, Diane. I have no interest in being your champion. Plus, I don't think I *could* be at this point in time. Mandy does have a nice all-around game, even if she *is* a handful out on the course."

"She's more than a handful. She's a monster who'll destroy anyone she sees as a threat to keeping that illegally earned 'championship' title."

"But she's won nine times in a row, so she's a seasoned competitor. The real deal, as they say."

"Believe me, there's nothing *real* about that broad. Her accent, her boobs, her butt, her claims of playing by the rules. They're all phony. Even her name! I had my paralegal run a check on a Miss Amanda Everett Manville from Charleston, South Carolina, where she claims to be from. But surprise! There's no such person!"

"She changed her name?"

"Yup. Dug a little deeper, and turns out that she's Angelina Teresa Fatabina from Bayonne, New Jersey. A town very divided, by-the-way, between the 'haves' and the 'have-nots'. Father was a sanitation engineer. Mother was a grocery store clerk. Young Angie got into quite a bit of trouble as a teenager. Ran with a tough crowd of kids. Had some skirmishes with the cops. Seemed to have straightened out when she attended beauty school."

"Straightened *out*? Wow . . ." Jody folded her arms across her chest. "Well . . . good for Mandy, or Amanda. Or Angelina."

"Her last date of employment was over fifteen years ago," Diane continued. "At a ritzy hair salon in mid-town Manhattan. I'm guessing that's where she hooked her husband, Monty. He used to travel back there for business, as I recall. She probably got the word that he belonged to a swanky country club in L.A. and snared him with some hot rolls in the hay. Monty's a nice guy. *Always* went for the sexy ones, though. His previous wife was a real hottie too. She cheated on him, then squeezed him for every cent he had in the divorce. We all watched it happen."

"Okay, Diane, I get the picture. So, Angie, or Mandy, was able to make a better life for herself. Good for her. And I really don't have the interest to play in any tournaments. Now I've got to get going. Great meeting you though." Jody opened the door of her car, slid into the seat, and started the engine of her car.

"Jody, please . . . hear me out! Listen to what she did to me!" Diane held the door from closing. "Four years ago, I was at the top of my game. I'd been taking weekly lessons and was beating Mandy at those Tuesday competitions. Word spread at the club that a new champion would soon be crowned . . . me! The pro shop even erected a grandstand on the 18th green for the crowd of members that were expected to be watching. But I'd made one *very* big mistake."

Jody looked up and turned off the engine of her car. "What was that?"

"I'd cheated on my husband, Ozzie. It was after one of those dinner dances. Ozzie was on a business trip, and I went stag. So did another member, the newly divorced Chad Morris. We sat at the same table, drinking, joking, and drinking some more. The evening culminated in the empty coatroom and our tryst was pretty much of a blur. The next day I was wracked with guilt because I really did love Ozzie."

"Oh my gosh, Diane! I can't imagine cheating on Derrick. That would destroy—"

"Then I followed my mistake with an even bigger one," Diane continued. "I went to church to confess my sin." She paused to stifle a sob.

"Why was that a mistake?" Jody asked.

"The mistake was that I confessed it to my trusted priest, our courtesy member, Father Norm O'Malley," Diane said, her tear-filled eyes now glaring. "He and Mandy were on civil terms back then. She knew I was a member of his congregation and promised him a brand-new Calloway driver if he could get some dirt on me. And he *did*. The morning of the Club Championship, I warmed up at the range and was ready to attack the course. Ozzie even insisted on caddying for me. The dear man was so excited. I'd picked up my scorecard from the stack in the pro shop and was about to hand it to him to keep score until something caught my eye."

"What?" Jody asked, now less concerned about whatever needed her attention at the office.

"On the card was a tiny stick figure drawing of two entwined horizontal figures and a sign with the word 'coatroom' above them. The bottom of the card had the words 'drop out now'. I knew who'd written it. Even if she was bluffing, there was no way I could play in the match with that woman. I told the rules committee I'd thrown out my back and would have to withdraw. A few hours later, Mandy was awarded her fifth club championship title."

"Diane," Jody began, shaking her head. "I have never—"

"And it only gets worse. That night, I was so distraught that I told the entire story to Ozzie—coatroom fling and all. He promptly divorced me."

"Oh, how horrific!" Jody exclaimed.

"I'm not her only victim," Diane said, pointing to the clubhouse. "Ask another member of our group, Laura Shaw, to tell you about Mandy's sixth club championship win. She got that one by telling Laura on the 10th hole that she'd seen her dog running loose on the street that morning. The poor woman ran from the course to find her dog safely penned in her back yard."

"I've never heard of a grown woman acting like such a—"

"Or ask Christine Fox about Mandy's fourth win. How she mentioned on the 12th hole that she'd heard a nasty rumor about Christine's husband fooling around with that hot little Gabriella from the cleaning crew."

Jody shook her head in disbelief. "I think I liked this club better when I played here as a child and saw no evil, heard no evil," she said with a sigh.

"Mandy's just part of the problem. It's really sad to see what's happened to this place over the past few years. I'm on the board of directors here, and I'm convinced our president, the honorable Newt Sizemore, is using the member's treasury as his own piggy bank. He's also paying pennies to guzzle down the club's valuable wine. In fact, I've got a meeting with a guy in a few minutes who I hope can help me fix that problem." Diane's cell dinged with a text. "Ah! He's on his way now!"

"Bye, Diane. I don't know what to say about all this," Jody said as she shut the door to her car, fired up the engine, and backed out of her parking space.

"Just say one thing! Say you'll go out there and beat that bitch!" Diane called out as Jody drove off.

•   •   •

"It's a pleasure to meet you Ms. Sharp!" The man in the lobby of the Bellstone clubhouse told Diane as he handed her his business card. "Malcolm Ramey from Wine Auctions West, at your service."

"Thanks so much for coming by," Diane said. "Ready to travel down into the deep dark dungeon?"

"Sure am. Blowing dust off vintages in historic cellars is my number one passion."

"Great! You'll be one of the last to see the old cellar before it's emptied out and turned into a storage area," Diane said while she led him past the dining room and into the bar where the massive new wine cellar was under construction.

"Wow!" Malcolm exclaimed. "Quite a project! Looks like motorized carousels are going in there too. I saw a cellar like this at the new Four Seasons in Dubai. This one does seem like overkill though for a country club."

"Tell me about it," Diane snapped. "Now you'll see the historic gem it's replacing." Malcolm followed her into the kitchen and down a staircase leading to the basement. After going through a small wooden door and down a series of stone steps, he felt the cold, humid climate of the underground cave. "This cellar dates back to the early 1920's," Diane told him. "It was carved out of the original building's granite foundation and can hold over twenty thousand bottles."

"Smells wonderful." Malcolm took a deep breath. "And the temp and humidity level down here are optimum for maintaining the integrity of the corks and structure of the vintages. You don't see wine storage environments of this caliber in Southern California much. Seems almost criminal to abandon it."

"Yup. In more ways than one," Diane said.

Malcolm started checking out the bottles. "Wow . . . Lafitte, La Tache, Der Pollerhof, Chateau Rothschild . . . all pricey stuff."

"This entire 200-acre property and the clubhouse was once the home of a movie mogul named Harry Bellstone," Diane began. "He was known as the king of those one-reeler comedies that accompanied the main feature in movie theaters back in the twenties and thirties. Nowadays, they just force a bunch of annoying commercials down our throats before the movie starts."

"That's why I'm hooked on Netflix," Malcolm said.

"Me too. So, this Harry fella was a serious collector of French vintages. He'd been stocking his cellar for years with booty from his wine-buying trips to Champagne, Burgundy, and Bordeaux. When Harry died, the founder of this club, a Mr. Forrest Wheeler, and a group of businessmen bought the estate, which included the wines in the cellar. Wheeler continued to add to the collection with wines from Napa, Italy, and Spain, thinking they would only appreciate in value.

He hoped that one day the members would use the proceeds to build a new clubhouse, redo the golf course, or just bank the money."

"Looks like he made some good investments," Malcolm said while he continued to check out the collection.

"Investments that are fast being liquidated——no pun intended. 'Cause the current Board of Directors are using this as their own private cellar."

"Uh-oh. Not good," Malcolm said.

"But I was lucky to get last year's board to authorize an appraisal of these bottles to determine exactly what we're sitting on here. And I need this done sooner rather than later."

"We'll get on it, Ms. Sharp."

"Great. Once I get your numbers, my committee and I can put accurate price tags on the wines for in-house consumption. We'll also decide which bottles to sell-off, though we may have some pushback from the current board."

"Sounds like you might have a fight on your hands. But we can get you top dollar for these bottles at our quarterly auctions. They attract serious bidders from all over the world."

"Great. So, get me that inventory, ASAP. Before these SOBs try to stop me."

"You got it. Just give me a week or two to get things rolling."

• • •

While Diane and Malcolm Ramey were down in the club's ancient cellar, President Newt Sizemore was lunching with Bradley Watchtower and Monty Manville on crab Louie salad and veal coq au vin in the building's book-lined boardroom. They'd started their meal with a glass of 1998 Screaming Eagle Cabernet. Forrest Wheeler had purchased the bottle at the time of the wine's release for less than $100. The fact that the bottle would have commanded over $2,500 on the resale market was of little consequence to those at the table.

"I handed over near every penny in the member's fund to your bookie yesterday," Monty told Newt. "Two hundred grand on the nose. Our balance is now a whopping one dollar and thirty-nine cents.

Besides having an accounting nightmare, we could all end up in jail. So, what now, chief?"

"What's now is, we're going after that little prick, Shorty Columbo! He's gotta make good on that bum tip he gave me on Guillermo, or we'll kick him outta here on his ass," Newt roared.

"Haven't you *heard*?" an astonished Bradley asked the president.

"Heard *what*?" Newt shifted in his seat, his eyes darting from one man to the other.

"He's already outta here," Bradley began. "The guy walked away from his membership two days ago. After five years on the waiting list of Los Angeles Country Club, Shorty Columbo's gambling connections achieved the impossible. They got a second-generation Italian-American from the Bronx accepted at the most exclusive blue blood club in the state."

"The Vegas mob fucked us!" Newt bellowed. "And we've gotta wipe up their mess!"

"No, Newt. We've gotta wipe up your mess," Monty said, his voice trembling. "You're the one who made that stupid bet. Plus, the wine cellar was originally supposed to be one story. Now it's two stories. It was going to have a nice wooden door. Now it's got a thirty-foot glass window with motorized shelves."

"You don't understand, Red. It'll all be—"

"I understand plenty!" Monty slammed his fist on the mahogany table. "After paying the deposit for the cellar, the two hundred grand we owed climbed to five hundred grand. And after paying off your loss, we're half a million in the hole!"

"Hey, calm down, buddy," Newt pleaded.

"I am calm! But I also think that old cellar is just fine! How'd we ever let you talk us into voting for this project anyhow?"

"I admit to getting a bit carried away here. But the finished product will be worth the few headaches, I *promise*."

"We've heard months of promises," Bradley added. "Now we're down to the wire."

Newt picked up his wine and slowly twirled the glass of deep purple Cabernet to encourage aeration. "That's why I've got a backup plan—and this one's a slam dunk." The president took a swig of the wine that was getting more flavorful by the minute as it continued to open-up in the crystal stemware. He paused to allow ample time for the liquid to permeate from the front palate through the mouth and linger on the back palate where he detected strong flavors of dark red berries, flowers, mint, and spices, all woven together as layers of fruit built effortlessly to the long seductive finish. "Oh, that's gorgeous!" he said to no one in particular. "Now hear me out, fellas. As you know, our dear Food and Beverage Chair and legal eagle bitch Diane Sharp is hell-bent on taking control of our wine collection. She's all hot and bothered about commissioning a complete inventory of the bottles in the old cellar. Well, I've been doing an inventory of my own, and it looks like we're sitting on upwards of 12,000 bottles. From what I've researched online, the best are worth between $3,000 and $9,500 per bottle. So, here's the deal; Norm O'Malley has a Chinese business contact, a Mr. Ning Chung, who pays top dollar for fine French wine and resells the stuff to his customers in the Far East. He swears that the Chinaman has always been a straight shooter—money up front, no returns, and no questions asked. O'Malley has already selected thirty or so of what he thinks are the most valuable bottles and is hammering out a sweet deal with Chung that should net us in the ballpark of the $200K we need to tide us over through next month. He's planning a second deal to happen in early July to bring in the $300K to pay off the cellar before Diane begins her inventory."

"Stealing from Peter to pay Paul," Monty interjected. "No dice, Newt. I'm not—"

"Just give me a sec here, Red." Newt held up his hand to silence the accountant. "As Norm explained to me, it's seamless. Says he can get one of his illegals from the church in here to remove the bottles. The priest will confirm that the money's been wired into the Bellstone account before he ships the wine off to China. No one here has any real idea at this point of what we're sitting on, so the stuff won't be missed. O'Malley thinks he can put this all together within the week, since time is of the essence."

Stunned at what Newt was proposing, Monty stared at the man before speaking. "Why the hell would Father O'Malley get involved with something as underhanded as this? The man's an ordained priest for God's sakes!"

"He'll do it because he'll do whatever it takes to keep on playing here for free, is why. Anyway, he's basically done the same thing for the Los Angeles Archdiocese by selling off vintage bottles from the church's ancient cellar downtown. Rumor has it he's put some nice change in the archbishop's pocket. Guess that's how he commands his hefty salary while spending 24/7 on the golf course."

"It just seems a damn shame that we have to sell off the only perks of our job, especially when you consider all of the work we do as officers on this board," Bradley said.

"I hear ya, Brad. But the times at this club are a changin'. With the membership questioning our enjoyment of the wines and Ms. Sharp on the warpath, we've got to make our move while we can. So, with your blessings, I'll give Norm the go-ahead to get this party started."

"Uh-uh. No way, Newt," Monty said with a shake of his head. "You aren't getting any blessing from me on this."

"I'm in," Bradley said before he drained his glass of the wine. "Sorry, Red, you've been outvoted."

"And remember guys . . . loose lips sink ships. Not a word to anyone!" Newt instructed as he refilled his glass. "By the way, this 1998 Screaming Eagle earned 100 points from Wine Spectator. Quite a damn good deal when you consider we're only paying twenty bucks between the three of us for the bottle. Now, bon appetite fellas!"

Five

Wednesday, May 9th 2011

"Hello, my love," Jody sang out to Derrick as she walked into the kitchen at seven-thirty on the morning after her golf game with the ladies. "What can I make my adorable husband for breakfast? Waffles, eggs benedict, cheese omelet?"

"Thanks, Jo. Just having some coffee." Derrick was sitting at the counter typing away on his computer. "Trying to finish up this bid for the liability policy for Newt Sizemore. Want to get to the office before eight, since I've got a twelve o'clock game with the Gamblers." He began to type a text on his iPhone.

"Sounds fun, babe! Hey, who're you texting so early?"

"Setting up a meeting with a lady I've been courting. Got some big assets. And from what I've been seeing, she doesn't have much coverage."

"Sounds like you've got a hot one on the line!" Jody said as she sliced up some peaches for her smoothie.

"I'll run over to see her after the game. Should be back for dinner though. Want me to pick up some Chinese on the way?"

"Sure, that'd be great. Hey, Derrick, I've got some hot gossip for you."

"What's that hon?" he asked, still texting.

"One of the golfing ladies I met at yesterday's luncheon was practically begging me to enter this year's club championship!"

"Why? What's it to her if you play?"

"She said Mandy Manville has pulled all kinds of nasty tricks on the other players to win the tournament in the past. Seems that woman has made some serious enemies."

"She sure looked like she had the members eating out of her hand at that dinner-dance."

"Yeah, she did. But looks can be deceiving, right? This lady also said that the board of directors are bad news. She even accused your friend Newt Sizemore of having his hand in the member's till. So, watch your step with that guy, will ya?"

"Sure. And I'll have him thoroughly vetted if we get to write that policy for him."

"What's happening over at that club anyhow?" Jody said as she shook her head. "I never heard about problems like that when Grandpa was around."

"It all sounds like the normal club stuff to me, Jo. Just concentrate on getting your golf game back and stay out of club politics. Every place has its group of complainers. Maybe they're jealous that Newt's a good golfer. Maybe they wish they had his money. Maybe they couldn't get elected to the board themselves. Who knows what's really going on with those folks?"

Jody pointed at the TV on the wall. "Derrick, look!" she cried out as Lisa Langheart, the reporter for the Los Angeles station KTLA, was standing in front of the Bellstone clubhouse doing a tease for her upcoming story.

*"**A member of the exclusive Bellstone Country Club is a sure bet to be playing alongside the nation's top-ranked professional golfers in Scotland this October. Meet the very talented lady right after the break.**"*

"This club championship thing is really getting big," Jody said.

"You should go for it, babe. It'd be a hoot to see you blow the nine-time champion out of the water. That would sure as heck get everyone's attention."

"I don't care about getting everyone's attention. And I don't think I'll ever have the heart for that kind of competition again," Jody said with a deep sigh.

"I hear ya hon, and I'm sorry." Derrick got up from his seat at the counter and gave his wife a hug.

"But . . ." Jody looked up at him with a smile. "It might be nice to get my game back for casual play. 'Cause I really did have some fun out there yesterday. Especially when the old swing showed up for a few holes."

"There ya go babe! I knew it wouldn't take long to get some of that fighting spirt back!" He went back to the counter and shut down his computer.

"Well, as Grandpa used to say, we've got to stop and smell the roses. 'Cause we only get to play one round in life. Work's pretty much under control right now. At the least, we could play with the other couples on Sunday afternoons. And one of the caddies even offered to help me sharpen up my game."

"Like I've been telling you, I'd love nothing more than for you to get your mojo on the course back." Derrick picked up his coffee travel mug and laptop. Jody followed her husband out to the garage.

"Hey, Derrick . . . one more thing."

"What's that, hon?" He opened his car door and put his laptop on the passenger seat.

"I was thinking . . . I was thinking that I might go off the pill this month."

"Oh, Jo . . ." He walked over and took her hand. "Let's not rush things, honey. We've got a lot going on right now without adding a child into the mix."

"Just come here for a sec." She led him out of the garage and pointed down the street of their Sherman Oaks neighborhood. "Can't you see us pushing a stroller down these sidewalks? There's a bunch of families with little ones here. And I was just reading that our Sunshine Elementary is one of the best schools in L.A. Plus, I could do most of my work from home before the kids go to kindergarten. And Derrick . . ." She playfully took his face in her hands and stroked his chin. "I so want a little boy with his daddy's cute chin dimple." She poked the dimple with her finger. "And I'm sure that cleft is a dominant gene. C'mon, what do ya say?"

"I'll say that we just joined the club, we still have repairs to do on the house, and work's getting crazier for me all the time."

"But thirty's coming up fast. I can just hear my biological clock ticking away! Can't we at least start thinking about having a family?"

"Sure, we can think about it. But all I can think about now is my beautiful wife who I'm just not ready to share with anyone else. Hey, how bout we have one of our date nights tomorrow? Maybe take in a movie?"

"Well . . . sure. As long as it's not based on a video game, like the last one you dragged me to. Maybe an old classic?" she said with eyes brightening. "There's a great one playing at the Luxor . . . I'll give you a hint: "Fasten your seatbelts. It's gonna be a bumpy night."

"John Travolta in *Urban Cowboy*?" Derrick asked with a yawn.

"You're thirty years off. Betty Davis in *All About Eve*."

"Whatever, you little goofball. And we can go see that if you want to. Now go give that caddy a call."

•　　•　　•

When Jody returned to the kitchen, the KTLA interview featuring Mandy Manville was on the TV. She was standing on the Bellstone golf course, wearing a tight-fitting pink polo shirt with matching skort, and holding a pink golf club. Reporter Lisa Langheart began her introduction.

"The still sluggish economy has caused the sales of golf club memberships nationwide to sag in the past few years. But one local lady is creating excitement at Bellstone Country Club here in Tarzana." Lisa held her microphone toward Mandy. ***"Before we talk about your chance to play in this year's Cialis Pro-Am, Mandy, can you share some of your secrets of success on the golf course with our viewers?"***

"I'd love to, Lisa," Mandy began. "First and foremost, ah would say that no matta what happens out thah—good shot, bad shot, the numba one rule is to keep a positive attitude! Nevah, evah allow negativity to creep its way into your game!"

"Oh, my god!" Jody called out at the TV. "Who are you trying to kid, lady?" While she shook her head in awe of the woman's gift for self-promotion, she rummaged through her kitchen drawer in search of Jackson's business card.

•   •   •

"Ok, put 'em here, Mrs. B, right in the heart," Jackson called out as Jody hit chip shots with her lob wedge into the baseball catcher's mitt he was holding. "A little higher, so it lands nice and soft. There it is. You've got it now. I'll back up to 100 yards, so you can do the same with your nine iron."

Jackson and Jody had been working on different short game drills in the Wheeler Garden practice area for the past hour. While Jody hit ball after ball into the center of the mitt, she began to feel her touch returning.

"Looks like you'd be in great shape for this year's club championship, Mrs. Benson. We've got another month to get ready for it. Any chance you'll decide to play?"

Through his long mane of hair, Jody could see Jackson's eyes sparkling with an intensity she hadn't noticed before. "To be truthful, Jackson, I'm not sure if I'm ready to compete again." While she spoke, she kept her eyes on the statue of her grandfather.

"What's your story, Mrs. Benson? Why are you so afraid to enjoy the game you were born to play? Not to mention showing off that beautiful swing."

"Why am I so afraid to show off *my* beautiful swing? Why are *you* so afraid to show off that face of yours? What's with that hair? And what's with working as a caddy? You've got a degree from Yale, for gosh sakes!"

"How did you know that?"

"Eddie told me."

"Of course, he did." He paused and cocked his head. "I'm starting to think there's a conspiracy going on here."

"Could be," she said with a wink.

"Okay, Doctor Benson. How 'bout we make a deal? I'll tell you what's keeping me from reaching my potential, and you can tell me what's keeping you from blowing us all away in the championship."

"Deal," Jody agreed.

"Heads or tails," Jackson pulled a quarter from his pocket.

"Heads."

He flipped the coin into his palm and slapped it on the back of his hand. "Tails. You first."

"Ok, well . . . my story's pretty short but not too sweet." Jody looked over at the statue again. "Thanks to my grandpa, golf was a huge part of my life ever since I can remember. He had me putting at the age of two. By ten, he had me playing in some local junior tournaments. After good runs on my junior and high school teams, I got accepted to Princeton on a golf scholarship. Grandpa was so proud of me," she said with a smile. "He used to fly out to the East Coast from LA for my matches in New Jersey, Massachusetts, Connecticut. He even came out to help coach our Varsity team. The other girls were thrilled to have a former PGA pro giving them swing tips. In my Senior year, we'd won our division and were playing for the national championship against Yale. It was the end of March, and the weather was cold and nasty, but Grandpa insisted on carrying my bag for me. I should have told him not to. I should have made him take a cart like the other girls and their caddies were doing. But he always said that the only way to feel the lay of a course is to walk it."

"He was right there," Jackson said. "You can't feel the lay of a course by riding over it in a cart. Any good golfer will tell you that."

"So, he walked eighteen long holes with my bag on his shoulders."

"I played that course back in the day. Can be tough. 'Specially in that wind," Jackson agreed.

"At the final hole, the match was tied, and it was my turn to putt. My ball was a good thirty feet from the hole, and my concentration just vanished. I looked over at Forrest. He made a gesture of looking at the hole, while he stroked an imaginary putter. Then he mouthed the advice he'd given me so many times before. He was saying, 'Trust your instincts'. I took a deep breath, looked at the hole, and envisioned my ball rolling into the center of the cup. I made my stroke, and the ball seemed to roll toward the hole with a glow around it, as if it were saying that my grandpa's words were golden. When it dropped in, my birdie putt cinched victory for our team. While my Princeton playing partner jumped up and cheered, one of our opponents on the Yale team, a huge, muscular Slavic girl named Ursula, threw her putter up in the air in frustration. It spun around toward Grandpa. He saw it coming, but the weight of the bag prevented him from dodging it in time and the face of the putter hit him squarely in the head. He slumped over and collapsed in a heap, bag and all. When I ran to him, he looked up at me and said, 'Always remember to trust your instincts, honey.' Those were his last words." Jody was silent for a moment. She took another look at the statue. "So, I'm sure you can understand why I gave up golf for a long, long time."

"Oh no! To have a moment like that marred by tragedy. And what happened to Ursula?"

"The police declared the death an accident. A few years later, Ursula went on to win a gold medal in the 2008 Olympics Javelin toss."

"What a terrible, crazy story," Jackson said.

"It did get better, though. For me, that is. I came back to LA after getting my undergrad degree. Worked in research for a while. I knew I needed a P.H.D. to advance in biological sciences, but I just didn't have the motivation. One evening a friend asked me to help her out with her golf swing, so I joined her at the driving range up the way in Studio City."

"That's a fun spot," Jackson said. "I'm over there most nights lately, trying to keep my swing in tune."

"I was trying to get my friend to increase her club head speed by swinging faster, not harder, ya know, by keeping her body relaxed, like a rag doll as some say? I started hitting some shots to give her the idea. When I turned around, I saw the cutest guy I'd ever set eyes on watching me. I somehow knew that he was the man I was going to marry."

"Sounds like love at first sight. Thought that only happens to men."

"More like lust at first sight. Seems like between my studies, golf, and my nights watching old movies on *TCM*, I was ripe for a real-live relationship. I did get some warnings about Derrick being a real party boy and a big-time womanizer from some friends that knew him. But after we got serious, he managed to convince me that he'd grown up and was ready to commit to one woman. With his love and support, I went on to get a doctorate in ornithology."

"Sounds like you're one smart cookie who got lucky with love. Wish I could say the same. Just wasn't that lucky or that smart."

"You're talking like your life's over. What are you, thirty?"

"I'll be thirty-four in August. And no, my life's not over. Just hit some speed bumps along the way."

"Drugs? Booze? Legal problems?"

"No, nothing like that. Like Eddie said, I went to Yale—majored in theater and creative writing. After college, I wrote and acted in a couple of plays in New York City. Small theater stuff, which led to a couple of small parts on 'the great white way', as they still call Broadway. That parlayed into some acting jobs in television, which brought me out to LA. Got my big break in 2009 when film director Marty Stadler gave me a plum role in *The Sphinx*, if you remember that film?"

"That's where I know you from! Jackson Lyons! You're that Jackson Lyons! Oh, my gosh . . . you were the time traveler who had to solve the seven riddles to save . . . what's her name? The tall red head with the gap in her front teeth?"

"Rene' Shelton," Jackson nodded. "My costar in the film."

"Yes! And that's one modern movie that I loved! I laid awake most of the night after I saw it. Retracing the clues to solve the riddles."

"Well, that's where my story gets complicated. Because almost from the first day of shooting, everyone on set realized we had big problems with the script. It was one of those overblown deals written by committee. Bad dialogue and a plot that didn't add up. But no one on set had the balls to tell the truth to the suits at the studio for fear that the money guys would pull the plug on the thing. I didn't want to make my Hollywood debut in a stinker, so I took it upon myself to do a rewrite. Stayed up all hours of the night for weeks; reworking scenes, making the riddles relate to each other, and adding in that crazy twist at the end. I showed my draft to Marty, and he was sold. To keep the studio folks from messing things up again, we re-shot scenes on a closed set, and Marty kept it all under wraps 'til we had a final cut of the film. We screened our masterpiece for the suits, and they went nuts. They loved it. The picture did about $175 mil at the box office, and I got some nice mentions for my acting in the reviews."

"You were great in it. And you wrote it too. That's pretty awesome!"

"I did a lot that was right. But I did even more that was wrong. I fell in love with Rene', who happened to be Marty's girlfriend."

"You didn't! Don't you know you're not supposed to *you know what* where you eat?"

"I'm proof of that. She ended up leaving him for me. And even though he'd been cheating on her with another actress, I'd committed a mortal sin in his mind. Though I'd saved his picture, I'd damaged his ego. He refused to give me the on-screen writing credit I deserved and did everything in his power to have me blackballed in the industry. And as the director of a blockbuster, he had plenty of power."

"But you gave him that power with your rewrite!"

"True. Still, no one would touch me as an actor or a writer, for fear of alienating Marty. He even threatened my agent, who, of course, dumped me like a sack of garbage. My fall from grace didn't sit well with Rene' either. She dumped me too. I was fortunate to have made enough money from the role and residuals to pay the bills while I finish up the screenplay I'm working on now—a comedy set in Manhattan. Either I'm totally insane, or this new script is pretty terrific."

"So . . . from movie star to . . . caddy?" Jody asked, her face scrunched in disbelief.

"I played here a few months back with an actor friend who's a member here. That's when I met Eddie. After we chatted for a bit, I asked him if he could use another caddy and he said sure. Sounds odd, but it's working out great. I have plenty of time to polish my script while waiting around in the caddy yard. And the characters down there keep my creative juices flowing."

"And dare I ask about . . . that Grizzly Adams look?"

"Ah! You noticed."

"Very funny, Jackson! C'mon, what's the deal with all that hair? Is it a disguise or something?"

"You might say that. It keeps me from being recognized while I watch the dynamics on the course and get some great inspiration for my next script which is set at a country club."

"Hmm, I see. So you're observing the Bellstone members from behind your own personal shrubbery. Kind of like the way I watch birds."

"Ha! I love it!" Jackson said with a laugh.

"So, the mentally challenged mountain man is really a brilliant artist who's creating his masterpiece by observing the bizarre rituals of a tribe of crazy golfers."

"At the very least, he's a writer who thinks there could be a great movie made about this beautifully landscaped nuthouse. The only problem is, I've burned through my one big contact in the industry, and it's damn near impossible to get anyone to read an uncredited screenwriter's script in this town."

"But Marty the director must have forgiven you for the Rene' thing by now. Didn't I hear somewhere that he'd married Uma Thurman? Why don't you reach out to him and try to patch things up? He knows you're a talent. And he owes you big time for rescuing a picture that would have sunk without you. Give the guy a call. Or at least a text."

"I don't know if I'm ready to do that," Jackson said while he tossed a golf ball high in the air and caught it with the mitt.

"C'mon Jackson! With your talent you could be somebody! You could be a contender!"

"Like Marlon Brando in *On the Waterfront*," Jackson said. "Do you always weave quotes from movies through your conversations?"

"Sorry! It's a habit of mine that tends to annoy my husband."

"Don't apologize to me. I find it endearing."

"Then, here's another one . . . same actor, but years later . . . "I'm gonna make you an offer you can't refuse."

"*The Godfather*, of course! What's the offer?"

"You promise me that you'll at least think about trying to patch things up with Marty, and I promise to consider entering this year's Women's Club Championship."

Jackson turned to the statue of Forrest Wheeler. "Did you hear that Mr. Wheeler? Your little girl might get back in the game! How cool is that?" He took off his hat and tossed it toward the statue. It landed on the beak of the bronze trumpet crane that sat on the man's shoulder.

"And you will get a shave and a haircut if you get a meeting with Marty, won't you?"

"If it's part of your offer, then I'll do it. And may I say, Mrs. B, that your eyes are as green as those glistening reeds in that lake over there?"

"And please stop calling me Mrs. B! It makes me feel like I'm the sweet old Aunt from that Andy Griffith Show I used to watch on Nick at Night as a kid."

"Will do, Jody. Now let's see you get out of the bunker." Jackson tossed some balls into a sand trap. "Then maybe we'll work on some long irons. I'm yours 'til noon when Eddie's sending me out on a loop."

"Sure. But I've gotta leave before that. Have some things going on at the office. Maybe we can work together on the weekend if you've got some time."

"For you, Mrs. B . . . I mean Jody, I'll make time."

• • •

"Okay, we've got six bottles of Musigny, 1963, worth $43,000," Father Norman O'Malley told Newt Sizemore as he scanned down the list of wines from the Bellstone cellar he'd compiled on his iPhone. "Six bottles of Haute Brion, 1972 . . . $59,450. Twelve bottles Chateau Laffite, 1982 . . . $53,780. Twelve of the Petrus, 1978 . . . $46,550. That's a total of $201,000 and change. Be sure to send me decent pictures of every one of those bottles, Newt. I need close-ups of all labels, back and front, to show authenticity, vintages, and condition of the ink and paper. I also need views of the fill lines to show if there's been any evaporation of the wine. Email the photos to my personal address, not the one that goes to the Church. I'll play hardball with this Chung dude to get top dollar for the lot. $201,000 like I just told you. No, I can't get more, unless we give him more bottles." The priest held the phone from his ear and rolled his eyes. "Newt . . . Newt . . . will ya please just listen? The guy's not stupid. If he was, he wouldn't be worth three billion dollars. Okay then . . . I'm putting my best man, Javier, a very capable illegal fellow we've been sheltering here at the church on the job. Yup . . . yup . . . you just make sure the bottles he's removing are in the designated spot we agreed on. And don't forget to email me the codes to the alarm. None of those security cameras in the back, are there? Not yet? You sure about that? Good. What's that? He'll be there at three a.m. when that useless security guard is sleeping like a baby. Okay, later, big guy." With that, Father Norm clicked off his phone in his office at the All Saints Catholic Church of Encino. Thanks to the ever-growing thirst of Asian billionaires for fine French vintages, he was making some nice change selling wine for collectors he'd connected with through his church to Chinese middlemen who purchased the bottles for their wealthy clients. Though they haggled endlessly with him over price, they always ended up spending exorbitant sums of money that was paid up-front before the wine shipped out.

The priest had already moved several hundred thousand dollars in rare vintages from Bordeaux and Burgundy that had been stored in the cavernous cellars of the Los Angeles Cathedral for decades. The money went directly into the personal account of the archbishop, earning Norm the promise that he would be shielded from any entities the church had influence over, such as the LAPD, the FBI, and certain government officials. Now, by doing the same favor for Newt and his cronies, Norm was proving his value to the powers that be at the club. Golf was Norm's passion and having access to unlimited play at a course as fine as Bellstone was worth whatever services he could offer to retain his Courtesy Membership for many years to come.

•　•　•

Norman Liam O'Malley had been a survivor since the moment he arrived on earth. He was born in the back seat of his 15-year-old mother's boyfriend's car in Boston on a ninety-degree summer's day in the year 1960. The panicked and heartless young father stuffed the helpless creature and the remnants of the birth into a brown paper bag and tossed the package into a nearby dumpster. It was nearly a day later that the muffled cries from the bag were heard by a 12-year-old paperboy who pedaled by the dumpster on his bicycle after finishing his route. Thinking the weakened cries were those of an abandoned kitten, the boy climbed into the container, followed the sounds to the bag, and opened it. Horrified by what he saw, he put the bag in his bicycle basket, pedaled to the near-by Saint Michael's Seminary, and banged on the door. The priest in attendance rushed the package to the city's Catholic hospital, where doctors treated the newborn for severe dehydration, but otherwise determined him to be healthy.

Fearing that if, and when the Godless parents were discovered, the infant would be returned to them, the priest; a Father Sean McKenzie, used his substantial clout with Boston officials to have the baby released to his care as a ward of the church.

The nuns from the local parish created a makeshift nursery in the convent, named the child after a much-loved deceased parish priest, and cared for him until he was ready to enter the boy's school run by the priests of Saint Michael's. Father McKenzie, by then the monsignor in charge of the seminary, treated little Norman like the son he never had. An avid golfer, the senior priest began taking the smart and engaging youngster along on his daily golf outings at the public course across the street from Saint Michael's. By the age of eight, Norman could play all eighteen holes with ease. When he was thirteen, he could often outdrive and even outscore his mentor. The boy also excelled at his studies and was well on track for a career in theology. But young Norman knew that all was not right at the seminary.

The boys at Saint Michael's warned each other to stay away from Father Lovett, one of the senior priests at the school. Many told stories about the priest fondling them or other boys with threats to torture the parish's beloved old dog if they broke their silence. When Norman was thirteen, he found himself alone with Father Lovett in one of the seminary men's rooms. Before he could make his exit, the priest grabbed him around the neck with one hand and thrust his other hand down the front of the boy's trousers. It was Norm's luck that the sound of someone approaching the men's room prompted the priest to release his hold, and the terrified boy made his escape.

During their next day's golf outing, the still traumatized boy told Father McKenzie about his encounter. He assumed that his mentor would have the offending priest removed from the parish, but Father McKenzie's words surprised him.

"Though this man is a deviant, and his actions are evil, you must use this experience as an opportunity, Norman." While the monsignor spoke, he surveyed the long, breaking putt he needed to sink for his birdie. "You will do the same as I did when I was your age, and another priest in power put his hands on me. Finding success in the church is much like finding success at putting. In both arenas, knowledge is power." McKenzie walked around the hole and studied the slope of the green near the cup. "I told the man that if he ever touched me again, I would call the city newspaper and describe exactly what he did to me and to many other boys. Not only did he leave me alone, he paid me $25 a week to insure my continued silence. You see, what I had gained from his actions was knowledge." McKenzie then returned to his ball, set his feet, and took several practice strokes. "Your position in the church will always be secure if you collect such knowledge and use it to establish and maintain an advantage over your more powerful adversaries." The priest executed a perfect putting stroke that sent the ball on a path to the center of the hole. "In this way, and this way only, will you achieve success in our most holy institution, Mother Church."

•   •   •

"Okay, Myth-ter 007, or whoever you are. Thith may be your shot at the big time!" The old caddy called Bones snapped the top of Jackson Lyon's laptop down just seconds before the writer could add a new piece of dialogue to his nearly completed screenplay. The remark would be the perfect cap to a scene between the story's bickering married couple when their rowboat tipped over in New York City's Central Park.

"Eddie neeths another man to carry for the Gamblers at twelve o'clock th-arp," Bones told the younger man. "Follow my inth-ructions to a tee! And don't th-crew up!"

The noon weekday Gamblers game was a long-running tradition at Bellstone. Players came and went throughout the years, but the group continued to play the highest stakes game at the club. To be invited into the group, new players had to succeed at impressing the other players with their skills on the course and their guts to bet big.

On that Wednesday in the second week of May, newcomer Derrick Benson joined the competition with Gamblers regulars Newt Sizemore, Monty Manville, and Bradley Watchtower. Bones, who'd been a regular caddy for the group since 1957, would be carrying Monty and Bradley's bags, as well as keeping track of the day's bets on the scorecard. Jackson, the group's newest caddy, would be carrying for Newt and Derrick. Five other foursomes would be following the president's group. While the men gathered on the first tee a little before noon, Jackson spotted Derrick's BMW640i pulling up to the porte-cochere. Derrick handed his car keys to Bernardo and sprinted up to the tee box.

"No hurry, Mr. Benson. We've got a few minutes 'til tee off," Jackson told his player. "By-the-way, I'm Jackson, and I'll be carrying your bag today." The caddy extended his hand.

"Good to meet you, my man," Derrick said as he returned the handshake. "Traffic was brutal on the 101 West. Glad I made it in time."

"For sure. Hey, I had the pleasure of working with your wife on her game this morning. I'm sure you know that she's easily got what it takes to win this year's Women's Club Championship."

"No doubt in my mind. I know she'd love to get back in the winner's circle. Plus, I'd be pleased as all heck to have a wife who's the ladies club champ! Any encouragement you could give her would be—"

"Okay fellas!" Newt bellowed. "We've got a Nassau going. There's $200 on the front nine, $200 on the back, and $200 overall with automatic presses. Monty and Brad are partners, and I've got the new kid on the block, Derrick Benson."

When the players and caddies had assembled on the tee box of the 1st hole, Newt crooked his finger to summon Bones. "Yes, thir?" the lisping caddy asked the club president.

"I need you to make sure this new mountain man caddy gets familiar with my system," Newt said with his voice lowered. "Don't want any problems out there."

"I'll get him up and running for ya, Mr. Thizemore. Don't worry, thur. Eddie thaz he's a good man."

Derrick was the first to tee off. His drive was a boomer. "Way to blast it, partner!" Newt shouted. "I love this guy!"

Derrick stood tall as he watched his ball roar down the first hole of the historic course. He was thrilled to be a part of the coolest group at one of LA's most prestigious country clubs. His main goal of the day was to impress the other men, so they'd make him a regular in their fold. He was a betting man, and golf was a betting man's game. Plus, any business he could generate on the course would help silence his boss when the old man complained that his time would better be spent at the office.

The two caddies walked down the first fairway with their player's bags on their shoulders.

"That young fella, Benson," Bones said to Jackson. "I've theen him before."

"You must've seen him out here," Jackson answered. "He played with the guys last Sunday."

"Nope, that wasn't it. I know that face from thum-where's else," the other caddy insisted. "It'll come to me."

On the 3rd hole, Newt hit a shot dangerously close to a stream that meandered through the course and flowed down to the Wheeler Garden. Bones and Jackson set off to hunt for the ball while Newt limited his search to the in-bounds side of the water hazard. After a minute of searching, Jackson spotted the president's ball, with his "NS" logo lying under the water.

"Think I see it here, Mr. Size—"

"Shhhhh!" Bones hissed at the other caddy. Jackson looked up at the old man, who signaled for him to watch Newt.

"Found it here in the grass guys!" the president called out to his competitors as he lay down one of the identical balls that he always carried to cover his errant shots. "Not a bad lie either. Guess I caught a break."

"Looks like you don't need it anyway," Bradley called out. "Your partner just chipped in for a birdie."

Newt was having a tough golf day, which he assumed was due to the six double Daniels he'd consumed at the bar the evening before. But thanks to Derrick's skills on the course, the younger man easily made up for the president's shortcomings, which enabled their team to double the bet with each two-point lead. On the 18th and final hole, a tough par four, Derrick landed his ball on the green in two. As the other players were all lying three, a one-putt by Derrick would pay off big time for the team of Benson and Sizemore.

"Okay Jackson," Derrick called out to the caddy, as he tossed him his ball for a wipe. "I don't know these greens yet, so I'm at your mercy for a great read."

Jackson pointed to a white speck on the grass that was halfway down the hill and ten feet left of the hole. "Pretend the hole is right here, Mr. Benson."

Derrick hit the putt as instructed. The ball traveled over the speck and continued rolling until it dropped into the cup.

"YES!" Derrick shouted, giving a fist pump.

"You closed those fuckers out!" Newt cried, causing all within earshot to look in his direction. "We're taking the money every way which way from Sunday!"

After settling the bets, the players walked off the green, while the caddies held back and slung the golf bags onto their shoulders. "Dancin' Bare!" Bones whispered to Jackson as the two men started their march toward the pro shop.

"*Dancin' wha*? What're you talking about, Bones?"

"Dancin' Bare. The thrip joint. That's where I know him from," the old caddy said as he pointed toward Derrick. "The guy's a regular. At least he *was* a regular when I was there. I haven't been in for a few months th-ince I've gone stone cold on the ponies. But I got a bet on a hot filly runnin' this afternoon down at Santa—"

Jackson stared at the haggard old man before cutting him off. "Mr. Benson? At a strip joint? I don't think so."

"I know tho. He had a thing goin' with one of the gals down there. A hot lookin' little redhead. What was her name? Annette? Amanda? Amber? Yeah, that's it! Amber! Heard she was even braggin' to the other gals that he was even gonna leave hith nasty bitch of a wife and marry her."

"Then it was some other guy. Not Mr. Benson," Jackson said with relief. "Mr. Benson is married to one of the nicest—"

"He alwath pulled up at the front of the place in a th-ilver BMW640i! Yeah! Itz all comin' back to me now."

Jackson stared at Bones. Then he looked at Derrick who was sharing a laugh with Newt. "Holy shit," he said through his long mane of hair.

When the players arrived at the pro shop, Bradley Watchtower called to Derrick. "Hey Benson! How about joining us for a steak and some drink in the men's grill?"

"No can do, gentlemen. Got a meeting in a bit with a client who needs my services. Here, check her out." He pulled out his iPhone and began to scan through his photos while Newt and Bradley came closer to peer at the screen. Their eyes popped at the image of a pole dancer in a G-string, with pasties on her enormous breasts. "I like to say that this one has some big assets and very little coverage," Derrick said with a chuckle.

"Whoa! Sweet Jesus lad!" Newt said while he enlarged the photo with his thumb. "You *do* know how to play!" He elbowed Derrick in the ribs and lowered his voice to a whisper. "Just how do you find time for that with your pretty wife waiting at home? Unless she's into that kind of stuff?" he asked with a curious squint. "We've got some other couples that like to swing right here at the club."

"No way," Derrick whispered back. "Not my wife. She's an old-fashioned girl who likes to cook and watch old movies." He looked up, surprised to see Jackson staring at him from a few feet away. "Oh, excuse us, my man," he told the caddy. "Just some boy talk." He reached into his pocket and pulled out one of the hundred dollar bills he'd won. "Here ya go." He walked toward Jackson with the bill in one hand and extended the other for a shake. "And thanks for helping me out today, pal."

The caddy ignored Derrick's hand and the money, while he backed away in disgust. "No thanks, Mr. Benson. Use it to buy your girlfriend some clothes."

•　　•　　•

Eddie, who had a clear view of the scene from the starter's booth, signaled for Jackson to come to his window as the caddy passed by on his way to the bag room. "Did you and Mr. Benson have a problem out there, Jackson? You know it's strictly forbidden for a caddy to be anything less than gracious to a member of this club."

Jackson pulled his hair back from his face and leaned into the window of the booth. "I found out that Mr. Benson is not conducting himself in a manner appropriate for a married man," he confided in a low voice.

"Is that so?" asked Eddie.

"He's been screwing a stripper and bragging about it. I wanted to knock the guy's teeth out."

"Oh, dear God—dear God in heaven!" Eddie put his hand to his forehead. "That's just terrible!" the old man stammered. "I've known Mrs. Benson since she was a tiny babe. That girl has a heart as big as the sky above us, and her grandfather was one of the greatest men I've ever had the honor of calling my friend. If I wasn't eighty-eight years old, I'd go out there and knock the fellow's teeth out myself."

"That guy must have her totally fooled," Jackson said.

"Well from what I've seen around here, the wives are usually the last ones to know." Eddie lit the stub of the cigar he'd been smoking, took a few puffs of the stogie, and flicked out the match. "She deserves to be told. One of us has to tell her." With the cigar fixed between his teeth, he looked at Jackson. "And it shouldn't be me."

•   •   •

"Benson Insurance, how can I help you?" Derrick Benson had phoned his office on his car's Bluetooth system as he drove out of the Bellstone parking lot.

"I know how you can help me, Shannon, you gorgeous thing!"

"Oh hi, Derrick," the receptionist replied. "How'd your golf game go?"

"I dazzled 'em. Won ten Benjamins that're burning a hole in my hot little pocket. Plus, the guys in the coolest group at the coolest club in LA are now official fans of Derrick the Dude. Anyhow, sexy stuff, is my dad around?"

"He's in a meeting right now but was looking for you a few minutes ago. You coming in?"

"Crap! I was supposed to be there now to meet with Stu Nelson at four. Oh, well, I'll be a bit late is all. Got a stop to make, first."

"A stop, huh? You've got a pocket full of cash, and you're ducking out on your meeting. On your way to one of those seedy strip clubs again, aren't you? You're so gross."

"Nope, don't frequent those dumps anymore. Got my own personal performer."

"Derrick . . . you're crazy! It was bad enough when you were twenty. But you're a grown man now . . . who hasn't grown up!"

"Hey, please, Shannon—no lectures! I've been a devoted husband for months now."

"That's hard to believe. You can't be faithful to any woman for that long."

"Believe it baby. Between work and golf, I haven't had the time or the energy for any real fun."

"And what if this woman makes trouble and Jody finds out? You didn't see me stick around after that Mona Wassman told me you were bonking her, did you?"

"And you broke my poor teenage heart, my love. But Jody won't find out. Amber's happy with our arrangement. She knows I'm a married man. It's no strings, no problemo. So if my dad asks for me, just tell him I'll be a bit late. *Caio bella.*"

Derrick clicked off his phone, determined not to let Shannon's negativity bring him down. When he turned off Ventura Boulevard and made his way onto the 101 Freeway toward Sepulveda, he cranked up the music of Bruno Mars until it blasted through the BMW's six-piece surround sound system.

"Cause your sex takes me to paradise, yeah, your sex takes me to paradise, and it shows, yeah, yeah, yeah"

He began to feel the familiar surge in his loins as he pictured Amber waiting for him in her North Hollywood apartment. Ever since the stripper teased him in her morning text about some big surprise she had in store, he'd been trying to imagine what that surprise might entail. She had such an exciting and creative sexual mind. The very first time they hooked up she invited another girl from the club to join them for their date. It was double the fun as the girls introduced him to the pleasures of ménage-a-trois.

His next visit began with Amber standing on her kitchen counter as he walked in the door. With a G-string covering her crotch and tassels dangling from her breasts, she proceeded to perform one of her dance routines set to the Katy Perry song about *"streakin' in the park, skinny dipping in the dark, last Friday night"*. She gave him a scare when she slipped on the tile and landed hard on that beautiful behind. But he kissed it and made it all so much better.

Now, trying to imagine what other treats the stripper might have in store was making him hotter by the minute. He remembered her mentioning that a sister was moving out from Arkansas and would be staying with her until she found a job and a place of her own. That scenario triggered a thought that caused his genitals to become rock hard. There was a very good chance that in just a few minutes, two sisters would be having their way with him.

Cruising down Sepulveda Boulevard, he spotted the billboard with the number to call for instant bail bonds and knew that Amber's apartment complex was just past the sign. After pulling into a parking space on the street, he raced up the building's exterior staircase and opened the door to her apartment.

"Honey, I'm finally home!" he said with a chuckle as he marched into the bedroom, ready to feast his hungry eyes on one, or even two voluptuous naked bodies. But what he saw stopped him dead in his tracks.

•   •   •

"Okay, Jody, I'm pulling up the flock of white trumpet cranes that landed at their usual nesting ground in Morro Bay last week, right on schedule."

Jody was working with Rob Trotter, her technical advisor at the field office of the Department of Fish and Wildlife. The two were in a room known as 'the studio' that was outfitted with a large computer screen linked to the main frames of the other agencies, universities, and societies that partner with Fish and Wildlife to pinpoint the locations of migrating birds in the western hemisphere. By fitting transmitters on the legs of the birds, scientists use satellites to track the exact routes the animals follow, and the stopover points they select for resting and refueling during the annual journeys to their breeding grounds. The birds and their locations are depicted by electronic blips with travel dates, and the data is integrated into Google Earth and displayed on the screen.

"Yup, I see the cranes in beautiful Moro Bay," Jody said as she pointed to the patch of the electronic blips on the California coastline.

"Yup," Rob said. "The adult cranes arrived at their nesting site on March 4th of this year, which is the same date as last year, and in 2009, 2008 and 2007. In past years, they remained at the site for the standard eighteen weeks before flying off with their young. That gave them fourteen days for nest building, forty-five days for the eggs to hatch, and seventy days for the young to mature enough to take flight."

"Sounds right," Jody agreed.

"Yeah, but here's what's wrong." Rob pulled up a chart on the screen. "This year, the birds took off just eight weeks after arriving, which would be only a day or so after the chicks had hatched. Barring a fire or another natural disaster, we've got to think these nests were raided. And for the entire flock of chicks to disappear at once . . . they weren't victims of wildlife predators. This had to be a well-planned poaching."

"Oh no, *not again!*" Jody said with a groan. "How many flocks of these guys have we lost this year, Rob? Twenty?"

"Twenty-three, to be exact. These cartels seem to be getting more sophisticated by the month. The cranes'll go the way of the passenger pigeon and the dodo bird if this keeps up."

"It's just too bad those chicks are too tiny to be fitted with transmitters," Jody said. "If the electronics were small and light enough, we could track whoever's raiding the nests right into those labs that cook up that anti-wrinkle serum."

"Someday, boss. The way technology's going, we'll be able to wire-up hummingbirds before long."

"Yeah, but 'before long' may be too late for this species," Jody said as she stared at the screen in frustration.

"On a lighter note, how'd your practice go this morning?" Rob made the motion of swinging a golf club. "That caddy help you any?"

"He sure did. The guy's quite a character. He's a great coach, and fun too."

"With what we see happening here, I'll take fun any day," Rob said.

On her way back to her office, Jody made a stop in the ladies room, where she discovered that her period had arrived right on schedule—twenty-eight days since the last one had started. For the past year, the familiar red stain on her underwear had left her feeling sad and empty by knowing that another egg had slipped away from her body. Another egg had lost its chance to fulfill its destiny to become a child that would drink from her breast, say its first words, take its first steps, and learn to ride a bike. And Jody's heart ached with the knowledge that she'd lost another chance to love a child with every fiber of her being.

When she came back into her office, her eyes fell on the picture she kept on her desk from her honeymoon in Hawaii. There was no doubt that she looked hot in her string bikini, and she was reminded of how ripped Derrick looked in those surfing jams he'd worn. Though the photo was only two years old, she couldn't help but notice that the washboard abs of the man she married had been replaced by a slight paunch. But she also detected something else that had changed. He had his arms around her waist, and he was looking at her with total adoration. It occurred to her that she hadn't seen anything close to that look for a long time.

•　　•　　•

"Where you been all this time, boy?" Chuck Benson asked Derrick as he walked into his father's office. "You're just getting your ass back to work now?" The chairman of Benson Insurance had been waiting for his son for over two hours.

"Like I told you, Dad, I had a golf game at noon," Derrick said. "Trying to drum up some new business at the club. I'm making some good contacts there."

"I'll believe that you're making some good contacts all right, but not on the golf course. You gettin' yourself into trouble again? And by-the-way, you look like you've seen a ghost! What's goin' on with you, son?"

"Nothing, Dad. Really. I just saw Stu Nelson's car pulling out of the parking garage as I pulled in. I was sick knowing that I must have missed our meeting. Thought you'd said six o'clock."

"No. I told you four o'clock. So, what you been doin'?"

"I told you, Dad. I had a golf game."

"Yeah, at twelve noon. We waited 'til four fifteen but had to go ahead without you. A round of golf shouldn't take more than four hours. Now you're strolling in here at six o'clock at night. You should be on your way home to your wife."

Chuck Benson knew his son all too well. During high school, Derrick seemed to screw up every chance he got. With his lackluster grades, he was lucky that his skills and talent on the golf course gained him entry to a decent college. During his first year at the University of Southern California, he was nearly thrown out of school for drinking and raising hell with his buddies in the dorms. The fact that the kid was blessed with his mom's pretty face and Irish charm seemed to save his ass every time. It also enabled him to get any girl who happened to catch his eye into bed. And that's what the senior Benson was most worried about that evening.

"Sorry, Dad. Should'a called to check in. My apologies."

"I'm just worried about what you're up to is all, boy. Don't forget that this girl is the best thing that ever happened to you. Having a classy wife like that on your arm can help you take this firm to the next level. The only reason I made you second in command here is that your brother married that fat piece of trash from Stockton. Plus, I'm expecting some very good-looking and very smart grandchildren out of your union."

"Me too, sir. Jody knows I'm anxious for kids. I'm just waiting for her to pull the trigger."

"Well, I'm glad to hear that, son. You married well, so don't fuck it up."

"I won't, Dad. You've gotta believe me. My main priorities these days are Benson Insurance and Mrs. Derrick Benson."

Six

Sunday, July 15ᵗʰ1985
26 years before the 2011 Bellstone Women's Club Championship

"Mommy, let me off here please," the little girl begged, as they rode through the grand entrance gates of Bayonne Country Club. "I don't want them to see our old car."

"Angela Teresa Fatabina! What on earth has become of you? You know your fatha worked his fingas ta the bone to buy this cah from Uncle Dominick! Just what would he think of ya for actin' like this perfectly fine station wagon isn't good enough for ya to ride in?"

Angie's mother stopped the 1967 Plymouth at the grand porte-cochere of Bayonne County Club. A few minutes later, Angie was standing in the club's practice area that had the kids from her neighborhood on one side of the grass, and the fair-haired, crisply dressed country club kids on the other. A man spoke through a megaphone.

"Hi, kids! I'm Brian, the golf pro here. Our club's young golfers and I would like to welcome you to Bayonne Country Club. Today is our member's way of giving back to the community that's been so good to all of their families. This morning we're gonna hit some golf balls. Later on you'll enjoy hot dogs and a swim in the pool."

Young Angie stared in wonder at the green grass covering the golf course that seemed to go on for miles. The endless beds of pink and white azalea bushes, the bags of junior-size clubs, and the piles of bright white golf balls made her stomach flutter with excitement. Then, Monique Wolfe ruined everything.

"Hey, I know you," Monique called to Angie. "You're that Italian girl from my history class! And you're wearing those plaid shorts I gave to the clothing drive last summer! They're way too big for you! Ha ha ha! My mom says that your daddy's a garbage man. One thing we can say about him is his business is always picking up! Ha ha ha!"

"*Always picking up!* That is *so* funny Monique," Shelly Greenbrier said amidst a flurry of giggles.

Then, looking and sounding like an angel, Randi Sharp came to the rescue. Wearing a pink and white golf ensemble, she had blonde pig tails, a turned-up nose, and she spoke with an adorable southern accent. On that day, young Angie thought that Randi was the prettiest and coolest person on earth.

"Hey Monique," Randi said to the girl. "Don't y'all be mean to Angie. She's the smartest gal in my biology class. And I stink at it! Miss Peartree says I'll have to take it again in summer school if I don't pull my grade up." Randi took her new friend by the hand. "C'mon Angie. Let me show you how to hit your wedge out of a sand trap, honey." She jumped into a nearby bunker. "Maybe later you can help me study for next Friday's bio test."

"Sure, I'll help you, Randi," Angie said as she hopped next to her friend in the sand.

Randi then dug her feet into the sand and stood behind one of the practice balls as she held her sand wedge. "Now watch how I do this, Angie. Hit through the sand, two inches in back of the ball," she said as she demonstrated the shot. The ball flew out of the bunker onto a near-by green. "Now you try." Angie swung the club into the sand, but the ball barely moved. "No Angie, you have to finish your swing. Try it again and finish the swing with your club pointed at the target." Angie followed her friend's advice by finishing her swing. The ball flew high into the air, landed a foot from the flag on the green, and rolled into the cup. "It went in the hole! It went in the hole! I think you'd be really good at golf if you started playing," Randi told her friend.

"But I'll never be able to play." Angie cried. "My parents aren't rich like yours. They're poor. They can never join a golf club, and they can never afford to give me lessons."

"You may be poor now, Angie. But someday you'll have enough money to play golf. And you'll beat all of the rich folks. I'm sure of it."

Seven

Thursday, May 10ᵗʰ 2011

"*Hola* Mama, *es* Marty! How was your shift at Walmart this evening? Not too many crazy parents killing each in the aisles over too few nerf guns? *Bueno!* And hey, Mama, I have a job! Security guard. No, it's only *temporario*. I'm filling in for Uncle Pepe here at Bellstone. I'll be here all night long. Mama stop crying! No, there's no danger. It's a country club full of rich people! *Buenos noches*, Mama. *Hasta manana.*"

Martin Rodriquez clicked off his cell phone and shook his head in frustration. Ever since his father was killed in the crossfire of Mexican drug gangs, the Army veteran's mother worried about her son non-stop. She worried about him being injured or killed during his two-year tour in Afghanistan. When he arrived home, she worried that he wouldn't find a job. Now that he finally had some night work, she worried about his safety. But safety was the last thing on Martin's mind as he sat in a golf cart in the Bellstone parking lot at eleven o'clock on a Thursday night. The stocky young man with the expressive face had loved golf since he was a youngster. His grandfather had been a caddy at Bellstone and had taken him from the age of six to play the course on the club's caddy family days. And on that night, even though Martin was just filling in as a night watchman, he was delighted to be back at the club in any capacity and was even more happy for the chance to earn some money.

Still living at his parent's house in the not-too-faraway town of Glendora, Martin was taking classes during the day at the local junior college with the plan of getting certified as an EMT within the next year. Knowing that night jobs were hard to come by, he felt lucky to have an in through his Uncle Pepe with Ace Officers, the company that provided security for the club. While Pepe was spending the week in Mexico, Martin was subbing for him with the hope that the temp job would lead to additional assignments through Ace. His uncle had assured him that the gig was a total piece of cake that involved no more than tooling around in a golf cart with a flashlight to make sure all was well on the course, in the parking lot, and around the exterior of the buildings. It would also allow him many hours of uninterrupted sleep in the cushioned cart. The only action he might encounter would be a fight between the two feral cats that hung out near the kitchen dumpster.

•   •   •

By two a.m., Martin was snoring away under a star-filled sky. At the same time, Javier Hernandez parked his 1994 Toyota Tundra truck just outside of the Bellstone guard house and ducked underneath the entry arm of the gate to avoid being caught by the club's security camera. He hiked up the two-mile drive to the dimly lit parking lot, crept to the rear of the clubhouse, and climbed the stairs to the loading dock. Dressed in black pants and a tee shirt, he carried a flashlight and two bags made of nylon netting that together could hold up to 50 bottles of wine. Guided by the flashlight, he disarmed the alarm and opened the back door of the kitchen with the security code that Father Norm had written down for him. After entering the building, Javier followed the route the priest had sketched out on the paper that took him through the kitchen and down the stairs to the basement of the clubhouse.

"Enemy attack! Take cover! Take cover! Move, move, move!" Martin cried out in his sleep. The ex-GI was having another nightmare triggered by his post-traumatic stress. Curled up on the seat of the cart, he whimpered and twitched in reaction to the gunfire and madness that filled every dream since he returned home. On most nights, his distraught mother would run into his room to shake him awake. But on that night, there was no one to hear his cries.

When Javier came to the door of the wine cellar, he checked his paper once more for the alarm code. He tapped it in, and the door to the cellar unlocked. After spending a good fifteen minutes loading the bottles that Norm had specified into the two net bags and slinging them over his shoulders, he hit the cellar's exit button and typed in the proper code. He followed the same routine leaving the kitchen, but in his haste, he mixed up the last two letters of that exit code.

• • •

"Enemy alert! Enemy alert!" Martin screamed while the alarm at his operating base exploded in his head. But this alarm had a different sound than the one he had heard a thousand times while on duty. It was more like a dinging bell. And the earsplitting noise didn't stop when he woke up.

When Martin regained his senses, he realized that the racket was coming from the back of the clubhouse. He grabbed his pistol and ran toward the loading dock. Though the security company did not arm their guards, he was taking no chances. After living through the hell of Afghanistan and seeing too many of his buddies picked off by Taliban soldiers, he never left home without a snub-nosed thirty-two strapped to his ankle. When he reached the loading dock, he looked up and saw the shadow of a figure with sacks on its back running across the concrete platform.

"Stop now! Put your hands in the air! Stop now, or I'll shoot!" Martin called out. "I said 'stop now', soldier! Stop with your hands up!" Hearing Martin's shouts through the alarm, Javier, who neither spoke nor understood any English, darted one way—then the other. Perceiving the movements as threatening, the veteran soldier took aim and fired a shot at the target. The bullet hit Javier in the stomach and sent him and the sacks packed with wine bottles flying from the platform onto the asphalt of the parking lot below. Martin, a Catholic, said several quick Hail Marys as he watched the bottles explode with an eruption of wine and glass, with Javier at the center of the fury.

Eight

Friday, May 11th 2011

The cell phone on Newt Sizemore's nightstand rang at five a.m. He rolled over and struggled to open eyes crusted with sleep while he cursed himself for not putting the ring on silent. When he picked up the phone, he saw the words "Mike Armstrong, Bellstone Country Club Manager" at the top of the screen.

"Newt, it's me, Mike," the manager's voice called out through the cell's speaker. "We have a situation here. Are you awake?"

"What's up Mike?" A wave of nausea rose in Newt's gut, in part from the two bottles of wine he'd consumed the night before, but also from the thought that Father O'Malley's plan must have gone terribly wrong.

"We had a robbery this morning—early, about three. A young Hispanic male tried to make off with a few dozen bottles from the wine cellar."

"How . . . how . . . how's that possible, Mike? And what would a Mexican kid want with some old wine?" Newt struggled to hide his panic as his mind raced to figure out how the screw up could have happened.

"He wasn't Mexican. The medics said he's from Guatemala. And it wasn't just 'some old wine'. The detective on the case ran some numbers on the bottles and they were all worth thousands. He's estimating that the total loss could be over a hundred grand."

"Loss?" Newt asked, relieved that the operation had succeeded, and the case would remain unsolved.

"Yes, loss," Mike answered. "The bottles were all smashed to smithereens. But that's not the worst of it. The security guard on duty shot the guy while he was trying to get away. The ambulance just left and the EMT's aren't sure if he'll make it or not."

Newt was getting dizzy from the waves of nausea pulsating through him. "Pepe shot a guy?" he cried out in a weakened voice. "That's impossible. He doesn't carry a gun."

"Pepe's in Mexico. His nephew, fresh from a tour in Afghanistan, was subbing for him. He had a pistol. It's a real mess, Newt. The place is swarming with cops. I suggest you get over here ASAP."

"Whaz going on, honey?" a half-asleep Noreen Sizemore slurred to her husband as he clicked off of the call.

"Trouble at the club. I've gotta run over there and straighten things out. Go back to sleep, Nor," Newt said as he hoisted his 245 pound frame out of bed.

"Those members are so lucky to have a good man like you taking care a-things, Newtie," Noreen assured her husband. "I hope these folks appreciate all the hard work you do for them." She grabbed her pillow and fell back asleep with a dreamy smile on her face.

• • •

Newt pulled into the parking lot of the club just as the sun was rising over the Santa Monica Mountains. Early bird golfers and arriving employees were standing in groups sharing the bits of news they'd picked up about the theft and shooting. Police had cordoned off the loading dock area with yellow tape. Crime scene investigators were picking out shards of broken glass and saturated wine labels from the nylon bag and putting them into containers as evidence. Martin was sobbing in the back of a squad car with his head in his hands, as he awaited his trip to the police station for further questioning. Newt spotted Mike Armstrong in a conversation with another man and walked over to them.

"Tell me what you know, Mike."

"Newt, this is Lieutenant Rocco Valentine from the Los Angeles Police Department. I've answered a lot of his questions, maybe you could help."

"Sure," Newt said. "How do you do Lieutenant? I'm Newt Sizemore––president of the club." He tried to keep his voice from cracking, and his hand from trembling as he offered it to the officer. The cop looked to be all business with his ramrod straight posture, closely cropped hair, and rippling abs that were visible through his white button-down shirt. His appearance posed a stark contrast to the disheveled club president with his puffy red face, bloodshot eyes, and sagging belly.

"How's it goin' Mr. Sizemore?" the lieutenant asked with a heavy New Jersey accent. "I've been tellin' your manager here that we've got an ID on the alleged thief from the license in his wallet. He's a Mr. Javier Hernandez. Appears to be an illegal immigrant from Guatemala. Has a North Hollywood address. His vehicle is still sitting outside of the gate, with his keys and wallet on the seat. Must-a entered the parking lot on foot with the intention of carrying the stolen wine out in those net bags you see on the ground over there. We have a unit on the way now to check out his address, and whatever else we can come up with. Hopefully, he'll survive the bullet in his belly and will be talkin' when he wakes up."

"I sure hope he will, Lieutenant," Newt said, nodding his head with concern. "We're all anxious to find out how in the name of God that fellow ever got in there."

"I can tell you now, Mr. Sizemore, that all signs point to this as an inside job. These restaurant and club kitchen robberies usually are. We know Mr. Hernandez had the alarm code to enter the buildin'. But he messed up the code on the way out and activated the alarm. Any idea who could have given him that code? A disgruntled employee? A club member? Or even an ex-club member?"

"Well . . ." Newt began. For a moment, he considered tossing out Shorty Columbo's name as a possible suspect. But if Shorty retaliated by telling the cops about Newt betting the treasury on a bum tip, he could find himself in serious trouble.

"Yes, Mr. Sizemore?" the lieutenant asked with head cocked. "Does someone come to mind?"

"No . . . no one, Lieutenant," Newt said as his right leg started to spasm. "We run a very tight ship here."

"Glad to hear it. But there's no doubt that the guy who took the bullet was doing a job for someone who knows just what bottles are in that cellar and how much they're worth."

"Oh, my dear sweet Lord above us, Lieutenant!" Newt said while the rolls of fat on his face morphed into a horrified expression. "To think that we could have a traitor within our ranks. It just makes me ill! Please, tell me what I can do . . . what any of us here can do to help you smoke out the rat!"

"Fahget about it, sir. That's our job. You can rest assured we'll be making one or more arrests and getting some convictions here, Mr. Sizemore. Based on the planning that went into the heist, and the value of the wine that was destroyed, I'd say we're looking at conspiracy and grand theft—charges that come with some serious jail time."

Acids began to shoot up from Newt's stomach to his throat, as the gravity of his situation set in. He spotted Father Norm O'Malley pulling into the parking lot for his usual seven a.m. tee off. The priest hopped out of his Lexus sedan dressed in green and red shorts, red socks, a red cap, and a green polo topped with a clerical collar buttoned onto the shirt.

"Please excuse me for a moment officer," Newt said to the cop. He walked off toward the priest at a relaxed pace so as not to arouse the officer's suspicion. When he reached him, he shot out his words in a furious hiss. "Do you know we could all go down in flames for this, O'Malley?"

"What's going on, Newt?" the priest asked as he surveyed the activity at the other side of the parking lot. "What are those black and whites doing here?"

"They're here because your 'very capable illegal fellow' fucked up the alarm code on the way outta the building! The alarm woke up the security guard who shot the moron, sending two hundred G's worth of wine running into the sewer. The kid is in the hospital, and the cops are already thinking it was an inside job!"

"Holy crap! That is a shame——but shit does happen, Newt! Well, you won't have to worry about the cops. I'll put in a call to the archdiocese to make the whole thing go away. The big wheels downtown owe me on several counts. But I did just email you and Monty to confirm that my contact Chung had his client, Li Fong, wire the two hundred thousand into the Bellstone account this morning. That wine is fully paid for. So, we've got to send some comparable selections out right away. I'm sure I can find plenty more bottles of equal value out of the thousands still down there. Otherwise, we'll have to send that money back pronto. We sure don't want to fool around with the Chinese mafia, or whatever this Fong guy is connected to."

Newt's face darkened from red to a deep purple as his already high blood pressure began to skyrocket. "I can't ask Monty to send out a check for that amount to a guy in China! He's already furious with me! And we can't send any more illegals in to steal the stuff either. Mike's talking to the Guard Rite guys now about installing security cameras down there this afternoon. Now, thanks to you, I've got to figure out a way to pay this Fong guy back, then cough up another several hundred G's for the tab on the wine cellar. And what about this kid who got shot? What if he survives and tells the cops who sent him down there?"

"Javier's no problem," Norm assured Newt. "He'll get a visit from his priest after my morning eighteen. You just figure out how to refund that money to Li Fong, and pronto."

"Whatever you say, Father O'Malley," Newt spat out. "Enjoy your round."

"I certainly will. Teeing off with Danny DeVito this morning. The guy can't play for shit but he's a great source of those filthy jokes that the archbishop loves to hear."

From across the parking lot, Lieutenant Valentine watched the conversation taking place between the two men with interest. "Who's that guy gettin' chewed out by Sizemore over there?" he asked Mike Armstrong.

"Oh, that's Father Norm. Father Norman O'Malley. He practically lives here."

●　　●　　●

At nine o'clock on that same Friday morning, Mandy Manville was lying back in her plastic surgeon's reclining chair under a blinding light. "Hold your face very still now," the doctor instructed. "I'm putting the needle in further this time—hitting the interior line of the neuromuscular tissue to give you more bang for your buck, as we like to say."

Doctor Marvin Feingold had been injecting Mandy's forehead and smile lines every six months for the past five years. For the first three years, the Botox delivered magical results. It took several years off of her face within minutes and the results lasted for months. But the past few sessions had left her disappointed.

"This stuff has lost its kick, Doc," she said as she ran her finger over her face. "We did this same drill only a month ago. But these furrows in my brow and these lines around my mouth came right back and are deeper than ever."

"We can only fend off the inevitable for so long, Mandy," Doctor Feingold said as he examined her skin with surgical eye loupes affixed to his forehead. "This stuff just can't keep working forever. Your skin continues to lose its elasticity. Especially with all those hours you log out on that golf course with our LA sun beating down on your face."

"Yeah, I get that. But I've been reading about some other treatments on-line. Said to be giving great results. Revitalift, Sculptra, Ultrasmooth? Any of those work better?"

"Don't think so. Botox is still considered the gold standard. But there *is* a new treatment that I've been hearing about. It's the hot drug in Brazil right now. Supposed to work its way right through the muscles of the face, and iron out the wrinkles while it tightens up the skin. I saw an item about it in one of my online journals. It's very pricey, and highly illegal in the U.S., 'cause the serum is made from the beaks of endangered baby birds. Those white trumpet cranes you see around here from time to time."

"Trumpet cranes, sure. Our golf club is full of them."

"It seems the birds are smuggled out of this country and taken to labs somewhere in Mexico that manufacture the serum and ship it off to countries down south. That's all I know about it at this point," the doctor said.

"Well, if there's any chance you can get some of that juice, grab it for me, will you Doc? I'll be playing in a televised Pro-Am tournament in Scotland in a couple of months. I've got to look dynamite over there. Whatever the cost."

"Don't count on it, Mandy. But how about taking one of those 'restorative vacations' to Rio? You'll come back lifted and can tell everyone you just got a good rest."

"No time for that, Doc. Plus, you're the only one I trust to mess around with this kisser."

"Thanks for your vote of confidence," he said as he held her chin up to assess the total woman. "Overall, I'm pleased with how you're holding up. This face and form still showcase some of my best work yet."

Mandy had been Marvin Feingold's patient since she arrived in Los Angeles. Through the doctor's artistry, her Romanesque profile that was a part of her heritage became ancient history when the surgeon enlarged her chin and shaved down her nose. Her thin lips were plumped up with silicon, and her plump thighs were slimmed down with liposuction. Her size 34B breasts became 36D's. To top off Feingold's work, her Beverly Hills salon changed her hair color from mousy brown hair to golden blonde.

"Now for the fun part," the doctor said as he fixed a small mask over Mandy's nose to give her a hit of nitrous oxide. "Just sit back, relax, and get ready for another sweet dream."

After Mandy's eyes had closed, she heard the voice of a thirteen-year-old girl cut through the chatter of kids at Bayonne Country Club on that summer day so long ago.

"Hey Randi!" Monique Wolfe called out as she and Shelly Greenbrier ran toward the sand trap where Randi and Angie were standing. "Brian said the poor kids had to stay on the other side of the grass! You're gonna get in trouble if he sees *her* here!" she said as she pointed to Angie. "Yeah, you're gonna get in trouble," Shelly said.

"Mind your own business you two," Randi warned the two girls. "Angie's gonna be a great golfer someday, so y'all better be nice to her!"

Mandy awoke to the sound of a flash, as a 400-watt surgical light bulb permeated her closed eyelids.

"Okay, you're doing great," the doctor told her. "The gas is wearing off, so this one's really gonna sting for a moment."

The needle went deep into her face, but Mandy's pain was eased by the thought that those who had snubbed her in the past would be pea green with envy when they watched her play in the Pro-Am. She even fantasized that her old friend Randi King would be sitting in the stands, her blonde hair glistening in the sun as she told her husband that she'd been a friend of Mandy Manville's long ago, when the golfer was still known as Angie.

"Okay, now one last poke in that smile line and you're free to go. Just take a nice deep breath."

"Jesus Christ! You're killing me, Doc!" Mandy cried with words contorted by her twisted mouth.

"Stay still for a few more seconds. Remember, 'no pain, no gain'."

Nine

Saturday, May 12th 2011

"Surprise honey lamb! I wasn't sure what you would thank, so I wanted to see your face when you seen me! We're due in six weeks! It's a boy! Now you can devorce yer wife and marry me! Congrats darlin'! You're going to be a papa!"

Derrick Benson drove up the 101 Freeway North toward Encino while Amber's announcement played out over and over in his head. When he'd walked into her bedroom three nights before, and saw that naked body, hideously deformed by pregnancy, he got the shock of his life. It had never crossed his mind that a woman he'd hooked up with for a little fun could try to saddle him with a child. He'd assumed that sex with Amber would be foolproof, the only cost would be a little cash for meals, and a hundred bucks or so every now and then for her to buy something special. At first, he'd claimed that considering her occupation, the chances were slim that he'd fathered her child. But Amber insisted that the child was his, and said she'd prove it with a DNA test after the baby was born. Terrified by that threat, he'd handed her every cent of his Gambler winnings and feared it would only be the beginning of years of child support payments.

On his way home from Amber's, Derrick phoned the Bellstone front desk and had Newt Sizemore called away from his dinner with the Gamblers. With nowhere else to turn, he hoped that the president would have a suggestion on how to make this nightmare go away. Newt was quick to offer the assistance of Father Norm O'Malley. Though the wine sale had been botched, the president still had confidence in the priest's ability to assist with the personal problems that the club's valued members might encounter.

• • •

It was late afternoon when Derrick parked his car and walked up to the entrance of the All Saints Church of Encino to meet with Father Norm O'Malley. His introduction to the priest on the driving range had been brief, and he had no idea how a man of the cloth would react to a married man who had impregnated a stripper. He was also skeptical that there was anything the priest could do to help him with his problem. When he pulled the massive doors of the church open, he felt his heart pounding, and had nervous perspiration spurting from the pits of his arms.

The cavernous cathedral was empty, save for an organist who was practicing his hymns on the medieval-style organ that had dozens of metal pipes reaching up to the building's elaborate ceiling. Derrick looked up in awe at the stained-glass windows with glorious depictions of Christ, the Virgin Mary, angels, and apostles, that all made him feel very unworthy of their blessings. Following Newt's instructions, he approached one of the confessionals, pushed a curtain open, and took a seat in the booth. A few moments later, he saw the shadow of the entering priest. When the sliding door between man of God and penitent opened with a sharp snap, Derrick felt his stomach churn with apprehension.

"Hey, what's up sharp-shooter? I heard you killed 'em last Wednesday!" the faceless voice exclaimed through the opening. "Three birdies! Wow! Newt told me he was high as a 747 after your match. Said you were bombing your drives three-fifty down the middle! Made a stunning putt on eighteen to take the all the money too!"

"Ahhh . . . thank you, sir, I mean, Father. Yeah . . . I . . . I had a great time with the guys!"

"Please, call me Norm. And I know you're not here to talk golf, son. Newt said you've gotten yourself into some trouble. How old is this girl? Does she live alone? And, more important, is she a Catholic?"

"Amber is twenty-three. She does live alone, and yes, I think she might be Catholic, though we never discussed her faith. When I asked her why she didn't have an abortion while there was still time, she told me that she was afraid of going to hell. I'd assumed any woman with a job like hers would be on the pill. But I guess that was also against her religion."

"Well, the fact that she's a Catholic is wonderful news!" The priest clapped his hands together. "That'll make our job a whole lot easier. I'm going to call in a favor from the Chicago Archdiocese. They have one of the most tightly cloistered nunneries in the country."

"Nu . . . nu . . . nunnery?" Derrick stammered.

"You heard right. Nunnery. Some of the oldest remedies are still the best course of action. But it's crucial that you have no more contact with the girl from this moment on. Got that?"

"Sure. Absolutely," Derrick said as a welcomed feeling of relief helped to relax his mind and body.

"Good. I'll arrange to send in a team to fetch your young lady and drive her out to the nunnery in Chicago where she'll be confined until the baby's born. No drugs, alcohol, or tobacco use allowed, of course. She'll receive the proper nutrition, have the opportunity to exercise, and she'll get plenty of spiritual guidance. The Catholic hospital in the city will provide for her prenatal care, and the delivery of the child. After that, the Church will place the child in a fine home with deserving parents. It'll all be perfectly seamless, my son. You'll be free and clear of the matter. To put it simply, your problem will simply disappear."

"D . . . d . . . disappear? But isn't what you're talking about against the law? Couldn't I go to jail for this?"

"The Church is ruled by its own set of laws. We answer to a much higher authority."

"But why? Why would you and the Church do this for me, Father? You barely know me, and I'm not even a Catholic."

"Two reasons," the priest said. "First, it's not like the Church doesn't benefit from these situations. They have a list of families that are more than happy to make a very substantial donation for a healthy newborn. It's a win-win on both ends. Second, Bellstone takes care of its own. And from what I've been hearing, you have a long road of exceptional comradery ahead of you at our great club."

"Wow . . . that . . . that means the world to me, Father," Derrick said. "I do feel like I've found a home at Bellstone."

"You certainly have. Now . . . have you got a key to this girl's apartment? These interventions, as we call them, usually take place at night when the women are sleeping. So, it's crucial that the rescue team has the ability to let themselves into wherever she lives."

"Yes. I've got one here, Father." Derrick pulled the key Amber had given him on their second date from his pocket and slipped it through the opening in the confessional.

"Great. At some point, the team might opt to give her a shot to relax her before escorting her into the transport vehicle. It's best to have her sedated until she's safely sequestered inside the nunnery. After that, the girl will have no contact with the outside world, save for her doctors at the Catholic hospital."

"I just don't know how Amber could survive being isolated like that. She's a very social—"

"Don't you worry, son. It won't be so bad for the girl. The nuns are all very nice, and she'll meet others in her situation. After the baby is born, she'll be free to return to LA, or she may elect to strip in Chicago. Some of the unwed mothers have even remained at the nunnery and taken their vows. Plus, the food at this particular convent is said to be outstanding."

"Oh, my God!" Derrick shook his head as the enormity of his situation finally hit him. "I don't know . . . I just don't know. Amber— a prisoner? She'll be terrified!"

"Would you consider sharing the news of the pregnancy with your wife, as an alternative? It would most likely challenge your marriage, but she might find it in her heart to forgive. I've even seen cases where the wife welcomes both child and mistress into the fold. Perhaps you could work out a joint custody situation?"

"No, no way," Derrick said, his hands gripping his temples. "Jody can never find out about this!"

"Then put your faith in the church. And allow this unfortunate chapter to someday become a distant memory."

Ten

Sunday, June 5th 2011
One month before the Bellstone Ladies Club
Championship

"Morning young lady! What can I do you for?" Sherrie Pickens, the head waitress of Albuquerque's Route 40 Café asked the young woman who had just taken a seat at the counter of the diner.

"I think I'll have the sausage, pancakes, and grits combo ma'am. And maybe a side of hash browns. Plus, juice and coffee," Danika Lane told the waitress as she studied the décor on the wall of the diner. There were colorful Native American weavings, ceramic plates decorated by the local Pueblos, and black and white photographs of the town in the 1800s. Handmade wooden frames held antique paintings of the tribe's most revered creatures that included bears, mountain lions, and large white birds with trumpet-shaped beaks.

Farther down the otherwise empty counter, a seventy-something-year-old gentleman looked up at Danika from his copy of the Albuquerque Journal. "Well, aren't you a sight for sore eyes, young miss!" the man exclaimed with a smile. "I just love to see a wholesome gal with a hearty appetite. They seem to be a dying breed out here these days, with so many folks into that fitness craze."

"Not me, sir," Danika answered. "Plus, I'm driving all the way to Los Angeles today. Been on the road since yesterday from my home in Little Rock, Arkansas. Slept a few hours roadside in my car. Don't plan on stopping, so this meal'll have ta serve as my lunch and dinner."

"Ya don't have ta bother sharing the nitty gritties of your life with Bucky if ya don't want to hon," the waitress told Danika. "He thinks spendin' the morning at the counter with a paper and cup a coffee gives him platinum customer status at this place. Allows him to flirt with every young gal that walks through the door. Plus, you'll find it a chore to converse with him, 'cause he don't hear so well."

"I heard that Sherry," Bucky replied. "And I'm not flirting with this young one. Ya know dang well I only have eyes fer one girl, and that's you."

"Well, aren't I the lucky one?" Sherrie said as she filled Danika's coffee cup with the steaming brew.

Bucky looked back at Danika. "What do you plan to do with yerself in Tinseltown, if you don't mind my askin'? Y'all want to get into the movies out there?"

"No sir," Danika told Bucky. "Looking to secure employment in my field of recreational vehicle sales. I'll be bunkin' in with my sister for a bit. She makes her livin' as a dancer."

"A dancer? What is she—a ballerina? Or is she on that *Dancing with the Stars* TV show?"

"Not in this lifetime, sir. Amber's an exotic dancer."

"What'd ya say?" Bucky called out with a hand to his ear.

"**An exotic dancer**," Danika repeated.

"Oh . . . you mean she's a stripper!" Bucky called back. "Well, I hope she doesn't try to talk you into falling into that line of work, young lady."

"No way in Halifax will she. First, I'm about fifty pounds too heavy to do those kind'a moves like she does. Though I do plan to get a bicycle and shed some of this weight when I git out to LA. Second, I'm a good Catholic girl. The only man who can see me in the altogether will be my husband. When and if I do ever get married, that is."

"Hah! I love it," Bucky chuckled before taking another sip of his coffee. "The stripper and her God-fearin' virgin sister. Both living under one roof. Would be a good set-up for one of those Hollywood movies!"

●　　●　　●

"Good morning, Mr. and Mrs. Benson! You two must be here for the Sunday game," Bob at the Bellstone front gate said to Derrick and Jody. "They're saying it's gonna be a scorcher! Almost ninety degrees and it's only ten o'clock. Be sure you folks drink plenty of water out there," the guard reminded the couple as he opened the entrance arm to let the silver BMW through.

"Thanks so much, Bob. You stay cool now," Jody called out to the man as they drove past him.

The Sunday couple's game was a long-running tradition at Bellstone. The cost was a ten dollar buy-in, and the pro shop paired up couples to compete in foursomes. After the round, the players would head to the bar to toast the winners.

"Good job setting up today's game, Jo," Derrick told his wife.

"No big deal, hon. I just emailed Rick at the pro shop, and he put us on the list. And, hey! My game is really coming together! I'm hitting the ball a lot straighter. And Jackson's been a huge help with my short shots."

"I can't believe that weird-looking caddy could be much help to anyone. But whatever works for you, Jo. I'm just glad you're getting out on the course. Ups my status here too. I've got a wife who's a stunning golfer and she's beautiful to boot! Who wouldn't be impressed? You're the dream of every guy here!"

"Oh Derrick, don't be silly. People aren't that superficial."

"In LA? You better believe they are!"

"I'm not getting back into golf to impress anyone," Jody said as Derrick pulled the car up to the porte-cochere. "I just want us to have something we can share together. Especially if we can't have a . . . you know."

"Oh please, sweetheart. Not that again. We just went through this," Derrick snapped as the reality of Amber's situation brought him back to reality.

The level of stress in her husband's voice worried Jody. When he turned the engine off she studied his profile. There were dark rings under his eyes, and the muscles of his jaw were twitching. She put her hand on the back of his neck and began to work her fingers through the tight muscles. "What's with you, Der? You haven't been yourself lately. Is there something going on you're not telling me about?"

Derrick put his forehead down on the steering wheel of the car to enjoy Jody's touch. He wished he could confide in his intelligent and sensible wife about the pregnancy. He wished he could tell her that on this very day, sometime after midnight, the priest was having the stripper whisked off to a convent in Chicago. Though Father O'Malley had assured him that the entire plan would be perfectly seamless, Derrick knew that, in the words of the poet, the best laid schemes of mice and men often go awry. And for the first time ever, he wished he didn't have a constant urge to have sex with every attractive woman on the planet.

"You're right, hon," he said as Jody's strong fingers helped to melt away his tension. "I haven't been myself and it's not fair to you. Dad's been breathing down my neck ever since we joined this place. I know the club's going to be a good thing for the firm in the long run, but he's gotta let me settle in and cement some connections. I just hope I can keep my sanity until then."

"Sorry, my love. I didn't mean to heap any more pressure on you by bringing up the baby thing." Jody finished up her massage with a rapid drumming of her fists on his back. "How 'bout if we just try to enjoy our afternoon?"

"Sure, you got it." He checked himself out in the rear-view mirror of the BMW and adjusted his baseball cap and Ray-Bans. "Let's go knock 'em dead out there," he said as he hopped out of the car and handed his keys to Bernardo.

•   •   •

When the Bensons arrived on the first tee, Derrick saw Jackson waiting for them with his and Jody's golf bag slung over his shoulders. He felt uncomfortable with Jody having any association with a caddy who knew about his fling with a stripper. But all discomfort vanished when he saw Mandy Manville sashaying up to the tee with her husband Monty to complete their foursome. Mandy's regular caddy, Armando, trailed behind with the Manville's golf bags on his shoulders.

"What a wondaful surprise ya'll!" Mandy gushed. "I had no idea we'd be playing with our adorable new membas today!" Despite the Los Angeles summertime heat, Mandy looked as cool as an ice cream cone. She wore a hip-hugging white skort, and a light pink polo shirt with the top three buttons opened to reveal a hint of her robust cleavage.

"The pleasure's all ours, Mandy," Derrick said with a grin that reached from ear-to-ear.

"I'd been hoping to have the chance to tee it up with your darlin' little wife again," Mandy told him. "Did you know that we played togetha a while back? She was such a good sport when she ran into trouble. Isn't that right, honey?" she asked Jody with her mouth turned down in a sympathetic pout.

"The truth is, Mandy, I actually enjoyed the chance—" Jody began.

"It's such a frustratin' game. I really felt for you," Mandy interrupted. "But let's just have fun today, and not worry about who wins or loses a couple of dollas, okay y'all?" She punctuated the question by flashing her $30,000 smile, designed by Dr. Marc Pearlstein of Rodeo Drive Cosmetic Dentistry. "And with the championship comin' up, I'm just trying to work on keepin' my focus, 'cause I'll sure need it over in Scotland with those crowds and the television crews coverin' the tournament. Of course, qualifyin' for the Pro-Am depends on how well I play in this yeah's championship, mind you. But enough about my game. Hey, Derrick! Monty says you're the new golden boy with those crazy Gamblahs! That so?"

"It might have just been a lucky day for me, Mandy," Derrick said with a mega-watt smile that Jody hadn't seen before. "I took some of your husband's money. But I'm sure he'll get it back from me this week."

"So, Jody," Monty asked. "How about you? Gonna duke it out with the ladies in this year's club championship? It's quite a big deal around here, as I'm sure you've heard." He turned to Mandy. "When is it, sweetie? I know it's coming up soon. I saw the sign-up sheet with your name on it hanging on the wall in the pro shop."

"July 6th, baby, just round the cornah. But I am in no way ready. And I wouldn't be surprised if Hope took the title this yeah. She's been practicing her little butt off lately, bless her heart."

"You should think about it, babe," Derrick said to his wife.

"I have been," Jody said. "Thanks to Jackson. He's made me an offer I can't refuse. Isn't that right, Jackson? Or should I say that I made *him* an offer?" Jody looked over at the caddy and winked.

"Oh, and what offer is that?" Derrick asked, concerned that his wife and the caddy might be getting too chummy.

"We've negotiated an agreement. He'll strongly consider getting his acting and writing career back on track if I strongly consider getting my golf game back in shape and entering the championship."

"You're thinking about entering the championship?" Mandy asked, taking a step back and cupping her hand to her mouth to express both surprise and delight. "How wondaful! You'll have a ball with the girls! But I must warn you . . ." She lowered her voice as if sharing a coveted secret. "Some of them can be awfully cruel out thah. I wouldn't want your feelings to get hurt the way mine did for the first few years I played."

"Don't you worry about Jody the Tiger," Derrick piped up. "She can give as good as she gets and then some."

"I think you're biased, babe." Jody smiled and tapped a playful fist on her husband's shoulder.

Derrick and Monty climbed the steps to the men's tee box where each hit their first shot. "Your turn ladies! Hit 'em straight!" Derrick called to the two women.

"After you, Ms. Club Champion," Jody said to Mandy, leading the way with her arm.

Mandy took her driver from Armando and walked to the women's tee box. She put her hot pink tee in the ground, placed a hot pink ball bearing the initials "MM" on the tee, and took a slow practice swing. She then hit the ball with a swing that showcased her stunning figure and caught the eye of every male golfer within sight of her. "I'll take it!" Mandy exclaimed as she watched her ball sail 180 yards down the middle of the fairway.

Jody took her driver from Jackson and teed up her ball. Without bothering to take a practice swing, she took her stance and readied the long muscles of her arms and legs for the strike. Under the rim of her baseball cap, her pretty-pink lips formed an expression that was all business as she executed a powerful swing that sent her club and shiny black braid twirling around her shoulders while the ball took off like a bullet. Though it started out straight, it took a sudden turn left and sailed over the trees of the first fairway and into the club parking lot.

"FORE!" Jackson bellowed to warn those in range of the outgoing ball. The caddy stood tall for a few moments to track the ball's path. "No painful cries or car alarms wailing. But it's out of bounds for sure," he said as he tossed a new ball to his player. "Better hit another one."

"Tough break, hon," Derrick said.

"Oh, what a dang shame! You didn't deserve that at all," Mandy said in a voice that exuded tragedy.

"It's okay," Jody shrugged. "I never liked that ball anyway."

Jody's second shot was long and in-play, but after hitting out of bounds, her chances of paring the hole were slim to none.

"I am simply dee-lighted to play with y'all today," Mandy chirped to Jody as the group walked down the first fairway. "Tell me sugah, how are those white trumpet cranes down at the lake doin'? Have they laid their li'l eggs by now?"

"Actually, their eggs are quite large, and yes, they laid them a couple of weeks ago," Jody said, pleased to hear Mandy taking an interest in the club's wildlife.

"That's wondaful news! How many babies will there be? And just when will they come out of their shells, so to speak?"

"Hmmm . . . let's see." Jody pulled out her cell to check her data. "Around two hundred or so chicks should be making their debut thirty days from now, which would be on July 5th."

"Well, what do you know! That's the day before our club championship! Must be a good omen for you, Jody-girl! I do so hope you decide to play in it this year."

"Well, I've heard it can get pretty interesting," Jody said as she walked over to Jackson who was standing by her provisional ball with a six-iron in his hand.

"Looks like 150 yards to the flagstick, Tiger," he said as he gave her a wink and handed her the club.

"Very funny, Jackson." Jody took her stance and hit down on the ball, sending it flying high in the air toward the flag stick.

"Beautiful shot!" the caddy said. "You can make that putt to save bogey."

"Ah! That felt good. I think I'm starting to like this game again," Jody said while she savored the sight of her ball that landed with a thud on the green. "In fact . . ." She gave Jackson a knowing smile before calling out to Mandy. "Okay, Ms. Club Champion, you've twisted my arm! I'll put my name on that sign-up sheet today." She turned back to the caddy. "Does this mean our deal is a go?"

"It's a go!" Jackson said while giving her a thumbs up.

After Mandy hit her ball, she walked up to the green to see Jody's ball sitting just three feet from the pin and wondered why she hadn't kept her mouth shut.

•   •   •

"Hey, baby girl! How's the ride going? You somewheres in Arizona? Be here ya think around seven? I'll be workin' real late, so the key'll be under the doormat. Got a Swansons fer ya in the freezer with fried chicken and corn. Brownie for de-zert. Bed's all ready for ya, so climb right in and get cozy when you're ready. What's that? Yup, I'm still workin' my little pregnant tail off, five nights a week. Gonna stay up on that pole for as long as I kin! The club has no problem with it. Boss says it's good for business 'cause the clients love the big boobs and belly. No, it's safe . . . doctor said so. Anyway, I'm happy as a hog in slop that you're coming to stay with me, Danika honey! Little Derrick's gonna be so lucky to have his auntie around to love him. Now, you drive real careful. We kin catch up in the mornin'. I love ya, sweetheart!"

Amber Lane clicked off her cell with tears in her eyes. Though she knew that her sister was a good driver, she couldn't help but worry that something could go wrong for Danika out on the road. After spending so many years apart, it was almost too good to be true that her only close relative was finally coming to live with her in Los Angeles.

She examined the carpet, the walls, and the counter of the one-bedroom apartment that she'd vacuumed, sprayed, and scrubbed in preparation for Danika's arrival. Offering only three hundred square feet of living space, it would be a tight squeeze for two. But it was larger than the cramped fifth wheel the girls had been raised in, and Amber was a much better housekeeper than the girls' cracked-addicted parents had been. Pleased with her work, the mother-to-be returned her vacuum to the closet and began to sing.

"Hey soul sister I don't want to miss a thing you do, Tonight. Hey-ey, hey-ey-ey-ey ey . . . tonight."

Amber took one last look around, put her key under the mat, and waltzed down the stairs toward the metro stop where she'd catch the bus that would let her off within walking distance of Dancin' Bare.

•   •   •

"If it wasn't for that bogey on the first hole, you'd have shot even par today," Jackson told Jody as he walked off the 18th green with the Bensons. "Not bad considering this was only the second time you've played an actual round of golf in seven years."

With Jody's score of eighty-three, and Mandy's disappointing eighty-eight, the Bensons easily beat the Manvilles, who would now be buying drinks for the winners in the White Trumpet Crane Lounge.

"You played lights out today, Miss Jody!" Mandy said as she and Monty caught up with the other couple after they'd paid Armando for his services. "What-evah kind of energy drink did you have for breakfast this mornin'?" I did wake up with a nasty headache, so I'm afraid I didn't play my usual game. And my putting was simply a dis-asta all day long. But my sweet Armando just showed me what I'd been doin' wrong. Y'all go along now," she insisted as she waved Monty and the Bensons off with her arms. "I'll be thah in a few."

"See you in the bar, honey," Monty said to his wife. He turned to Derrick and Jody. "And I'll see you two in the bar, also." He headed for the men's locker room.

Derrick gave Jody a congratulatory hug. "That's my girl! You got your game back in record time. I'm super-proud of you for taking us to the winner's circle today, hon."

"Don't thank me, babe. Thank Jackson. He's my coach," Jody said as she pointed to the caddy, who still had the couple's bags on his shoulders. "Now you be a witness, Der, and remind him that he has to keep his end of the deal we made if I play in the championship."

"Hon, between my job, my golf game, and my beautiful wife, I have no time to worry about what caddies do or don't do," Derrick said as he handed Jackson a hundred-dollar bill for his services. "You get that, don't you, Jackson?"

Jackson ignored the question and turned to Jody. "Don't worry. I'm keeping my promise to you, Jody. Unlike some folks around here, I don't lie to women." He turned and walked back to the caddy yard.

Jody looked at Derrick. "Why are you so rude to Jackson? He's been nothing but supportive by helping me with my game."

"You wouldn't understand, babe. It's a guy thing."

"Why wouldn't I understand? Try me."

"He got out of line with me a couple of weeks ago during a Gambler's game. Made some accusations."

"What? You're kidding, right? What accusations could he possibly have made? Did he call you a cheater or something?"

Stunned by the question, Derrick stared at his wife. "Now, why would he call me a cheater? Everyone who knows me would never, ever, think I'd cheat on you!"

"That's not what I meant! I was asking if he accused you of cheating at golf!"

Aware that he was stepping into dangerous waters, Derrick rushed to change the subject. "Let's just talk about the fact that my gorgeous wife is once again an amazing golfer. You just beat the Bellstone nine-time Woman Club Champion by a mile! There's no doubt that Mandy will be handing her crown over to you in July."

"I wouldn't count on that, Der," Jody said with a shake of her head. "Mandy's a seasoned competitor. And I don't have a compelling need to be the club champ. But I've been thinking that entering the tournament and playing the course my Grandpa founded would be pretty cool. And maybe . . . just maybe . . ." she looked at Derrick and smiled. "Maybe playing in that championship with the skills he taught me and the integrity he instilled in me would . . . in a way . . . bring a part of him back to me. And I'll admit it . . ." She took his hand in hers and swung it back and forth as they walked. "I am looking forward to taking part in a real competition again."

"I like what I'm hearing, Jo," Derrick said with a smile. "So, get your name up on that sheet before we leave today. Don't want to miss any deadlines."

The couple came upon Tournament Rock on their way to the clubhouse and Jody paused to look at her grandfather's name. She then noticed a pair of white trumpet cranes that were busy pulling insects from the bark of the massive oak tree that towered above the rock.

"Look Derrick!" she pointed to the tree. "The cranes are feeding on gold-spotted oak borers. See those guys that are about a half-inch long each, with gold spots on their back? And the birds seem to be doing a good job of keeping the population of the pests in check. If the insects were out of control, the bark of the tree would have deep cracks, and sap would be leaking out from the inner part of the trunk. Good news, huh?"

"Uh huh. Sure, hon," Derrick answered with a yawn.

"Just to be safe, I think I'll have Brett, the tree guy at the office, inspect the health of all the oaks on the property, same as they're doing at some other golf courses and parks in the area. Probably should get the approval of the club's board to bring Brett in here. Maybe I should set up a meeting with that Newt fellow and the head of the club's Greens Committee that oversees the course. What do you think?"

"I think . . . I think that's a great idea." But Derrick wasn't thinking about gold-spotted oak borers or meetings with any Committees. He had spotted Mandy walking in the distance and was focused on her breasts that merrily bounced along with every step she took. His eyes then settled on the cheeks of her derriere that were perfectly packed into her curve-hugging white skort as she marched through the door to the pro shop.

•   •   •

"Ah! Mrs. Manville!" Rick Lightfoot exclaimed when Mandy walked into the shop. The head pro was sitting on a stool while finessing his resume on the computer behind the counter. With the championship drawing closer, he'd ramped up his pursuit of head-pro positions at Arizona country clubs. "I was hoping you'd stop by! The kilt-style skorts you wanted to wear on the course in Scotland arrived late yesterday." He jumped up to retrieve a garment bag from the wall behind him. "We do have a problem though, as they all look a bit too long," he said as he unzipped the garment bag, removed the skorts, and held them up on their hangers. "But I'm sure Maggie can arrange to have them altered if they fit you otherwise."

"We've got bigger problems than that, Lightfoot," Mandy snarled as she pointed out the window. "That goody two-shoes Jody Benson woman just ate me alive out there. The little nerd acted so polite and nonchalant about beating me when I knew she was savoring every moment. Then she had the fucking nerve to tell me that she plans to play in this year's championship. First of all, she's practically a professional. And this is strictly an amateur event! Second, she's a brand-new member! And I'm sure there's some rule here about players having to log a certain number of rounds before they can compete in the most important tournament of the year."

"She was a college player, not a professional, Mrs. Manville," Rick said as he replaced the garments in the hanging bag. "And the rule about having to log a certain number of rounds doesn't apply to new members. I'm afraid there's just no way for me to stop her from playing."

"Well, you'd better find a way fast! Or Jody Benson will be our 2011 Women's Club Champion. And your plans of landing a cushy job at a club in Arizona will go up in smoke!"

Rick sat back down on the stool, removed his glasses, and tugged at the skin of his forehead to calm another tension headache while Mandy stood at the counter with chest heaving. When her eyes floated over to a mirror on the counter of the shop, she froze in horror. The strain of the past few hours had taken a serious toll on her appearance. Deep lines were etched around her eyes and mouth, her hair hung limp, and her shoulders were hunched in defeat. Horrified at the image, she labored to smooth her skin with her fingers, and pulled a lifting comb from her purse to fluff up her hair. She then carefully reapplied her lipstick, thrust out her chest, and found her brightest smile before she marched out of the shop.

• • •

"She moves her body like a cyclone.
And she makes me want to do it all night long.
Going hard when they turn the spotlights on.
Because she moves her body like a cyclone.
Just like a cyclone."

"C'mon Amber—you're moving more like a light breeze than a cyclone!" the skinny old man at the bar shouted over the strip club's muffled sound system while Amber tried to keep up with the song coming through it. "We're payin' for live—not half dead entertainment at this joint. Plus, I'd ask ya for a lap dance, but ya might crush me!"

"Hey, Mickey, give her a rest from you needlin'," scolded Scats Malone as he looked up from the daily crossword puzzle he'd been working to solve. "How'd you like to shake your booty with a kid packed inside your belly like she's doin'?"

"Thanks, Scats," the stripper called out as she rested against the pole to catch her breath. "I swear to the good lord above me . . . this job ain't gettin' none easier."

After gyrating to the strip club tunes playlist for three hours, Amber Lane was ready for the first break of her shift. It was only four o'clock in the afternoon, but her energy was depleted. She was in her seventh month of pregnancy and was already carrying twenty extra pounds on her petite frame. Plus, the 100-degree heat outside was no match for the club's cheap air conditioning system. She knelt on the chipped linoleum floor of the stage to gather the small pile of dollar bills that her clients had tossed at her, threw a cover-up over her G-string and pasties, and gingerly walked down the few steps to join the smattering of regulars sitting at the bar.

"May I buy you a drink, Amber?" It was that nice Marvin Squirtfeld, who had never missed a "Dancin' Bare Sunday" as long as Amber had been at the club.

"Thanks, Marveen, but I brung my own protein shake like I always do. No alkehol for me with little Derrick growin' inside." Amber patted her swollen belly and bent down from her stool to pull a thermos from her tote bag.

"Hey, Buckets!" she called out to a man hunched over one of the tables behind the bar. "Like I told youz before, put that cigarette out, or I'll have Lou toss you outta here." Buckets McKracken was an emaciated old man with onset emphysema who refused to believe that the Los Angeles smoking regulations applied to strip clubs.

Marvin turned to the stripper. "Amber, you know, I've been thinking . . ." he said as he wound a paper napkin round and round his plump index finger.

"What chu been thinkin' about Marveen?" The stripper took a spray bottle of organic cleanser and disinfected the bar before setting her thermos down on the yellow Formica surface.

"Well, I know I'm not what you might call handsome," said the pudgy and bald accountant with sad beady eyes and only the faintest suggestion of lips to outline his one-inch-wide mouth. "But I do have my own business. Mind you it's small, but it brings in a steady income. And my two-bedroom home in Van Nuys is fully paid for. What I'm trying to say is . . ."

"What yer tryin' to say is what you already said before, Marveen. I 'preciate the offer, but as I told ya, my heart belongs to another." Amber clasped her belly and looked over at the door of the club. A smile crossed her face, as her mind drifted back to that night almost a year ago. The night Derrick walked into Dancin' Bare for the very first time. When she spotted the man with the curly dark hair and that dimple in his chin, the two of them locked eyes and she felt as if she was up on that stage for him and no one else. Her show began with an arms-only climb up and down the pole. She followed that up by performing a pirouette, a Russian split, a shoulder mount, and a stunt known by those in her industry as a "Chinese flag". After taking a moment to catch her breath, she topped her routine off with a cross-leg climb up and down the pole. The crowd went wild, but through the thunder of the applause and cat calls, she saw only Derrick as he came forward and slipped a Benjamin in her G-string. She leapt off the stage to give him a lap dance, and their romance took off from there.

Looking at the lowlifes sitting at the grimy tables around her, Amber felt like a princess now that she was carrying the son of a rich guy in her belly. Derrick drove a flashy car, he always had a pocket full of cash, and his beautiful bad-boy face made her heart skip a beat every time she looked up, or down at him during sex. He was the man she had always dreamed she would marry—her Prince Charming who would whisk her away from her grind of a job and seedy apartment, to carry her over the threshold of a mansion every bit as beautiful as the ones on *Keeping up with the Kardashians* and *The Real Housewives of Beverly Hills.*

Revitalized by a welcomed burst of energy, Amber stood up from her stool and gave Marvin a peck on his bulbous forehead that was glistening with nervous perspiration. "Thanks fer askin' though Marv," she said as she removed her cover-up and made her way back up on the stage.

•   •   •

"I see y'all have already ordered," Mandy chirped as she took her seat at the table to join Monty, Derrick, and Jody in the club's climate controlled White Trumpet Crane Lounge. She looked up at the waiter who was putting drinks on the table. "My usual please, Mario."

"Pink cosmopolitan. Coming right up, Mrs. Manville," the waiter assured her.

"And how might ah little winnahs be feelin'?" Mandy asked. She gave a smile to Derrick as she caught his eyes landing on her breasts that were snuggled in tight against the fabric of her pink polo.

"We're still a bit hot," Jody told her. "Must be ninety-five out there in the sun." She wiped a bead of sweat from her brow and took a long sip of her sparkling water.

Mandy shook her head and made a clucking sound. "I don't know what sent my game into the latrine today. Just bad puttin', I suppose. Plus, this heat just fried my focus. Kept me from shootin' anywhere neah what I usually do."

"We all have good days and bad days, Mandy. That's golf!" Derrick said with a wink.

"Yup. And who was it that said, 'Golf is a good walk spoiled'?" Jody added. "Wasn't that Mark Twain? In spite of all the new equipment, it seems the game hasn't gotten any easier since he played."

"I guess it hasn't," Mandy agreed. "I should just be thankful to have such young and fine-lookin' opponents to play against out thah." She gave Derrick a sly grin, then looked at her husband. "And aren't you lookin' just like a boiled lobst'a, Monty! Did you use that SPF 50 I brought you?" She took Monty's chin in her hand and pointed his face toward the Bensons. "With that fah skin, my red-headed boy has ta be so cah-ful during the summah time!" She tilted her head toward Derrick. "And speakin' of hot, my li'l Ferrari seemed to be ova-heatin' on the way heah this mornin'."

Monty gave his wife a confused look. "That seems strange, hon. Didn't Fillipo just give your car a tune-up last week?"

Mandy shook her head in disbelief of her husband's ineptitude. "If you hadn't insisted on drivin' over here in that borin' old fogie Lexus, you'd a seen what I'm talkin' about."

"For you, Mrs. Manville," Mario said as he set her pink colored cocktail in a tall-stemmed glass on the table.

Mandy gingerly plucked out the slice of lime and took a long sip of the frothy concoction. "Monty's scared a ridin' with me," she told the Bensons as she dabbed at the froth on her lips with a napkin while using utmost care to avoid smudging her lipstick. "Says I missed my callin' as an Indy 500 drivah."

"Well, you've sure got the right rig for the track, Mandy," Derrick said.

Mandy cocked her head. "Hey Derrick. You couldn't be as clueless as my husband is when it comes to automobiles. Is there any chance you'd agree to take that li'l F-car down the hill for a spin to see if you think it's safe for me to drive it back home?"

"Hmmm . . . tough call." He put his finger to his chin. "Well, it'd be quite a sacrifice to fire up a Testarossa. But heck, I'll be a martyr!" Derrick sprung out of his chair and offered his hand to Mandy, who rose from her seat.

"Oh, you darlin' boy! Thank you ev-ah-so! We'll be back in two shakes of a jackrabbit's tail, y'all." Mandy handed her keys to Derrick, and the two of them dashed out of the bar.

Still seated at the table, Monty turned to Jody. "Didn't those two seem a bit anxious to take off in that car?"

Jody rolled her eyes and shook her head. "I sure don't get this fascination folks have with muscle cars. And I hope this test drive doesn't give Derrick any ideas. He's already got a pretty slick ride."

Newt was sitting at the bar nursing his third double Daniels of the day. When he turned toward Jody, she waved at him. "Hello there, Mr. Sizemore!" she called out. "Remember me? I'm Derrick Benson's wife, Jody? We sat at your table at the White Trumpet Crane Spring Fling last month?"

The large man gave her a smile, rose from his bar seat with his drink, walked over to the table, and grabbed Monty's shoulders while looking at Jody. "Well of course! I couldn't forget a pretty face like that. Could I, Monty?" The other man winced at Newt's touch.

"That young buck husband of yours has quite a golf swing," Newt continued. "I hear you do too."

"Thanks! We're really enjoying the course and comradery here," Jody said. "Hey, Mr. Sizemore, I'd like a word with you . . . if you've got some time?"

"I've always got time for our young and attractive members. And please, call me Newt."

"I'll leave you two to discuss your business," Monty said as he stood and headed to the bar.

The president took a seat and leaned toward Jody with hands clasped. "Now, what can I do for you, sweetheart?"

"Well Mr. Size . . . I mean, Newt . . . I'm employed by the California Department of Fish and Wildlife, and I'd like to set up a meeting with you and the members of your Greens Committee, to talk about potential threats to the trees and the wildlife on the golf course."

Newt sat back in his chair. The smile dissolved. "Threats? Just what kind of threats are you talking about?"

"That's what the meeting would be about. To address specific concerns—"

"We don't want or need any 'meetings' with outside entities about how we maintain our golf course," he interrupted. "Especially if 'addressing these concerns' is going to cost us an arm and a leg."

"Please let me finish, Newt. There are a number of issues we need to educate you and the other board members about with regards to the ecosystem on the club's property."

"Just tell me what these 'issues' are right now, darling, if you're so damned concerned."

"Umm, well . . . Newt, sir, they center on the relationship between the oak trees, the white trumpet cranes, and an insect called the gold-spotted oak borer. Ya see––"

"Yes, yes," Newt interrupted her. "Get to the point."

"The oak trees in California are dying by the thousands due to an insect that bores near the interface of the xylem and phloem of the trunks."

"Can you humor me by talking in plain English, please? We don't all have fancy degrees in the sciences from ivy league colleges back east, like yourself."

"Okay, sure, Newt." Jody took a deep breath. "The pests damage the tree's vascular systems that transport water and nutrients from the roots to the leaves." Before she'd finished her sentence, Newt began to wave his index finger in a circular motion as a gesture to wrap up whatever point she was trying to make. "Which eventually kills the trees," Jody continued while the president craned his head toward the bar, looked at his watch, and rolled his eyes in annoyance. "But we're lucky here," Jody said as beads of perspiration dripped from her forehead onto her nose and cheeks. "Because we have a large flock of white trumpet cranes that feast on these insects during the spring and summer months." Sensing that the man was about to get up from his chair and walk off, she began to speak at a faster pace. "Even so, I'd like to get your board's permission to have our tree guy come out to examine the health of the oaks on the property, which are an invaluable part of the ecosystem."

Ignoring her, Newt held up a finger and called out to the bartender. "Hey Mario!"

"Be right with you, sir," Mario answered while he set cocktails down at a nearby table.

Struggling to make her point, Jody spoke even faster. "The oaks are home to various species of birds and other beneficial insects." After taking a quick pause to inhale, she summed up her request at rapid-fire speed. "I'd also like to discuss the club's commitment to protect the white trumpet cranes—that are crucial to protecting the health of the oaks."

"Protect those damn birds from what?" Newt barked as he sat forward in his chair, his face darkening from red to deep purple. The bartender, who had arrived at the table, slowly backed away to the bar as the president continued his tirade. "How about protecting us golfers from those noisy varmints? I damn near missed a putt today with the way those creatures were screaming at me from the sky!"

"They weren't screaming at you . . . Newt," Jody said. "They were sounding their mating calls, just as they've been doing in this very spot for hundreds, maybe thousands of years."

"Well, they've been crapping all over the cars in the parking lot for years too," Newt shouted while banging his fist on the table. "And not one of us has taken a shotgun to them yet, as far as I know. Though I wouldn't blame any of our fed-up members if they did."

Monty, who had been listening from the bar, was appalled by his friend's behavior. "Whoa, easy there, Newt. No need to get angry at the woman."

"I am angry," the president shot back, the veins on his neck visibly throbbing. "We can damn well do what we want to those pests on our own property."

"Actually, you can't," Jody told him. "White trumpet cranes are a federally protected species. It's illegal to interfere with their welfare in any way."

Newt stood up and shook an index finger at Jody. "Wait a doggone minute, young lady! Who do you think you are to just waltz into a club that's been minding its own business for sixty-some-odd years, and start telling us how to run things?"

"I didn't 'just waltz into this club', sir," she said with a half-smile, her eyes twinkling. "My grandfather founded Bellstone, and I've been coming here with my family since I was a baby. And if it wasn't for my grandfather, this entire property would probably be a housing development."

"She's got you there, Newt," Monty said. "Now sit back down, lower your voice, and let her finish what she's trying to tell you."

"Go ahead then," the man said as he sat back down in the seat, folded his arms over his chest, and shook his head in annoyance.

"Thanks, Monty," Jody said before turning to Newt. "The bottom line is that the oaks need a healthy population of cranes to survive, and the birds need our help more than ever before."

"And why would that be?" Newt asked. "They all look too darn healthy to me."

"They need our help because the entire species is being threatened by poachers who sell the newly hatched chicks for use in the black market."

Newt tilted his head and squinted his eyes. "They sell the chicks? To who? Those things are much too small to fry up."

"They're sold to companies in the South American cosmetic industry who use them to make a serum that removes wrinkles. It's kind of like Botox."

"Well, you could slap me silly. Those creatures are good for something." Newt shook his head in amazement. "And what kind of money are they getting for them?"

"That's not the point of this discussion, Mr. . . . . Newt. Again, what I'd like to do is to set up a meeting with your board about these issues."

"Sure, darlin'. Believe me, as president of this club, I share your concern." Newt sat forward in his chair and placed a hand on each knee. "Just tell me how many of those little fellas we might have down at that lake."

"We don't have them yet. The eggs aren't due to hatch until the first week of July. But each pair of birds lays two or three eggs, so the flock should produce about two hundred chicks in total. My team at Fish and Wildlife will be doing whatever is needed to ensure the safety of these chicks in the Southern California area, which includes this property."

"Ya don't say." Newt's anger had dissipated, and he sat back in his chair deep in thought. "And please do excuse me for exhibiting such exuberance during our conversation, my dear. I'm sure you can understand why I get extremely emotional about this very special place we have here. Though I will admit that I've been as guilty as the next fellow about taking our most precious treasures for granted at one time or another." He stood up to leave. "It was nice talking to you, Joanie."

"That's Jody, Mister . . . Newt. And as I said, I'd like to meet with you and some members of your board soon."

"Let me get back to you on that. We'll stay in touch." Newt walked away.

Jody looked at Monty with eyes narrowed and head tilted. "What do you make of that guy? He went from angry, to fascinated, to having no interest in what I had to say—all in less than two minutes."

"I can't make any excuses for Newt, except to say he's got a lot on his plate lately. I'm head of security here, and you've got my permission to do whatever you have to do to protect those birds. And those oaks."

"I appreciate that, Monty. But just so you know, as a federal agent, I'm authorized to enter any public or private lands to protect the wildlife under our jurisdiction. I was only asking for a chance to educate those in charge about the fragile ecosystem here."

"I get where you're coming from." Monty looked at his watch, and then toward the exit of the room. "Guess we have a few minutes before our spouses return. How about I buy you a drink, and you can tell me your secret for hitting the ball so far."

•   •   •

"No sign of any overheating yet, Mandy," Derrick said as driver and passenger buckled up and Derrick revved the Ferrari's powerful engine.

"Well, that *is* a relief. I do *so* appreciate your help on this."

"Trust me, the pleasure is all mine!" Derrick said as he shoved the car into gear. It roared out of the parking lot and down the two-mile-long private road leading to Bellstone's gated entrance. The propulsion of the motion caused Mandy to sit back and thrust her chest forward as the shoulder straps of the belt lifted and separated her bosoms until each partially exposed breast threatened to pop from her Wonderbra.

Catching Derrick's eyes on her chest, Mandy was pleased to see a bulge forming in the crotch of his golf shorts. Steadying herself against the motion of the car, she leaned toward the driver. Then, using fingers sporting long lacquered nails, she worked with skilled precision to open his belt buckle, unzip his fly, and grab what had become a very sizable erection.

"Feels nice," Derrick said with a moan as his penis enlarged in both length and width.

"Tomorra night, Safari Inn," Mandy instructed. "I'll text you the time and room numba. Now let's head back to the bar befoah my engine ovaheats."

•　•　•

While Amber Lane was doing a slow twirl on the pole at Dancin' Bare, her sister Danika fulfilled her longtime dream of coming to Los Angeles. She had been dreaming all year about arriving at Amber's apartment building that she'd imagined would be set on a beautiful street with stately palm trees, ocean views, and movie stars on every corner. But when Danika pulled up at her sister's address on Sepulveda Boulevard, there was no ocean within miles, and the street was lined with row after row of stark boxy buildings that had crumbling stucco exteriors, prison-like bars on the windows, and homeless people camped on the trash-filled sidewalk.

She found a parking spot around the corner from Amber's building and began to unload her 1996 hunter green Honda Civic that was packed with black plastic garbage bags holding all of her worldly possessions. After dragging the bags up the stairs, she let herself into the apartment with the key Amber had hidden under the mat and looked forward to having a nutritious meal and relaxing after her five-day journey. Knowing that her sister wouldn't be home for hours, she ate the microwaved fried chicken and corn that Amber had left for her while she sat at the metal foldout dining table and flipped through the motor home catalogues that she'd brought with her from Little Rock.

It was close to ten p.m. when Danika changed into her sweats and climbed into the bed she would be sharing with her pregnant sister.

She quickly fell asleep with the happy thought that she'd soon be touching her sister's round belly and feeling the kicks of her unborn nephew.

The next thing she remembered was waking to a lit room and her wrists being tied together with a scarf. A man standing over her stuffed a gag in her mouth, jammed a syringe in her arm, and pulled her out of bed while a woman rummaged through Amber's closet. Danika's eyes began to lose focus, and the intruders, who were conversing in Spanish, trundled her down the stairs, and pushed her into the back of a dented black Bonneville sedan along with a duffel bag filled with clothes from the closet. The doors to the car were slammed shut and locked. Still aware of her surroundings, Danika felt for her cell in the pocket of her sweatpants. With her bound hands, she attempted to pound the screen through the fabric of the sweats to alert one of her contacts with a pocket call or text. She lost consciousness as the car took off with a jerk down Sepulveda Boulevard and made its way onto the freeway.

• • •

When Amber walked in the door of her apartment at two thirty a.m., she saw her sister's catalogues on the kitchen table and her dinner dish soaking in the sink. Though exhausted after dancing on the pole for hours, the young mother-to-be was filled with a rush of warm emotion knowing that the one relative she loved was with her, especially now that little Derrick was on the way. She crept into the bedroom and gingerly curled up near the edge of the bed so as not to wake her sister and fell into a deep and peaceful sleep.

• • •

Danika gained consciousness nearly halfway into the thirty-hour drive from Los Angeles to Chicago and heard the Latin sounds of Enrique Iglesias, Don Omar, and Noel Torres blasting through the single speaker of the car's radio. Sometime during the drive, the gag had been removed from her mouth and the ropes had been cut from her wrists.

She was still groggy from the sedation when the car pulled into a rest stop where she was roused and escorted to a bathroom. After relieving herself, she was helped back into the car, and given a meal of milk, fruit, and a hamburger. When the Bonneville pulled back onto the highway, she could hear the woman passenger in the front seat verbally assaulting the man behind the wheel in Spanish. Over and over in accompaniment to the flamenco rhythms, acoustic guitars, and soulful lyrics of the tunes on the radio, Danika heard the woman say, *"No embarazada. Gorda! Gorda! Gorda!"* Having only studied French in school, she was clueless as to what those words might have meant.

Eleven

Monday, June 6th 2011

"Danika? Danika? You here, Sissy?" When Amber woke up at noon on the Monday after her sister's arrival, Danika was nowhere to be found in the small quarters. The stripper opened the apartment window and was met by a rush of the hot and dirty North Hollywood air, along with the roar of traffic on Sepulveda Boulevard. She poked her head out in the street and yelled, "Danika! Danika! Danika!" But her cries were no match for the rush of the never-ending parade of cars, trucks, and motorcycles on the street below.

"Where'd ya go now, little girl?" Amber cried out in disbelief. While growing up in a household with drug addicted parents who provided little or no care for their children, she'd often served as Danika's surrogate mother. Always the more adventurous of the two girls, Danika would sometimes disappear for days from the family's fifth wheel, leaving her older sister sick with worry. Now, Amber couldn't help but be annoyed that Danika would venture out before the two had spent any time together. After she called her sister's cell several times but got no answer, she checked her text messages and saw the letters *zzzwwwoooo* that Danika had sent around one a.m. As Amber's text-speak vocabulary was limited to OMFG (Oh My Fucking God), BJ (Blow Job), and LHU (Let's Hook Up), she had no clue what her sister's message meant, making her feel very much over the hill.

When Amber left for Dancin' Bare on Monday afternoon, she was not all that worried about Danika's whereabouts. But after walking in her door at two-thirty a.m. on Tuesday and discovering that her sister hadn't returned, her annoyance turned to concern. And when she awoke at eight a.m. and still no Danika, she knew that her sister had to be in trouble.

Twelve

Tuesday, June 7th 2011

"Bye Jo! See you tonight! Love you!" Derrick Benson called out to his wife as she drove off to work for an early morning conference call with Senator Diane Feinstein about her global warming project. When he walked back into the kitchen to grab his coffee mug and laptop to take to the office, his cell dinged with a text from Amber. Though the stripper had sent him a flurry of texts throughout the previous weeks, he'd followed Father Norm's advice and immediately deleted them all. But this one caught his eye:

Amber: *My cister Danika came to cee me Sundy but she disapeered and I've caled the police. Pleeze halp me find her!*

An icy chill ran from the back of Derrick's head to the base of his spine as he feared that the sister's disappearance was related to the priest's plan to kidnap Amber. With trembling fingers, he punched in the number that Newt had given him for the priest. After a few rings, Norm's recorded voice came on with the words, "You've reached Reverend Norman O'Malley of All Saints Church. For church-related matters, contact my assistant, Mary at 818-555-1960. For anything golf related, leave me a message and I'll get back to you shortly." Derrick dialed Norm's number five more times in a matter of minutes. With each unanswered call, his panic seemed to double in intensity.

• • •

After nearly a day-and-a-half on the road, Danika began to emerge from her drug-induced haze. The morning sun was heating up the city as the car exited Interstate 80 and began to wind its way into downtown Chicago. It turned onto the city's Lakeside Drive and pulled into the parking lot of a large white building surrounded by manicured gardens. Danika's captors helped her out of the car, guided her up the steps of the building, and knocked on an old wooden door with a brass plaque inscribed with the words "Sisters of Saint Mary". The door slowly opened.

"Welcome my travelers. We've been expecting you," said an elderly woman in a black and white nun's habit. "I'm Sister Agnes. I can take charge of this young woman now. Bless you, children of God for delivering her to us safely."

"*Que tengas un buen día hermana,*" the woman passenger called out to the nun as the couple walked back to the car.

Sister Agnes turned to Danika. "Come, my child. It's nice and cool inside. So much better for you—in your condition." She led the girl into a dimly lit entrance hall where an oversized bible lay open on a table. A framed reproduction of da Vinci's painting, The Last Supper hung on the wall.

"Sister!" a still woozy Danika cried out to the nun. "I haven't been delivered! I was kidnapped! Those people drove me in their car for days! I don't know why I'm here, and I don't feel well. Please help me!"

"We are going to help you, Miss Lane. You're safe here. There's no need to be afraid. You're in God's hands now. All of your sins were washed away when you entered these doors."

"Sins? What sins?" Danika asked. "And how do you know my name?"

"Follow me upstairs. I'll show you to your chamber, where you can rest. Then you'll have a nice healthful meal with a big glass of milk."

Too tired to argue, Danika trudged behind the nun up a wide staircase to the second floor where she entered a room with an iron bed and a table that held several metal devices laid out on a white cloth. A crucifix hung on the wall over the bed. The sounds of cars, buses, and sirens from the street and sidewalks below rose through an open window. A large fan hung down from the ceiling and rotated in a furtive effort to ward off the brutal heat of the Chicago summer. Danika lay down, relieved to be on a bed after being curled up in the backseat of a car for what seemed like an eternity—and fell into a deep sleep.

•   •   •

"Beautiful drive, Father! Way to start the round!" The priest and actor Joe Pesci had teed off at seven a.m. to stay ahead of the Tuesday ladies group that would soon take over the course. Though Pesci was a betting man, he, like most of the good golfers, especially the Catholic ones, were afraid to take money from a priest. Plus, as few of the other Bellstone members were able to beat Father O'Malley, the stakes of any games played with him were usually limited to bragging rights for the winner.

"What's new in your world, Father? Put out any major fires lately?" Pesci asked as the two men rode together in a cart up the fairway of the first hole.

"One of our newer members was in a fine mess last week," the priest said. "But I was blessed to get things under control for the poor fellow." The priest looked over at the diminutive actor who always seemed to have a different statuesque blonde waiting for him at Eddie's booth at the close of each round. "Now tell me what's new with you, Joseph."

"Got a new Scorsese film shooting week after next on the Paramount lot with Stallone and Nicholson. Just wanna get my putting in shape before filming. The three of us are playing in the Pebble Beach Pro-Am during a break in the shoot. We'll have some big bets going on the side during that one."

"Well, as we've all learned . . . drive for show, putt for dough," the priest reminded the actor.

•   •   •

After sending a frantic text to Derrick, Amber searched up and down the streets near her apartment building for Danika's car. When she found her sister's hunter green Honda Civic with its Arkansas license plates in a parking spot on a nearby side street with two tickets tucked under the wipers on the windshield, she immediately put in a call to the Van Nuys Police Department. The cop on desk duty assured her that an officer would be by that afternoon to investigate her report of a missing person.

•　•　•

"Hello child," Sister Agnes said as she gently shook Danika by the shoulders to awaken her after the girl had slept for less than an hour. Two other nuns stood by the bed. One of them wore a white lab coat and had a surgical headlight affixed to her brow.

"Who . . . who are they?" the drowsy girl asked the nun.

"This is Sister Mary Grace," the nun said as she pointed to the woman in the lab coat. "And this is Sister Inez. Sister Mary Grace will give you a gentle examination. Please don't tense up, Miss Lane. You must trust in us, and in the Lord. No one will harm you or the babe."

"I don't want to be examined. And what do you mean by, 'the babe'? There's no babe," Danika pleaded in a voice still weak from the heavy doses of sedation. She tried to sit up, but Sister Agnes pushed her back down and kept a strong hold on her shoulders while Sister Mary Grace snapped on surgical gloves and locked metal gynecological stirrups into place at the foot of the bed. Then, in one move, she pulled Danika's sweatpants away from her sizable belly, slid them down her legs, and tossed them onto a chair.

"WHAT ARE YOU DOING? LEAVE ME ALONE!" Danika cried while Sister Inez forced the girl's feet into the stirrups and Sister Mary Grace began her probe.

"HELP! NO! PLEASE NOOOOOOO! NOOOOOOOO!" Danika yelled at the top of her lungs.

"You must relax, Miss Lane!" Sister Agnes told the girl.

"Did the priest say when the child is due?" Sister Mary Grace asked over the racket.

"In several weeks is what he told Mother Kathleen," Sister Agnes called out.

"PLEASE STOP! WHY ARE YOU DOING THIS?" Danika screamed as she twisted her pelvis to curtail the probing.

The old nun bent toward the girl's ear. "The Bible says that fornication without the sanctity of marriage is a sin. Your child deserves to be saved by a union that abides by the rules of the Lord."

"FORNICATION? WHAT FORNICATION? WHAT THE FUCK ARE YOU TALKING ABOUT LADY?" the furious girl shrieked at the woman.

Sister Mary Grace stood up and peeled off her gloves. "I'll go no further. This girl is not with child. She's just fat. What's more . . . she's a virgin!"

"Oh, my dear Lord," Sister Agnes cried out as she looked through the window toward the heavens.

•　•　•

After finishing eighteen holes with a more-than-respectable score of 78, Father Norm walked back to his car to check his messages before sitting down to his favorite lunch of Crab Louie in the Men's Grill. He planned to sneak in another eighteen that afternoon with his golfing buddy Justin Timberlake, and then pop over to the church for an hour or so before heading back to the club for dinner with Newt and a couple of guys on the Bellstone board.

When he picked up his cell, he saw six missed calls from Derrick Benson, and five missed calls from Sisters of Saint Mary. A screen full of missed calls was the last thing that he wanted to see right before lunch. He took a moment to skim through the messages that Derrick and Sister Agnes had left, and realized that a monumental mix-up had somehow occurred. After alerting the Grill that the chef should hold off on the preparation of his meal for a good ten minutes, Father Norm called Chicago.

•　•　•

With the discovery that Danika was not pregnant, the confused nuns scooted out of the bedroom and slammed the door behind them. Danika arose and tried to open the door, but finding it locked, she returned to the bed. Still partially sedated, she fell back asleep. An hour later, she awoke to the sound of a cell phone ringing in the hall and heard Sister Agnes conversing with someone she addressed as Father Norm. The call continued with a lot of whispering from the nun, interspersed with several "oh dears" and "oh Lordys" before she bid the caller goodbye. Within the hour, Sister Agnes and Sister Inez returned to the bedroom, helped Danika out of the bed, picked up her duffel bag, and escorted her out of the convent and onto the curb of Lakeside Drive. Standing on the curb, Danika soon heard the familiar refrains from the Latino radio station and saw the black Bonneville sedan pull into the parking lot of the convent. The same driver and passenger that had brought her there that morning got out of the car and directed Danika into the back seat of the vehicle. In a matter of minutes, the three of them were speeding down Interstate 80, heading west.

"Where are you taking me now?" Danika asked her captors. "I want to go back to my sister's home in LA."

"Si, Los Angeles. No bambino," the woman said with a satisfied smile, as she made the motion of rocking a baby in her arms.

"Now I get it," Danika told the woman. "You thought I was my sister! And so did those nuns! *But why?* And *what* would they want with my pregnant sister?"

The woman passenger turned toward the back seat and shrugged. *"No entiendo."*

Danika fished her cell phone out of her pocket and saw that it had lost its charge. During this second, seemingly interminable ride, she had no sedation, no escorts to the rest room, and her hamburgers were accompanied by coke instead of milk. Once again, the woman passenger delivered a torrential tirade in Spanish to the male driver and repeated the same refrain of *"No esta embarazada. Esta gorda! Esta gorda! Esta gorda!"*

Thirteen

Wednesday, June 8ᵗʰ 2011

At seven o'clock on Wednesday evening, more than a day after she called the always-overwhelmed North Hollywood Police Department to report that her sister had gone missing, Amber heard a knock on her door. She opened it, mindful as always to keep the chain of the lock in place.

"Lieutenant Rocco Valentine of the North Hollywood Police, here to investigate the report of a missing person," the cop said as he passed his badge through the partially opened door. "I'm looking for a Miss Amber Lane."

Amber removed the chain and stepped into the outside hallway of the building.

"Please officer, you must halp me! My sister, Danika came to stay with me last Sunday from Arkansas. I know she was here while I was at work because her suitcase and thangs are in my apartment. And her car is parked around the corner with a bundle of tickets. But she wasn't here when I got home early Monday mornin'. And she hasn't shown up since! I never got to see her. Not even once!"

"Ok, first some questions, Miss Lane. Please state your place of employment."

"I'm an exotic dancer at Dancin' Bare, just up the way on Sepulveda, sir. I couldn't even go into work today, being as I am so distraught."

Valentine nodded. "Ah, Dancin' Bare. Been there on some calls. Quite the playground for some real shady characters."

"It pays the bills, sir." She patted her belly. "More important than ever now with my li'l guy comin'."

The cop nodded. "And I need the name and address of your closest relative. Other than your sister, of course."

"Hmmm . . . that would have to be my baby's daddy—a Mr. Derrick Benson. I don't have his address, but he tells me he's a member of Bellstone. Did you hear of it? That golfing club over thar in Tarzana?"

"I sure have, ma'am. Another playground for some real shady characters. That Benson fella doesn't seem like he'll be much of a daddy if he allows his baby's mama to work in that strip club."

"That's all gonna change real soon, officer. When he devorces his wife and marries me."

"Oh yeah. Sure, he will, miss. Just as soon as Angelina Jolie divorces Brad Pitt for me."

"Holy macaroni, officer! You know Angelina?"

"No, just funning with you. Now, could you give me a description of your sister?"

"She's got red hair, and near ta five-foot-eight inches tall. She must weigh in at about one hundred eighty pounds." While Danika spoke, the officer looked down at the street below to see the black Bonneville sedan stop at the curb. When the door opened, Latino music poured out, and a heavy-set young woman carrying a black duffel bag stepped from the car. "And by one eighty, I'm being most gen-rous, sir. She's prob-ly more closer to two hundred. My sister is fat, which is really too bad cause she's got such a perty face!" While Amber unleashed a fury of sobs, Valentine kept his eyes on the other woman, who was now climbing the stairs to the apartment.

"Does she have blue eyes?" Valentine asked. "A splattering of freckles across the nose?"

"Why, yes she does," Amber said. "How'd ya know that, officer?"

"I believe she's right behind you." Amber spun around and saw her sister.

"Danika!" she cried out. "Dear God, girl! Where in sweet Jesus were ya?"

"It was awful, Amber! They took me right from your bed and drove me in a car for days! After some poking and prodding of my insides, they put me back in the same car and took me all the way back here!"

"Who took you, Miss Lane? And where to?" Valentine asked.

"To Chicago. I think it was a convent. Two Hispanic people—mentioned Guatemala. There were nuns . . . a Sister Agnes, a Sister Mary Grace, and another one. They thought I was having a baby. I heard Sister Agnes on the phone to someone. I think she called him Father Norm."

Fourteen

Friday, June 9th 2011

"Mr. Fuentes will be with you in a moment, Mr. Sizemore. Please take a seat in the lobby." Newt had arrived at the 35th floor of Century City's Fuentes Tower for a meeting with Emilio Fuentes of Fuentes Pan American Cosmetics. "You can go in now," the receptionist advised. "Please follow me, sir."

"With pleasure darlin'!" Newt trailed after the raven-haired beauty in the shiny black latex dress that hugged her tiny waist before it stretched out to accommodate her huge buttocks that seemed to float behind her down the hallway. She stopped at a spacious corner office with glass walls and motioned for Newt to enter.

"Buenos dias, Senor Sizemore," Emilio Fuentes said as he rose from his desk to shake Newt's hand.

"Howdy Emilio! I can call you Emilio, can't I? By the way, partner, the views in this place are hog wild!" Newt's eyes remained fixed on the backside of the receptionist as she walked back down the hallway, cocking his head to follow her as she turned a corner. "And what ya see through the windows aren't bad either!" He strolled closer to the glass walls of the corner office. One side of the building towered over the legendary Los Angeles Country Club. The aerial view of the golf course was so clear that the Texan was able to spot a familiar-looking swing that belonged to a player teeing off on a hole that ran along a lake. "Hey . . . looks like that prick Shorty Columbo down there." Newt cupped his hands to his mouth. "Knock it in the water, you asshole!" The Bellstone president turned to the other side of the wall that gave him a sweeping picture of the Pacific Ocean stretching all the way to Catalina Island.

"Just like sitting in a Boeing 787 Dreamliner," he said. "First class, of course." Newt cupped his hands to his mouth again. "This is your captain speaking. We are now cruising at an altitude of twenty thousand feet over the Pacific Ocean. Cocktails will be served in the main cabin."

Emilio Fuentes folded his arms over his chest and shook his head. "I'm on a very tight schedule today, Mr. Sizemore. What's the point of this meeting?"

Newt took a seat on the sleek white Hermes sofa that stretched the length of the office wall. "Sure, Emilio. Just trying to start a fruitful relationship off on a light note. But I'll get right to it. I've heard rumors that you're one of the largest suppliers in the Southern hemisphere of those drugs being lapped up by the cosmetic surgery industry. My sources are saying that you send in Botox and other pricey potions to those palaces in Rio de Janeiro, San Paulo, and other hot spots in Brazil that offer a fountain of youth to anyone who's got the do-rae-me to pay for it."

"That's right, Mr. Sizemore. Now how may I help you?"

"Well, Emilio . . . I have quite a bit of inventory you'll find very interesting that's sitting right on my property. And I'm offering it to you first. For the right price, of course."

•   •   •

"I got a feeling, that tonight's gonna be a good night. That tonight's gonna be a good good night. Ooooo hoooo."

The sounds of the Black Eyed Peas pulsated through the BMW640i's surround system and the Bavarian Autosport tires squealed with fury as Derrick twisted the car down the spiral ramp of the parking garage next to his office building in downtown Los Angeles. At five forty-five p.m. on a Friday that had been filled with stress thanks to his dad's ambitious new plan to up the firm's sales, he was ready to blow off some steam by meeting up with Mandy.

"I know we'll have a ball if we get down and just lose it all."

Derrick's life had become a complicated juggling act as he tried to meet the demands of his job, spend quality time with Jody, and establish himself as a regular with the Gamblers by playing golf and hanging out in the Bellstone bar for hours each week. Plus, the Amber brouhaha had nearly pushed his sanity over the edge. He was relieved to hear that after the convent plan went bust, Father Norm had come up with a simpler resolution to the problem. The priest assured him that he would arrange for some deacons from the church to pay Amber a visit when the child was born and offer her a hefty settlement to give the baby up to a loving couple.

"Let's paint the town, we'll shut it down. Let's burn the roof, and then we'll do it again," Fergie and her bandmates demanded as Derrick drove north on the 101 Freeway to his rendezvous. Drumming his fingers to the beat of the music on his top-of-the-line perforated leather steering wheel cover, he called Jody on the car's Bluetooth system.

"Hey babe! How's my girl doing?"

"Fine sweetheart! Even better now that I'm talking to my adorable husband."

"That's what I like to hear."

"Hey, Der! Went to the farmer's market during lunch and got some fresh pasta, local veggies, and killer-sharp cheeses for ya. Gonna whip up a fabulous new recipe I found online for dinner."

"Oh babe, bad news," Derrick said in his saddest voice. "I meant to tell you this morning. Dad wants me to meet some high roller dude at that Coach House restaurant in Burbank in a bit. Had me studying up on the guy's company all afternoon. I'll try to keep it to drinks, but I may get sucked into dinner. You cool with that?"

"Well . . . I guess I have to be. I'll save you a portion, just in case."

"You're the best, Jo!"

"Oh, and Derrick! I got some rocking-cool news today! I'll tell you about it later!"

"Great hon! Love you! And Jo?"

"Yeah?"

"Ya know, I'm really looking forward to watching you blow the other women away in that club championship."

"No guarantees there, Der. Though I am getting kind of psyched about getting the old competitive juices flowing again. But what really has me excited is that I'll be seeing my handsome husband later tonight! Have a good meeting!"

The call ended and the satellite radio kicked in, only now with the melancholy words of Rihanna.

"Just gonna stand there and hear my cry? That's all right because I love the way you lie. Love the way you lie."

Without the Black Eyed Peas to keep him pumped, Derrick felt a bit guilty about lying to his sweet, pretty, and accomplished wife. But when his cell dinged and a text from Mandy popped up on the screen, his guilt was erased by the surge of blood that flowed into his loins.

Mandy: *The Naughty Nurse has you on the schedule for 6 pm sharp 2nite/Safari Inn/ room 221*

"Oh, Miss Mandy, you are a trip and a half," he said out loud, shaking his head at the phone. It occurred to Derrick that Mandy was at least ten years older than Amber and several years older than Jody for that matter. But there was something exciting to him about the idea of having sex with an older woman. The rush hour freeway was bumper to bumper, but he enjoyed his time on the road by trying to visualize what Mandy looked like under those skin-tight golf clothes.

After exiting the 101 West at Barham Boulevard, he drove up Olive Avenue past the NBC Studios where Jay Leno taped "The Tonight Show". He realized how lucky little ole Burbank was to first have Johnny Carson, and then Jay, who added color to the town by filming comedy bits at local gas stations, residences, and Universal City Walk, where he shot his famous "Jaywalking" shtick.

Derrick's thoughts returned to his still-swollen genitals, as he pulled into the Safari Inn, and parked beneath the motel's 1960s-style sign comprised of a giant yellow surfboard. He ran up the outdoor stairs and followed the numbers on the doors down the walkway until he reached 221. The door was ajar. He peeked through the crack like a kid stealing a glance at a pile of gifts on Christmas morning.

• • •

Jody threw the tomatoes, onions, garlic, and red peppers from the farmer's market into the food processor to make her pasta sauce. Moray mushrooms were sautéing in the frying pan with chopped parsley and olive oil. Pecorino, Burrata, and Provolone cheeses were chopped and ready to be tossed into the bowl of fresh *al dente* pasta noodles. She wondered what time Derrick would come home from his client meeting and hoped it wouldn't be late. Her period had finally ended, and she was looking forward to a romantic dinner for two, followed by some glorious lovemaking.

•   •   •

Though the partially open door, Derrick spied Mandy waiting for him in a tiny nurse's costume comprised of a G-string with a medical symbol, a push-up bra, a white cap, and white high heel sandals.

"Do come in little Derrick," she cooed through the opening. When he entered the room, she looked up and down his body and shook her head. "Oh, me-o-my! You're a very, very dirty boy tonight, aren't you? Tsk, tsk, tsk . . . whateva have you been up to? We can't let you be examined by the Dirty Doctor lookin' like that! Step over to me heah and we'll get you out of those play clothes and into a nice warm tub for a cleansin'."

"Yes ma'am," Derrick said as he stepped toward Mandy with his heart beating a million miles per hour.

She pulled his polo shirt over his head, unbuckled his belt, and unzipped his fly. "Now you take off these filthy trousers," she instructed. He stepped out of his khaki pants and she guided him into a waiting bubble bath where she proceeded to wash him with a sponge, giving extra attention to his private parts by meticulously lathering up his penile shaft and scrotum with a soap made from the oils of peppermint and Ginkgo biloba. When she was satisfied with her work, she helped him out of the tub, patted him dry with a towel, and escorted him to the bed.

"You can wait here, young man. The doctah will be with you momentarily." She went into the bathroom and shut the door. Minutes later, the "Dirty Doctor" appeared. She was holding a clipboard with a pencil and clad only in an unbuttoned lab coat with a stethoscope hanging between her breasts.

"Good evenin' Mr. Benson. I have you down for a complete physical tonight, which will require me to examine every orifice of your body. It may cause some discomfort, but I trust you'll also enjoy some moments of pleasure. So please lay back and make yourself comfortable," she said as she pushed him down on the bed.

"I'm all yours, Doc!" Derrick said as he opened her lab coat and looked up to see if the real things were as magnificent as he'd fantasized. One glance confirmed that his imagination didn't begin to do them justice.

"I'll be followin' up my examination with a stress test. It's all standard medical practice, mind you. And quite safe," Mandy assured him as she walked over to dim the lights in the room.

"Help yourself, Doc. I'm always up for as much stress as a woman like you can provide."

•   •   •

When Derrick hadn't come home or called by nine, Jody served herself a bowl of her steaming pasta concoction, poured herself a glass of organic pinot noir, and sat down at her computer. She logged into one of her favorite research websites run by scientists at a university in Ontario that focused on the latest advances in conservation efforts throughout the world. After scanning down the recent posts, she clicked on an article about a revolutionary new development from a Canadian company called Band Technology that promised to yield a breakthrough in the tracking of migratory birds.

•   •   •

Derrick lay on the motel bed in a state of exhaustion after undergoing an extensive physical exam that included a series of tests to determine how many times he was able to ejaculate in an hour. The doctor stood over him writing notes on her clipboard.

"That was incredible!" he said while he fought to catch his breath. "I think I'm in love!"

"Shush now, sir!" Mandy scolded. "I don't want the doctor-patient relationship to exceed its appropriate limits."

"Oh, you *are* a hoot lady. I've gotta see you again next week. How does Monday work for you? Or how about Monday, Tuesday and Wednesday?"

"There's no need for any follow-up, sir. Your respiration, heart rate, and oxygen levels are all excellent. Howeva, I'll recommend that you get a second opinion from Hedda, the Head Professional on anotha night. She often touches areas that I tend to miss."

"Don't think you missed a thing, but she's welcome to give it a shot."

Only then did Mandy break character. "But you must first promise to do me one tiny favah, my love."

"You name it baby! I'm your slave."

"Aw, honey lamb! I just knew I could count on you to help me!" She tossed the clipboard on the floor and bent down to give him a hug, her breasts pressed into his chest. "I've had so much on my plate these past few months with preparin' to go to Scotland and all, that my golf game is just not up to pah—no pun intended. It's just my bad luck that I'm fah too busy to get it in shape for this yeah's club championship."

"But it seems like I see you playing golf and taking lessons at the club almost every day."

"That doesn't help me one itty bitty bit. I just have too much on my mind to focus on playing my best. And you know as well as anyone, that golf is mostly mental. Don't you, my sweet li'l puppy dog?"

"Sure, I do," he said as he pointed to his crotch. "And I want you to save some of that focus on keeping little Derrick here hard and happy."

She leaned over and kissed his flaccid penis. "That's why I need you to make sure yaw wife doesn't play in the championship this yeah. 'Cause there is a possibility, with the way I'm so distracted, that she could win and I would lose my invitation to play in the Scottish Pro-Am. And that would just be a da-zas-tah for the other club members, mind you, many of whom have already booked their flights and accommodations to Scotland to watch me play. So, can you please have her take her name off that sign-up sheet in the pro shop, sugah? If you say 'yes' right now, you'll get a special preview of your date with Hedda the Head Professional." She took his now throbbing penis in her hands to ready him for another blow job.

134

"Yes! Yes! Yes! I promise to make sure she doesn't play, Doctor, or Hedda, or whoever you are," he said as his words turned to moans of pleasure.

•   •   •

When Derrick hadn't come home by ten thirty, Jody changed into her red silk nightie from Victoria's Secret and climbed into bed. She flicked on her reading light and opened the book *It Takes a Village to Raise a Child*, by Hillary Clinton. Before she got through the first page, she heard Derrick's car pull into the driveway.

"Here's my gorgeous man," she said as he neared the bedroom.

"Hi, honey. I'm so sorry for missing what I'm sure was a delicious dinner."

"Love means never having to say you're sorry, Der. You know that."

"That's an easy one. Ali MacGraw to Ryan O'Neal in *Love Story*, right?" Derrick asked as he hobbled toward his wife with his penis smarting from Mandy's exuberant nibbling.

"You got it. Hey, you're limping babe. That trick knee acting up again?"

"Seems to be. I did a lot of running around today," he said as he sat on the bed beside her.

"My poor, hard-working husband. But I'm sure that meeting will be worth it in the long-run."

"Maybe. But it was *bor-ing!* I had some bad steak with this strictly blue-collar dude who talked on and on about his factory in Burbank that makes some type of widgets for airplane engines. He wanted to know what kind of coverage he needs in case a plane goes down." He picked up Jody's hand and kissed it. "All I could think about was my beautiful wife waiting at home for me."

"Well, now you're here. And, hey . . . here's my big news! I was going to tell you while you were driving, but thought it was better for you to focus on your meeting."

"You're always thinking of me, Jo."

"I'll get my payback in a few," she said with a wink. "Anyhow, Senator Feinstein has invited me to Washington this October to address her subcommittee in person! She selected my report over those of all the other regional directors in the state! I'll be hanging with the big boys at Fish and Wildlife National Headquarters for a whole week!"

"Oh wow—that's wonderful! I'm so proud of my amazing wife. You'll take D.C. by storm!"

"Yeah, it's pretty darn cool. But for now, I can't wait to ravage this guy in front of me with that sexy Cary Grant dimple in his chin." Jody pulled back the blanket on the bed to reveal the lacy nightie that hugged the curves of her body. "Come to mama bear, papa."

"Oh honey, that's sweet, but I'm totally beat!" He covered his mouth and feigned a yawn. "Can I get a raincheck for tomorrow night, when I can devote every ounce of my energy to the woman I love?" He took some locks of the long dark hair that had fallen across her brow and placed them behind her shoulders.

"Well, I guess so." She gave him a mischievous smile. "But you'd better bring your A-game, mister! I'm a woman with needs, you know."

Derrick took a moment to clear his throat. "Hey, speaking of A-games, Jo, there's something I need you to do for me."

"Anything for you, Der. What is it?"

"Would it be too much to ask you to take your name off of that club championship sign-up sheet?"

"Wha?" she asked, stunned by his question. "Take my name *off*? *The sign-up sheet?* You told me to me put it *on!* You're kidding, *aren't you?"*

"No, honey, I'm not kidding. I'm serious."

"But when you called from the car . . . just a few hours ago . . . you said you couldn't wait to watch me blow the other women away!"

He took another lock of her hair and curled it with his fingers. "I know Jo, but things have changed. You can play in it next year. Trust me—it's better to sit this one out."

"What are you talking about? You've been practically begging me to get my golf game back since before we joined Bellstone. This makes absolutely no sense."

"It does, and I'll tell you why." He lowered his head, inhaled deeply, then looked up at her with a somber expression. "Newt called me in the car about it tonight, babe."

"Newt? You're listening to that buffoon? You do know he's a buffoon, don't you Derrick?"

"He may well be, hon, but he *is* a potential client. He mentioned that some of the members would resent you beating Mandy Manville and ruining her chances of playing in that Scottish Pro-Am we've been hearing about. It seems a bunch of them have booked non-refundable tickets to fly to Edinburgh and cheer her on at St Andrews. Plus, he thinks it'll be great PR for Bellstone to have a lady member as a contender at a pro event like that."

Derrick gently released the curl he'd crafted. "Sorry sweetheart. It just wouldn't be a good move for you politically to play this year."

"Wait, Derrick . . . aren't you the same guy who told me I should just work on getting my game back, and stay out of club politics?"

"Guilty as charged!" He put his hands in the air for emphasis. "But we're new members, sweetheart. I don't want us to raise any eyebrows or cause any controversy."

"Raise eyebrows? Cause controversy? What's going on here, Derrick?" Jody sat up on the bed and backed away from him. "And why are you bringing this up now, at ten thirty at night? Something weird is going on, I can feel it."

"Nothing's going on, honey. I promise you." He took her arm and gently stroked it. "I'm under a lot of pressure while I'm trying to impress my Dad by having a banner sales year. And getting some business through the club is a big part of that. So, just tell me you'll think about bowing out. That's all I'm asking."

"All right, then. I'll give it some thought." She slid back down on the bed.

"Thanks, Jo. I love you so much." He took her in his arms, kissed her lips, and made a supreme effort to generate his fifth erection of the evening.

Fifteen

Wednesday, June 29ᵗʰ 2011
Eight days before the Bellstone Ladies Club
Championship

"Get ready for a preview of how your new bottle transport system operates." Hank Beaumont, the head contractor for Famous Cellars was demonstrating how the machinery in the new wine cellar would display and deliver the club's extensive wine collection to their members and guests. With the project's completion date just two weeks away, the officers of the Bellstone Board were watching a test of the system on the last Wednesday in June.

The construction of the mammoth new wine cellar, which was eating up nearly half of the square footage of the bar and the White Trumpet Crane Lounge, had been a major topic of conversation among the club members. The two-story structure would consist of motorized shelves that would keep thousands of bottles in rotation from the basement to the first floor and back again. This elaborate carousel was capable of both vertical and horizontal movement to take the bottles on a constant tour of the cellar's circumference while the traveling vintages would be displayed through the thirty-foot glass window in the dining room of the clubhouse.

"Each bottle is coded in the computer with a number and letter," Hank explained to the group as they watched the dozen or so demo bottles move through the soon-to-be-stocked cellar. "When the vintage is chosen from the wine list though an app on their phone, the designated bottle is showcased with a red light to enable the diner to watch his selection as it travels to the retrieval window in the dining room."

Many of the club's members were shocked that the board had approved such a costly project, especially one that required drastic alterations to the historic clubhouse building. Those with a more intricate knowledge of the club's shaky finances wondered how many thousands of dollars a month it would cost to run the cooling system and the motors that moved the shelves. Plus, several members who were involved in the construction business were skeptical that a project of such scope could really be completed for the $250,000 that Newt Sizemore claimed it was costing.

In his column for the club's June newsletter, Newt stated that, "the new cellar will make Bellstone the most sought after golf club in Los Angeles, and attract the upscale element desired to insure the long-term fiscal soundness of the club". But as word leaked out that a brass plaque would be fixed at the cellar door with the words, "Dedicated to 2011 President Newt Sizemore", many members began to dismiss the structure as another vanity project of a president determined to leave his mark on Bellstone.

While the members of the board were watching the demonstration, Food and Beverage Chairwoman Diane Sharp steered the president into a corner. "Okay, Sizemore," she began. "I still don't know how you and your cronies managed to weasel this monstrosity through here. I sure as hell had no say in the matter."

The six-foot three man looked down at the woman with his beefy lips twisted into a satisfied smile. "Those of us who attended the January meeting voted unanimously for the project, while you sat on a beach in Maui, Diane. It's all spelled out in the minutes."

"Maybe so, but I'm not standing by while you winos help yourselves to the rest of the priceless bottles in the old cellar. Per approval by last year's board, Wine Auctions West is coming in here during the second week of July to do an inventory and an appraisal of the entire collection. We also intend to revamp the pricing on all of the wine before you and your friends consume every drop."

"Guess your legal practice is slow these days if you're spending hours on this busywork. But go for it, Diane!" he said as he barged past her.

•   •   •

"Okay men, we're nearing the home stretch, and the cellar's looking awesome," Newt told Monty and Bradley when they met him in the boardroom after the tour. "And hey, guys, I'm willing to admit that I have to take some of the blame for our shaky financial situation here."

"Shaky?" Monty asked, his face darkening with rage. "We're 300 grand in the hole! Some of the blame? It was *you* who made us approve the new cellar. *You*, who went way over budget. *You* who acted on Shorty's bogus tip. *You* who cooked up that disastrous fake wine cellar robbery! Goddamn it, Newt, you deserve all of the blame for this mess!"

"Hey, settle down there, Red. I never said our year on the board would be easy. We're in this together . . . three men in a rowboat. Not the first time we've navigated some rough waters. And you can bet it won't be the last."

"So, what's your plan, big guy?" Bradley asked him.

"I need a bailout, fellas. And to show my commitment to what we're doing here, I'll double whatever you guys can help me out with."

"Well, I'm sure not happy about that, Newt," Bradley said. "But I'm willing to scrape together seventy-five grand to kick in and call it a day. That's the best I can do with the market still in the shitster."

"Alright, alright, ya got me," Monty said with his hands in the air. "If I sell what's left of my stocks and empty out my savings, I can pony up the same." He turned to Newt. "But you've got to come up with the other one hundred fifty. If not, we've got to come clean about our mistakes to the rest of the board and take our punishment—whatever it may be."

"I'll make it right. No worries," Newt insisted.

"No more using the member's fund to place bets?" Monty asked him. "No more underhanded sales of club property?"

"*Transparency* will be my new mantra. You have my word."

"And what about this Fong dude?" Bradley asked. "When and how does he get his two hundred thou back for the wine that was never delivered?"

"I'm on that too, fellas. Consider it a done deal," the President assured the two men.

•   •   •

"What the fuck? Are you out of your fucking mind?" Mandy asked Monty, while he was preparing her favorite meal of veal scaloppine with mushroom Marsala sauce. "Do you think I'd miss out on the chance of a lifetime because you and your idiot partners screwed up? It's not my fault you let that fat piece of shit talk you into building that stupid wine cellar. Now *we're* expected to pay for it out of our own pockets? And you're telling me I can't go to Scotland?"

"C'mon hon," Monty pleaded with his wife as he sautéed the mushrooms, Marsala, capers, mustard, salt, and pepper before adding the veal he'd fried to the mixture. "We're both at fault here for overspending. How about all your plastic work? The Ferrari? And golf lessons up the ying yang? My club bill quadrupled after we got married. Between airfares, hotels, and meals, that trip would cost us at least ten grand. We've lost big in the market, and now we've gotta help bail Newt out. Sorry about Scotland, sweetheart, but we've gotta start living within our means."

"I didn't marry you to live within means," Mandy snapped. "And I'm going to Scotland if you have to beg, borrow, or steal to send me. So, figure it out, asshole."

Monty sat at the kitchen counter in his red bib apron with his face in his hands as his wife stormed into the garage and slammed the door behind her. Before he could follow her out to calm her down, he heard the explosive engine of the Ferrari fire up and roar down the street of their usually tranquil Encino neighborhood.

Within seconds, Mandy was racing down Ventura Boulevard where she put the pedal to the metal and gunned the ferocious machine onto the 101 Freeway. "Why didn't I dump that pasty-faced loser years ago?" she screamed over the roar of the engine. As the car gained speed on the freeway, she thought about all of the sacrifices she'd made for the past ten years to retain her championship title. The lessons, the hours of practice, the tournaments, the dedication to the sport. Nearly blinded by tears, she wondered how, just when she was so close she could taste it, Monty could dare to suggest that she turn her back on the glory she'd fought so hard to attain.

She checked her Tiffany watch and saw that she was late for her meeting with Jorge at the Wheeler Garden. The two of them often met there after the bag boy finished his shift around seven p.m. when the course was clear of golfers. She'd been thinking about putting a stop to her dates with him anyway. But with her frustrated state, she'd wait for another day to give him the boot. He was a beautiful, twenty-one-year-old, well-endowed kid, who, unlike her husband, always seemed to have a hard-as-a-rock hard-on. Plus, he was a master at giving her the confidence she needed to believe she was at the top of her game. As she exited the freeway to make her way up Winnetka Boulevard toward the club, it occurred to Mandy that the Mexican immigrant might also be useful in another arena.

Sixteen

Thursday, June 30th 2011
Seven days before the Bellstone Ladies Club Championship

"Hey, I didn't know my girl was playing golf today! No work for you, hon?" Derrick was surprised to see Jody walk into the kitchen on a Thursday morning dressed in a blue polo shirt, white Capri pants, and golf shoes.

"I've decided to take the morning off and play eighteen. Just going out solo," Jody said as she grabbed a banana and dropped it into the blender. "Things are gonna get crazy next week with my D.C. trip coming up, so I figured I'd play some hooky and work on my swing." She opened the door to the pantry and took out a bag of multi-grain bread. "I'll be at the office by two."

"Sounds great!" Derrick walked over and took his wife in his arms. "Hey, before I take off, can we talk about my request from the other night? Have you thought about . . . ya know . . . about taking your name off that sign-up sheet?"

"No, not yet. I'll think about that tomorrow."

"I know that one! Vivien Leigh in *Gone with the Wind*."

"Yup, one of my favorites," Jody said as she put two slices of bread in the toaster.

"Well hit 'em straight then, Scarlett O'Hara. See you tonight. Love you!" Derrick gave his wife a kiss and walked out the door.

●   ●   ●

When Jody arrived at Bellstone, she saw Jackson getting out of his car in the far corner of the parking lot that was designated for caddies and other employees of the club. In contrast to the pristine rows of Italian sports cars, Mercedes, Range Rovers, Jaguars, and Porsches that lined the member/guest parking area nearest the clubhouse, the far corner of the lot was packed with rusty and dented rides with chugging engines that could be heard from the first to the last tee box on the golf course. They rumbled, roared, and filled the air with exhaust when the drivers pulled into the lot or fired them up on the way out. Jackson's brand-new Audi wagon looked totally out of place among the rows of beat-up sedans, worn-out Japanese compacts, and other weary jalopies.

Dressed in a green golf shirt, tan pants, and golf shoes, Jackson was pulling his golf bag from the back of the car when Jody rolled up. She called out to him through her open window.

"Hey Jackson, what's happening?"

"Hi, Jody! Teeing it up as a guest today."

"That's great! Who're you playing with?"

"Remember I told you I have a friend who's a member here? He's Trevor Studley, the actor. Says he's got some time between films this week and called me for a game." Jackson threw his bag over his shoulder. "Hey, why don't you join us? The Stud is a great guy to play with. Easy on the eyes too, the girls say."

"Trevor Studley?" asked Jody, her eyes wide. "*People Magazine's* 'Sexiest Man Alive'?"

"The very same one. But try not to tease him about it. He's tired of all the ribbing we've been giving him on that."

"Not a word," Jody promised. "But how could he have time to play any golf with all the millions of girls he's got chasing him?"

"He's a golf nut! If he had to choose between being a movie star or a golfer, I swear he'd take golf any day."

"Do I have time to run home to do my hair and make-up? *Just kidding!* Sure, I'd love to join you guys, if you don't think he'd mind."

"Nah. See you on the first tee in ten."

•　　•　　•

"A woman?" Trevor Studley asked with disbelief when the two men were on the 1st tee box. The actor put his ball down and drove it 250 yards down the fairway. He turned back to Jackson. "You sure we want to play with a woman, Jack-o?"

Trevor Studley was considered the hottest film star of 2011. Evoking a young George Clooney, the actor stood six foot two inches tall, had jet black hair, a chiseled chin, and a winning smile.

"This is no ordinary woman, pal. Trust me," Jackson said as he smashed his own drive 300 yards down the fairway. "And here she is now. Jody Benson, meet Trevor Studley."

"How d'ya do, Trevor?" Jody asked with hand extended. "Sure you don't mind if I join you, fellas?"

"Not . . . at . . . all," Trevor said as he grasped her hand and held it for a moment. He took in the sight of her pink lips, pearl white teeth, and dark lashes framing emerald-green eyes.

"Ok then! Guess I'm up!" Jody teed up her ball on the men's tee box. The slender but shapely woman made her usual full shoulder turn and hit the ball with a force that sent it flying down the fairway—— farther than Trevor's but stopping short of Jackson's drive.

"*Wow! Jeez!* I've never seen a woman hit a ball like that!" Trevor said.

"Oh, I bet you say that to all the girls you play with," Jody told him while she gave Jackson a wink. "You guys go ahead. I'm gonna hang back for a sec and send a quick text to the office."

As the two men walked up the fairway, Trevor made a confession to his friend. "I think I'm in love, bro."

"Great news, my man! Who's the lucky girl?"

"She is." Trevor pointed back at Jody. "She's exquisite! And what a swing! What's her story anyway? She seems too down-to-earth to be living in La La Land."

"She's a scientist. A bird doc, to be exact. Works for the government. Tracking migratory birds, among other things. Just did a report for a Senate subcommittee on global warming."

"Oh my God! She's brilliant, she's beautiful, she hits the ball a mile, and she's not a neurotic actress! What more could I want in a woman?"

"Sorry, Studley, she's taken," Jackson told his friend. "Guess her wedding ring was hidden under the golf glove."

"Should-a known. That's one lucky guy."

"No, actually . . . that's one real asshole."

Jody jogged up the fairway to join the two men. "Sorry guys! No more texting. Promise! By-the-way, what's today's game?"

"How about best ball? A dollar a hole?" Jackson suggested. "We don't want to stress Mr. Studley's wallet. He only starred in three major films so far this year. Poor guy."

"Maybe fifty cents a hole would make him more comfortable?" Jody asked.

"Enough you two . . . just hit your balls," Trevor said.

Jody flew a shot high in the air with her nine iron. "Get in the hole," she called out to the ball. It stopped on a dime, just two feet from the pin. "Or just close works too."

It was Jackson's turn to hit. He missed the green and walked off to look for his ball in some heavy rough.

Trevor turned to Jody. "I assume you're aware that our friend over there who's lugging golf bags for a living is one of the most talented guys in Hollywood. It's no secret in the biz that he saved Marty Stadler's last picture with his ghostwriting. We're all waiting for him to get back in the game. And to lose that ridiculous beard and mane of hair."

"Yes, your pal is quite the curiosity around here, Trevor. Let's hope he gets back on the horse sooner rather than later. *Whoa!* Great shot there, Jackson!" Jody called out as the caddy hit a stunning low screamer from under a tree. The ball rolled up to the green and snuggled right next to her ball.

"Ah, togetherness. Isn't that sweet," Trevor said. "So, Jackson tells me you're a bird biologist, huh Jody? You're a big muck-ety-muck at Fish and Wildlife?"

"Yup. I spend my time in the trenches fighting illegal developers, poachers, and other enemies of migratory birds."

"Well, you certainly don't look any the worse for the wear." He peered at her face and checked her out from the front and behind. "No battle scars that I can see. I think you're one of the prettiest ladies I've ever laid eyes on . . . if you don't mind me telling you."

"Hmmm . . . mind? Me . . . mind? *Not hardly*. And coming from a guy in your line of work, I'd say that's pretty darn flattering!"

• • •

"Hi, babe! Sorry I'm late! You must be starved," Jody told Derrick when she came home from the office at eight o'clock that evening.

"Nope, I'm fine, hon. Dinner's in the oven." How are you? How was your golf today?"

"It was fantastic! And you won't believe who Jackson and I played with!"

"Jackson? He's a *caddy!* Members don't play with *caddies!*"

"He wasn't a caddy today. He was a guest of *People Magazine's* 'Sexiest Man Alive' Trevor Studley! They're old friends!"

"What? A major film star and that burnout caddy are friends?"

"Yup. And don't call Jackson a burnout. That's not nice."

"Okay, okay. So, you and the guy who's not a burnout caddy played with Trevor Studley."

"We did. And guess what Trevor told me? Jody looked in the hallway's large mirror. She turned her face and form every which way to see what the actor was talking about. "Hmmm . . . not bad."

"What's not bad?"

"Trevor told me that he thinks I'm one of the prettiest ladies he's ever laid eyes on! How's that for a compliment? Think about all the hotties that fellow must get his hands on! Huh babe?"

"Wow! I mean, *WOW!"* Derrick said, taking Jody in his arms. "The Sexiest Man Alive" thinks my wife is one of the prettiest ladies alive! Now *that's* impressive!"

Seventeen

Friday, June 31ˢᵗ 2011
Six days before the Bellstone Ladies Club Championship

"C'mon, C'mon! Move it assholes! C'mon, C'mon! I'm already late!" Mandy was sitting in her car at ten o'clock in the morning on the last Friday in June, trying to make her way from the San Fernando Valley to Beverly Hills in the summer traffic that was getting worse with each passing day as tourists streamed into the already clogged West Side of Los Angeles. For the second time that month, she was on her way to see Dr. Feingold.

"Back so soon Mandy?" the doctor asked when he saw her in the waiting room. "Come on in, and let's chat." He led her into his private office where the walls were covered with autographed photos of smiling patients with beautifully rounded breasts and masterfully lifted faces with perfect chins, eyes, and noses.

"Doc," Mandy said with a voice shaking in frustration. "Every time I look in the mirror, I see the thousands of dollars I've poured into this face going down the drain. These wrinkles just keep getting deeper. I need a magic potion to make me look twenty-five again before the Scottish Pro-Am. I'm going to be on worldwide television! Those high-def cameras are unforgiving. I'm sure you've seen how awful those girls on *60 Minutes* look."

"First of all, those 'girls' on *60 Minutes* are mostly in their 60's and 70's. And second, yes, I have seen them. They're all my patients, and I think they look darn good for their age if I do say so myself. Especially when you consider that they work their tails off traveling around the world to do those stories each week."

"Enough about them. What I'm saying is I need a miracle. And I do have some thoughts about how to make that miracle happen. With your help, of course."

"If you're talking about getting your hands on some of that serum from baby white trumpet cranes that I'd mentioned, I did email a colleague of mine in Rio de Janeiro about it. The guy said he's seeing amazing results on lines and furrows that were previously resistant to Botox. He even referred to the stuff as a fountain of youth. Said he'd email me some before and after photos of patients he's used it on. From what he explained, the newly hatched chicks are harvested and smuggled to processing labs in Tijuana that extract the amino acids from the beaks of the birds. Seems that the acids are what give their trumpet shaped beaks the amazing elasticity to grow so large in such a short time. The labs then create the serum from the acids and ship it out to the suppliers. The harvesting and lab work is all done underground here and in Tijuana, but the Brazilian government is nowhere near as regulated as the U.S. is when it comes to contraband goods. So once the serum gets to Rio, it's sold on the open market. He gave me the name of his supplier but said that the guy has been out of the stuff for a while now, 'cause the birds are scarce and very valuable. Too bad! I'd really love to get a batch for my other clients. A few are quite high profile."

"Okay so hear me out, Doc. I pulled some info on the stuff up on Google last night." She slid her finger down the screen of her phone. "Here, listen to this . . .'Due to the $1,000 price that the chicks of these majestic creatures can yield for their use in the cosmetic industry, the birds are becoming a hot target for poachers'. You email that supplier," Mandy instructed. "Tell him if he can set up a deal with a lab that'll pay me top dollar for them, I have a fellow who can round up a couple hundred of those birds. That supplier also has to send some of that serum our way."

"Are you sure you can pull something like that off, Mandy? I can't have my good name tainted by any funny business. Ya know that, don't you? But I'm probably free to import the stuff from Rio. I haven't heard of any bans on it yet."

"I can get those birds down to Mexico if your distributor can take it from there. Just need the help of one knucklehead, and I'll be good to go."

• • •

"Mornin', boss!" Rob Trotter said to Jody as she walked into his office the day after her game with Jackson and Trevor Studley. "Hope you enjoyed your time on the links yesterday. Got any big fish stories to share? A hole-in-one, maybe?"

"Got a better story than that, Rob. I played with . . . maybe the hottest guy on the planet, Trevor Studley."

"Oh wow! Not a word to my wife about that. Kate's been trying to get me to take up golf and join your club. If she heard Studley's a member, she'd force me go into the private sector so we could afford a place like that."

"Don't worry Rob. My lips are sealed."

"Cool. Anyway, I called that Band Tech company in Canada yesterday that you read about on-line. They sent us a Fed Ex with a sample of their new tracking device. It just came in. You have time to take a look at it?"

"Of course!"

Rob opened a small box. Using tweezers, he lifted out a tiny plastic band. "Ta-dah! The latest development in avian satellite tracking technology! It's small enough for a finch, or birds that weigh less than an ounce. The manufacturers say the flexible loops will fit the legs of the trumpet crane chicks, and they'll stretch as the birds grow with no impact on flight performance. They're waterproof, shock resistant and weigh just half of a gram. And the best part is that they're only thirty bucks each. The models we've been using on the adult birds cost $3,000 and weigh three ounces. That's progress for ya! We can lift the chicks right out of the nests to band them. No messing around with tranquilizing darts, so we can wire up a lot more birds for a lot less money."

"Thanks for following up on this, Rob! You're a rock star!"

"Don't thank me. You found them. I thought our first step would be to try the hardware out on the cranes in that little lake at your country club when those eggs hatch. We can wire up a bunch of the chicks and let the satellite sit on them for a few days. A protected environment like that will allow us to work out any possible kinks with this new technology before be we take it on the road."

"Sounds like a plan. Order a couple dozen of those little gizmos to start." Jody's phone dinged with a text message. "Hmmm, seems I've got a visitor in the lobby. Anyway, get set to beam them up, Scotty! Get it . . . Scotty? Do ya know who said that?"

"Captain Kirk on *Star Trek*."

"That was an easy one!" Jody called out as she walked down the hallway to meet her visitor.

•　　•　　•

When Jody entered the lobby, she was puzzled to see the Bellstone head pro Rick Lightfoot seated on a sofa. Instead of wearing his usual golf attire, he appeared ill at ease in a dark blue suit, a green dress shirt, and a brown tie. He stood up to shake her hand.

"Good day, Mrs. Benson."

"Hello, Rick! Please sit down. So, whatever brings you out here?" she asked as she joined him on the sofa.

"I'm terribly sorry to bother you at work and all, Mrs. Benson," he began as he pulled off his eyeglasses, bowed his head, and pinched the skin on his forehead together with his fingers. "But I have a rather unconventional favor to ask, and I didn't want to bother you about it at the club."

"So . . . you're . . . disturbing me at work with it, instead?"

"I am, and I'm sorry." Rick pulled his phone from his pocket. "But maybe some pictures of my family would help to explain my situation." He thumbed through his photos and held the phone up for Jody to see one. "Here I am with my wife, Millie, and our boys, Teddy and Chuckie. Both are at the community college here in Glendale."

"Oh, they all look so . . . nice," Jody said as she looked at a portrait taken at Kmart of the smiling family in dress clothes against a backdrop of the Matterhorn. "You must be very proud of them."

"I sure am. And you may have heard that Millie and I have our hearts set on relocating to Arizona. We're ready for less stress, less traffic, less expense. And now that the boys are out of the house, we feel it's time."

"Good for you, Rick. But . . . why does this involve me?"

"It involves you because I've been Mrs. Manville's golf instructor since she took the game up twelve years ago. And for her to win this year's Club Championship and get to play in that Pro-Am in Scotland would really help my chances of securing a head pro position at a top-notch country club in Arizona."

"Oh no, not *you, too!*" I've already been told that I could piss off some members by playing in the championship. Now, I could keep you and Millie from changing your lives. C'mon . . . it's just a little tournament for Pete's sake!"

"It is for you, Mrs. Benson, but not for Mrs. Manville. And if you play anything like you did last Sunday, she won't stand a chance. So please—"

"Let me take a wild guess . . . you want me to take my name off that sign-up sheet. Am I right?"

"I know it's a lot to ask. But it would mean so much to Millie and me. And you'll win plenty of titles, Mrs. Benson. You're a great golfer."

"Okay, okay, *uncle!* I can't fight the lot of you. And I've got more important things to worry about right now. So, go ahead and erase my name from the sheet."

"Thank you, Mrs. Benson." Rick extended a hand that was sticky with nervous perspiration. "And please feel free to stop by the pro shop soon. I'd be happy to give you a complimentary lesson."

"Not much point to that now, is there?"

• • •

"How's it goin' Mr. Armstrong? Appreciate ya takin' the time ta see me today!"

"My pleasure, Lieutenant. I thought we'd chat in my office."

Mike Armstrong greeted Rocco Valentine in the front lobby of the Bellstone clubhouse. The cop was there to update the manager on his continuing investigation of the wine cellar robbery and shooting. When the two men reached Mike's office, Valentine helped himself to a seat on the sofa.

"So, tell me lieutenant, have you got any leads in this crime?" the manager asked.

"As I told ya, Mike . . . I can call you Mike, can't I?" Valentine put his feet up on the coffee table next to the sofa. "We sent the remnants of the thirty-six wine bottles and labels that we were able to peel off the pavement to a wine auction house for analysis. Now, hold onto your seat, Mike. Turns out that because of the year and appellation of the vintages, and the current state of the fine wine market, the stolen bottles would have fetched well over $250,000 on the auction block."

"Holy cow! What was in those bottles, anyway? Gold dust?"

"That's what I said." Valentine nodded his head in agreement. "I mean, I love wine, red or white, but $7.99 for a bottle is my limit."

"Think I'll just stick with beer," Mike said.

"We know this job wasn't the work of an illegal tryin' to make some fast cash," the cop continued. "It was planned from the get-go by someone who had access to those wines, had the alarm code, and knew their way around the cellar. And let me tell ya straight out, Mr. Manager. I've been in this racket longer than I'd like to admit, so I've got a pretty good nose for who's clean and who's dirty. You look like a Jersey guy ta me. Would Parsippany be a good guess?"

"Close . . . Hackensack. Born in Newark, though."

"Ah! We got some guys on the force from Newark. This cements my hunch that you're on the level, Mike. And the kitchen guys I talked to earlier know nothin' 'bout this. They all seem like good amigos."

"They are. Every one of them," the manager agreed.

"But that Texas-born president with the hangdog expression." Valentine shook his head. "He was hidin' somethin' all right that morning of the theft. And how about the verbal spankin' he was giving to that Father O'Malley out in the parking lot? That priest doesn't keep his Courtesy Membership by baptizin' member's babies in the club's swimming pool, now does he, Mike?"

"I really don't get too involved in the relationship between our Courtesy Members and those on the board of this club. They seem to have their own system in place. I'm just a hired hand here. Have always made my living by serving the more entitled folks of our beautiful city."

"Yeah, it's a kingdom that caters to the rich, for sure. Kind'a reminds me of Pompeii, LA does. At some point, it's all gonna blow. Then it's every man for himself, rich or poor."

"Well, hopefully the volcano won't erupt until my pension kicks in," Mike said.

"I'm with ya on that one." The lieutenant stood up. "Thanks for your time, Mike. I'd like ta talk ta some others at this paradise, includin' a Ms. Diane Sharp. She'd left me a message about a big hunk a money that was wired into the club treasury from a Li Fong in Hong Kong. Just might'a been enough to pay for that stolen wine. But first, I'll see if I can get some inspiration from the good Father O'Malley. He around here today?"

"Oh yeah, he's here all right. Today and every day. He usually finishes his morning round at about twelve thirty. Comes in for lunch and heads out for his second eighteen by two. But fat chance of getting any info from him that Mr. Sizemore hasn't given to you already."

"Just wanna get a read on the guy, is all. Thanks for your help, pal."

• • •

It was a few minutes past noon when Valentine took a seat on a bench near the clubhouse to wait for the priest. The cop had an expansive view of the 18th hole, a par four, where he spotted two men in the distance readying to tee off. One had the distinctive penguin shape that Valentine remembered from the parking lot. It was the priest, wearing a striped polo shirt with a clerical collar. His smooth as silk golf swing sent the ball speeding down the center of the fairway. The second player stepped up and hit what also looked to be a solid drive, though it lacked the distance of the priest's ball. As the twosome got closer, Valentine recognized the other man as the actor Chandler Dane, one of the stars of the hit TV medical drama, "Intensive Care". After the players hit onto the green, Chandler two-putted for a bogey. The priest walked around the hole to assess the break of the green. He took his stance and made several practice strokes, rocking only his shoulders back and forth, while keeping his head and the rest of his body perfectly still. He then rolled the ball into the hole for a birdie. The two men shook hands and Chandler drove off in the cart toward the parking lot as the priest headed for the clubhouse. Valentine stood up to greet him as he approached.

"Nice birdie, Father. How'd ya shoot today?"

"It was a good morning for me," the priest said with a serene smile. "Four birdies, two bogies. Shot two under. Are you a golfer, Lieutenant?"

"You know who I am?"

"You're Rocco Valentine, the LAPD's best detective. But are you a golfer?"

"Grew up playin' back East. Now I play the publics as often as I can. Try to go off-hours to avoid the crowds and get the twilight rate."

"Do you compete?"

"The LAPD has a couple of fundraising tournaments each year. Fun stuff, ya know. Nothin' serious."

"And I'll bet you win them. Don't you, detective?"

"Got a few trophies."

"So, you must share my belief that golf is the greatest game of all. A gift from God, as I like to say."

"Yeah, well, the places I play aren't as heavenly as this track."

"You'll have to join me for a round here at Bellstone sometime. As my guest, of course."

"Thanks, Father. That's very tempting."

"Now, what can I do for you, Lieutenant?"

"I'm lookin' into that wine theft and shooting. You must'a heard plenty about it."

"Naturally. Not much happens at the club that I don't hear about."

"Yeah, I figured. I understand you've got one of those Courtesy Memberships. You must help the top brass out a lot for a sweet privilege like that."

"I lend a hand when they need help."

"Sounds like they do need help. And plenty of it. It's no secret around here this fancy wine cellar that's under construction is goin' way over budget. Makes one wonder if someone on the hot seat tried to sell some of the club's pricey wine off to pay for the overages."

"You've been reading too many detective novels, Lieutenant. Bellstone is one of the richest clubs in the country. I'm sure there's plenty of money to fund the project."

"Maybe so, Father. But this kid who carried the wine out of the cellar . . . the one who got shot . . . he's an illegal from Guatemala. And he just vanished into thin air after recovering from his wounds. I've heard your Church has a program to shelter Guatemalan illegals. A bit of a coincidence, don't you think?"

"No I don't, detective. Our families are all good Christians. None of them would jeopardize their chance of gaining citizenship by committing a crime."

"That so? It just happens that I'm investigatin' another case involving Guatemalans who take things that don't belong to them. Only this time they kidnapped a young woman right out of her sister's bedroom while she was sleeping. Imagine how scared that poor girl was! Ya know what else is too close for comfort? That crime may be tied to another member of this club. Small world, isn't it, Father?"

"Yes, it's small, though it's anything but simple, Lieutenant. I'd like to commend you on your excellent police work. I'm comforted knowing that my local tax dollars are being spent on hardworking public servants like yourself with such creative imaginations."

"And the powers-that-be at this fine club must be comforted to have a man such as yourself, who's able to move heaven and earth to solve their most pressing problems."

"I think you're giving me more credit than I deserve."

"In any case, I'm sure our paths will cross again." Valentine extended his hand to the priest. "I hope you have another great round this afternoon, Father."

"God willing, Lieutenant. Though I find it a challenge to maintain focus when I play with Larry David on Wednesdays. He whines like a little girl about every shot he hits, good or bad. But I suppose I should give thanks if that's my worst problem in life."

Valentine walked back to his car to make a few calls before questioning the kitchen staff. He also planned to take another look around the club's existing wine cellar before his meet with Diane Sharp. He no sooner got to his car before his phone buzzed and he saw the name of his supervisor on his screen.

"Hey, Keith, what's up?"

"Yo Rocky! How've you been buddy? We've got to make some time to tee it up again soon. You hit the links lately?"

"Just hacking it up at the publics. Playing okay though, shot two under at Balboa in Encino last week. How can I help you, Captain?"

"Listen, Rocco. I need you to back off from that Father Norm over there at Bellstone."

"Back off? The guy's a walking felony! And he's acting like he's got the power of the Almighty behind him."

"That's 'cause he does. The order came straight from the DA, who got the request from the Archbishop himself."

"What the fuck? I just walked away from him, not five minutes ago! What does he have on those big shots to get me yanked so fast?"

"Don't wanna know and either do you. Word on the beat is the guy had some dirt on the Boston Archdiocese that landed him a plum gig out here where he can hit the links year-round. Must have a garage packed with negatives showing those big shots doing some very ungodly acts."

"He's got that kind of power and he's using it so he can play golf twice a day? Doesn't make sense."

"Whatever floats his boat. Just give the guy his space."

• • •

After leaving Dr. Feingold's office, Mandy Manville was winding her Ferrari up Coldwater Canyon Boulevard through the Santa Monica Mountains on her way to Bellstone for a one o'clock golf lesson with Rick. She was still on edge, as she hadn't heard back from Derrick about whether he'd been able to get his wife to pull out of the club championship.

"What I do for this sport," Mandy said to herself while she gingerly touched her jaw that still ached from the half dozen blow jobs she'd given him. Now she could only hope that the guy would make good on his promise that he'd convince Jody not to play. Though he was adorable to look at, he annoyed her by the way he followed her around like a love-sick puppy dog. When her phone buzzed and she saw Derrick's name on the screen, her stomach fluttered with anxiety.

"I hope you have good news for me," she said.

"Let's just say that my date with Hedda the Head Professional is a go."

"Yippee! You're awesome!"

"I'd like to take all the credit, but your golf coach ran a guilt trip on Jody that must have sealed the deal. Anyway, she seems okay with sitting out this year. So, text me the day, time, and place, and I'll be there. Ciao babe."

"I'll be in touch," Mandy said with a satisfied smile as she clicked off the call. She had no intention of going through that rigmarole with Derrick again as she'd gotten what she needed from him. "I'm gonna win! I'm gonna win! I'm gonna win!" she cried out as she slammed the Ferrari into fifth gear and thundered up the private road leading to the Bellstone parking lot. "Now, I just need to sweet talk one asshole, and it's next stop Saint Andrews!"

When she downshifted the car into the parking lot, she caught sight of Newt walking toward his white Cadillac. It was parked, as always, in the spot with the sign "Reserved for Club President". She shifted into a higher gear, roared up in his direction, and hit the brakes just inches from the man. Startled, he jumped backward to avoid being hit. The electric window on the car slid down.

"Hey Newt, I've got a proposition for you!" Mandy said, not realizing that it was nearly impossible for him to hear anything she was saying over the roar of her idling engine.

"Would ya shut that contraption down?" the president barked, holding his hands against his ears. Mandy turned off the engine, got out of the car, and walked over to him.

"Howdy Newt darlin'! I'm as happy as a bee on a bluebell that I've run into you!"

"You almost did, lady! I've had enough of you and that damn car around here!"

"Oh shush, big guy," she cooed. "Monty told me all about what's goin' on with your wine cellar debacle. So you and I need to cozy up and have a heartfelt talk about our little money problem heah."

"And why would I want to talk about that or anything else with you?"

"Because, I have a plan that can bail y'all out of this mess and finance my trip to Scotland. Which, as I don't have to remind you, is to the benefit of this heah club."

The president cocked his head. "Whatever might you be jabbering about, my dear?"

"It just so happens that those birds in the lake down thah are sittin' on some valuable assets. And when those assets hatch, they'll be worth a whole lot more than chicken feed. Now, I've had a convasation with our bag boy, Jorge. He and a cousin of his are willin' and able to remove the little ones from their nests and delivah them to a place in Mexico that will pay top dollah for them. But we'll need your help to make sure those fellas have safe access to round up those birds. Give the maintenance guys a mornin' off or somethin'. You and I can go in on this fifty-fifty, which should give you and Monty enough to cover what you owe on that cellah and pay for my trip."

Newt craned his neck up, looked to the left, and then looked to the right as if waiting for some higher authority to explain her ridiculous request. After a few moments, he spoke.

"Lady, you must be out of your mind to think that as the president of this club, I'd allow something as criminal and immoral as that to take place on these grounds. First of all . . . those birds are protected by the United States Department of Fish and Wildlife. And any actions that interfere with their well-being are strictly illegal. Second, the trumpet cranes are the symbol of Bellstone, and destroying their offspring would be a sacrilege to the spirit of this great club."

"Oh, come on now, Newtie. I've always thought you were cute as a button and smarter than a city fox. And when a fox finds a loose chicken in his very own lair, he grabs it." She gave him a wink and reached out to tickle his bloated neck with her fingers.

Newt backed away and wagged his index finger at her. "Don't you dare try using your cheap come hither shit with me. Consider yourself warned—if any harm comes to those precious creatures, all fingers will be pointing at you, you washed up whore."

In a matter of seconds, Mandy's eyes narrowed, her face darkened, and her lips twisted into a hideous sneer. "Where the fuck is this 'holier than thou' attitude coming from Sizemore, you fat fucking excuse for a club president?" Her voice had risen to a shout, and her accent now screamed of one from Bayonne, New Jersey. "I know all about your way of doing business. And I also know there's nothing you wouldn't stoop to, to un-fuck the fuck-ups you've made in the 'spirit of this great club'. And, by the way, asshole . . . you're not getting a dime from my husband!" She stormed back to her Ferrari, fired up the engine, and roared up to the porte-cochere to have Bernardo park her car.

Lieutenant Valentine had walked into the parking lot after wrapping up his meetings in the clubhouse. He'd caught the end of Mandy's tirade and watched with interest as she got out of her car, handed her keys to Bernardo, and strutted off toward the pro shop in her form-fitting pink capris and clingy white polo.

"Some kind'a club these folks are runnin'," the cop said to Bernardo. "On my first call to the place, I saw that president give hell to the priest. Now, it's the Texan himself who's taking the heat, and from one tough talkin' Tilly!"

Bernardo rolled his eyes and nodded his head in agreement. *"Si, senor.* This place is crazy!"

"Who's that red hot tamale, anyhow, Bernie boy? I didn't expect to see a feisty Jersey girl in this neck of the woods!"

"That's Mrs. Manville, and she's a Southern *senora.* Speaks with a real sexy, how you say—drawl? Most of the time. But you sure don't want to get on her bad side."

"I'd love to get on her bad side!" the cop said. "I'd love to get on her good side too! Any side'll work just fine for me."

Eighteen

Saturday, July 1st 2011
Five days before the Bellstone Ladies Club Championship

"Push, Miss Lane. You're doing great. Now give me one last big effort. The head is crowning! Almost here . . . almost here . . . here he is! Congratulations! Your son has arrived."

The obstetrician held Derrick Junior high in the air for Amber to see, before he handed the newborn to the delivery room nurse who cleaned and swaddled him in a tiny blanket. Danika, who had served as her sister's labor coach throughout the delivery, had tears of joy running down her cheeks.

"Oh sissy, I do love you," Amber said in a weak voice. "Thank God you came back after that awful kidnappin'." She reached for Danika's hand. "I am so lucky to have you in my life."

Danika wiped the new mother's brow with a cool washcloth. "I'm the lucky one, Amber. To have a sis in LA and a brand-new nephew. And hey, that nice Marvin from Dancin' Bare is still waiting out in the lobby for news of how you and the baby are doing. That was real kind of him to drive you here. Told me your water broke while you were up on that pole."

"It sure did, honey. Marvin saw the puddle, climbed up on the stage, and hustled me into his Camry. He made that little four cylinder take off like a NASCAR car to the emergency room."

"Seems like a responsible fella. I think he's sweet on you." While Danika spoke, the nurse placed the infant on Amber's chest. "Bet he'd make a real good daddy for little Derrick."

"Derrick Junior already has a daddy, sissy." Amber gazed into her newborn's face with the cleft in his chin that he'd inherited from his father. "When my honey sees his little boy here, he's gonna leave that witch he's hitched to now, and marry me. I know that in my heart."

The new mother carefully guided the nipple of her breast into Derrick Junior's mouth. When the baby began to suckle, she was overcome by an incredible rush of love for her son and the baby's father. As the milk began its steady flow from her breast, there was a light tapping on her shoulder. It was the delivery room nurse.

"There are some gentlemen here, Miss Lane. They say they're deacons from the Catholic Church and would like to have a word with you—if you're up to it."

"The Catholic Church?" A wave of terror shot through Amber as the horror of Danika's kidnapping came rushing back.

"No! No! No!" she cried out. "Don't let them near my baby, please! Danika, call 911 now!"

"It's all right, honey, we don't need to call the police," the nurse assured her. "No one's going to hurt your baby. And you certainly don't have to see anyone if you don't want to." She hurried out of the room to send the deacons away as Amber clutched little Derrick to her chest.

Nineteen

Monday, July 4th 2011
Two days before the Bellstone Ladies Club Championship

"I'm gonna take two weeks gonna have a fine vacation. I'm gonna take my problem to the United Nations. Well, I called my congressman and he said quote 'I'd like to help you son but you're too young to vote'. Sometimes I wonder what I'm a-gonna do, but there ain't no cure for the summertime blues."

The band calling themselves The Monkees were playing the songs of summer at Bellstone's 4th of July celebration. While the group paused between tunes, the party's DJ made an announcement.

"Happy birthday America! The Bellstone high dive contest begins in five minutes."

The club's annual outdoor festivity featured a barbecue with corn on the cob, hamburgers and hot dogs, and a dance floor next to the band. Lawn games included an egg toss, a potato sack race, and a tug of war where members were divided into teams to pull a giant rope across a finish line. There were inner-tube races, swim competitions, and a diving contest in the Olympic-sized pool that had one of the last remaining high diving boards at any country club in California.

Derrick and Jody were lounging in their bathing suits on chaises by the pool as they watched the swim races and chatted with Monty Manville and several other members. Mandy was in the pro shop trying on kilts that she might wear in the Scottish Pro-Am.

"The high dive contestants will be scored by our panel of three judges on a scale of one through ten, with ten being the highest. A trophy will be awarded to the winner," the D.J. told the crowd.

Jody nudged Derrick with her toe. "Hey babe, this contest was always my favorite part of the 4th here at Bellstone."

"Presenting our first competitor, Mr. Roy Martin, who will demonstrate what he calls, 'the bomb'," the D.J. said.

Weighing no less than 275 pounds, Roy Martin climbed up the ladder to the high dive and executed a titanic cannonball that soaked half of the audience with a shelf of water that rolled up and out of the pool. While viewers jumped from their lounges with drinks in hand, the judges held up scores of 0, 1, and 1.

"Next up . . . Mr. Brian Murphy will attempt a forward free position somersault."

After reaching the top of the board, the next diver, who had a roll of fat hanging over his Speedo, waved to a group of his beer-drinking friends below who threw their fists in the air and shouted, *"Murphy! Murphy! Murphy!"* The diver attempted a couple of bounces, sprung only a few inches up from the board, and hurled himself downward to execute the somersault as his friends sung out *"Go! Go! Go!"* But the weight of his stomach prevented his legs from achieving the thrust needed to execute the move. To the chants of *"No! No! No!"* he landed on the surface of the water with a belly flop that elicited a sharp cracking sound. The spectators responded with a series of moans, as the judges held up cards marked with 0, 1, and a very generous 2.

Derrick howled and grabbed his abdomen. "*Oh man*, that has *gotta* hurt!"

"Hey babe," Jody said to her husband. "Did you know that my grandpa had that high dive installed back in the early 1950's?"

"I did not," said Derrick, who was on his eighth beer. Rather than focusing on his wife, he was more interested in chatting with the guys about the future of the Los Angeles Lakers.

"Grandpa was on the Pasadena High School diving team, and even had a shot at the Olympics," Jody continued. "Gave up diving when he decided to focus on becoming a pro golfer."

"Ya don't say," Derrick said, pretending he'd been listening to her.

"When the golf course was under construction, Forrest had the estate's original pool refurbished, and ordered the high dive from a company in Omaha, Nebraska, of all places. He taught me some pretty cool dives from up there after our summer golf outings." Not sure if Derrick had heard her, she nudged him with her toe. "Did you hear that, Der? I used to do some pretty cool dives from up there."

"Oh, sure, hon . . . you did high dives. Cool!" He gave her leg a pat and jumped into the other conversation. "The Kobe Wan Kenobi is invincible. I'd bet the farm he'll be winning rings for LA well into his forties."

"Sorry for being such a bore, Der," Jody said out loud to herself while looking up at the high dive, deep in thought. "Hmmm . . . maybe this'll interest you." She hesitated for moment, then stood up and headed for the deep end of the pool. With her flat abdomen, ample bust, strong straight shoulders, and thick black braid, she created a pretty picture for the crowd in her red, white, and blue striped bikini. After speaking with the DJ, who nodded, she approached the high dive and started her climb up the ladder. Monty, who had been watching her, alerted Derrick and the rest of the group.

"Hey, Benson! It looks like your wife is gonna try to show those losers how it's done!"

"Wha . . . how'd she get up there?" Derrick asked as Jody reached the top of the ladder and stepped onto the board.

"Ladies and gentlemen . . ." the DJ announced. *"We have a late and final entry to our contest. I'd like to present Mrs. Jody Benson, who will perform what she calls a full twist followed by two backward somersaults."*

All eyes were on Jody as she took her position at the end of the board with her back to the water. She extended her arms in front of her and after a moment's pause, bent her knees and sprung backwards up and out from the board. She seemed to fly like a bird as she twisted and turned through the air and compressed her body as she spun into the first, and then the second somersault—before she sliced into the water without a splash. When she came up for air, it was to the sound of thunderous applause, loud whistling, and even a standing ovation by some in the crowd. The three judges each held up their cards while the DJ cried out, ***"Ladies and gentlemen . . . Jody Benson has scored three perfect tens! Come and claim your trophy, Jody!"***

"That is one spectacular woman," Jackson Lyons said out loud. The caddy was carrying for some of the Gamblers who had opted to forego the 4th of July festivities for a high stakes round of golf. He'd spotted Jody from the 18th green as she'd stepped onto the board. "And she's married to that cheating S.O.B.," he said, shaking his head.

Derrick stood up to greet his wife as she walked back to the chaise with her trophy in hand . "Honey, that was . . . that was . . . ta . . . ta . . . terrific!" he stammered as he held his arms open to embrace her. But the beers he'd consumed caused him to stumble before he caught his balance and had to settle for giving her a peck on the cheek. "You . . . you knocked everyone's socks off."

"I wasn't trying to knock anyone's socks off. I was hoping for my husband to show the slightest bit of interest in me," she said as she grabbed her towel and walked away.

"And you suc . . . suc . . . ceeded!" he called out after her.

•　　•　　•

On her way to the clubhouse, Jody spotted Jackson and ran up to him with her trophy in her hand, and the towel knotted over her hips. Having shaken her braid loose to allow her hair to dry, a mane of wavy curls cascaded down her back and the chlorine from the pool had given a near fluorescent cast to her green eyes. When she approached him, Jackson thought she resembled a splendid and exotic creature from the deep.

"Happy 4th of July, Jackson," she said.

"Same to you, Jody. That was quite the dive."

She held up her trophy. "Thanks. I was just trying to get someone's attention."

"Well, that's one way to do it."

"Listen, Jackson, there's something I have to tell you. I feel awful about it, but—"

"No!" he interrupted, shaking his head. "Don't tell me. Don't tell me she got you to drop out. She'd go to any lengths to do that, you know. Please don't give in to her."

"Don't blame her. Mandy's the one who convinced me to sign up in the first place. She really seemed like she wanted me to play in the tournament. But some of the other folks here feel I should drop out. I think it's in everyone's best interest for me to just step away."

"I don't get that at all. How is it in anyone's best interest to fix a club championship by telling the real champion not to play?"

"Please understand why I have to do this, Jackson."

"And please understand why I hate the fact that Forrest Wheeler's granddaughter has been pressured to sit out Bellstone's most important women's tournament for no good reason," the caddy said as he turned and walked toward the parking lot.

Jody headed toward the clubhouse to change into her clothes. When she pulled open the doors, she stopped at the life-size portrait of Forrest Wheeler that hung in the lobby. "Am I doing the right thing, Grandpa?" she asked as she looked into the eyes on the painting. "What would you, who taught me to play a game with honor and integrity, tell me to do?"

On her way to the locker room, she passed the nine portraits of Mandy Manville and saw the empty frame on the wall where the painting of the 2011 winner would soon be hanging. She noticed that the brass plaque below the frame had already been engraved with Mandy's name.

"You've won the match two days before it begins, Mandy?" Jody said out loud. "Not in my grandpa's club! If you're going to be the champion, you have to earn it fair and square."

Jody turned and ran out of the clubhouse. She spotted Jackson on the far side of the parking lot and called out to him. But her voice was drowned out by the music from the band. She pulled out her phone, texted the words *"WE'RE ON!"* and hit send. She saw the caddy pull his phone from his pocket and turn back toward her with a thumbs-up.

• • •

"I like the tartan plaid of this one," Mandy said as she turned left and right to check herself out in the full-length mirror of the pro shop. "What do you think, Maggie? Does it make my ass look flat?" She was modeling one of the kilts Rick had ordered for her. Shop assistant Maggie O'Grady stood in attendance with alternate styles draped over her arms, and Rick sat at his desk scanning his computer to find more kilts for Mandy to choose from.

"I think you look like a lass with a great ass in that one, Mandy," Jody said with a chuckle, as she entered the shop.

Mandy spotted her in the full-length mirror and turned around. "Well, look who's here! It's Jody-girl! Do you really think it suits my poor li'l ole booty?"

"I do," Jody said. "To a T."

"Thanks, honey-bunny. Hey . . . I was so sad to heah that you've chosen not to play in this yeah's championship, 'cause of your busy job and all! But I do wish you'd change your mind, sweet cheeks. We'd have a supah-fun time! Any chance you would reconsidah?"

"That's why I stopped in. I *have* reconsidered. And may the *best* woman win," Jody said with a wink. She walked over to the sign-up sheet and wrote her name where Rick had erased it. It took a few seconds for her words and actions to register with Mandy and Rick, but when they did, they were both too stunned to speak. "All right then . . . I'd better hit the range," Jody added as she headed for the door. "I've got a lot of practicing to catch up on with our 'super fun time' just two days away. Thanks so much for your encouragement, Mandy. And happy 4th to you all!"

When Jody walked out the door, a furious Mandy turned on Rick. "How the fuck did that happen?"

Twenty

Tuesday, July 5th 2011
The day before the Bellstone Ladies Club Championship

"Mission accomplished, boss lady!" Rob Trotter popped into Jody's office at nine-fifteen a.m. "The cranes were sitting ducks, no pun intended. We fitted twenty-five of the two hundred or so newly hatched chicks at your golf club with the mini transmitters bright and early this morning."

Rob displayed a photo he'd snapped of one of the hatchlings on his cell. Safely tucked in its nest, the baby crane was a ball of white fluff with shiny eyes and a tiny, trumpet-shaped yellow beak. A plastic loop as thin as human hair held a minuscule transmitter on the chick's leg.

"The loops caused no problems with the chick's mobility," Rob told Jody. "And the adult birds took no notice of our hardware. They just kept feeding their young as usual after we slipped the gear onto those tiny legs."

"Good work Rob! I'm keeping my fingers crossed that this technology'll be a game changer for us."

"I, for one, am cautiously optimistic," Rob said. "Heading into the studio now to confirm that the satellite is picking up the correct location of these little guys. And *here's* something else that's cool!" he added as he showed Jody the screen on his cell phone. "There's an app that lets you download the data. So, once we get this system up and running, we can track the flocks from anywhere we have cell service."

Jody looked upwards. "Thank you, Steve Jobs!"

"Amen," Rob added. "So, if these poachers strike again, we can follow them from our security vehicles, and email the coordinates to local law enforcement for assistance."

"Super-duper, Rob! I'm glad to see that *this* government entity is finally entering the 21st century! I was telling Kurt in the D.C. office that these gizmos could be a major breakthrough for the entire department."

"I agree. Hey Jody, will you be around tomorrow? Some of the support guys from 'Band-Tech' are going to take me through the new software upgrades in the studio."

"I've got a golf tournament in the morning. But I should be back in the office by one thirty or so."

"Oh? Is that the tournament your golf pro was trying to talk you out of playing in last week? The one he wants his star student to win? You've decided to play in it, after all?"

"I have. Long story."

"You'll have to tell me about it sometime. Over a glass of wine."

"Better make it two glasses."

"Sure! And hey . . . be sure to give it all you've got tomorrow, Captain! And go boldly . . . where no woman has gone before!"

"Will do, Commander. "At the least, I'll give my opponent a run for her money."

Twenty-one

Wednesday, July 6th 2011
The morning of the Bellstone Women's Club
Championship

"Ok Lisa, we're rolling. Quiet on the set! Action!"

"This is Lisa Langheart of KTLA news. I'm standing on the grounds of LA's historic Bellstone Country Club, where Amanda 'Mandy' Manville is expected to qualify for golf's biggest pro-amateur tournament, The Cialis Open at Saint Andrews golf course in Scotland. Odds are that the outcome of this morning's tournament here will earn Mandy her tenth consecutive Woman Club Champion title. And that title will enable this lady to tee it up with Tiger Woods or other top PGA professionals in October."

"How was it, Steve?" Lisa called out to her producer. "Too many audio pops?"

"No, that was great, Lisa. Let's set up our shot of Mandy teeing off."

Bellstone Country Club was a scene of activity and excitement on the morning of its Women's Club Championship Tournament. Along with the KTLA news team, several area newspaper reporters and photographers were there to cover the event. Over two hundred spectators, many wearing plaids, tam o'shanter caps, and kilts to celebrate their upcoming trip to Scotland, had shown up at an early hour to watch the match. A band of bagpipers decked out in formal Highland dress was assembled on the first tee box, piping the tune *Scotland the Brave.*

Because Mandy was going for her tenth consecutive club championship title, which would be followed by a spot in a Professional

Golf Association of America sanctioned tournament, a representative of the group was in attendance to audit the tournament. The official would make sure that all necessary requirements were being met in the staging of the event, and that all rules of golf were followed during the competition.

Though twenty women would be playing in the tournament, the spectators were only there to watch the two top competitors, Mandy Manville and Jody Benson. Both women would tee-off at eight a.m. By seven thirty, Jody and the other women were warming up on the driving range.

"Okay, young lady, are you ready for the big event?" a familiar voice called out as Jody hit her last range ball. She turned and saw a man with a face she knew she'd seen before, though she wasn't sure where. When he picked up her golf bag and threw it over his shoulder, she made the connection.

"Jackson! Is that *you?*"

The caddy's long beard was gone, and his once cascading blonde hair was now short and waved back from his forehead. With his turquoise eyes and a sexy smile that revealed two rows of perfect white teeth, Jackson was every bit as great looking as he had been in his role as the time traveler in *The Sphinx*.

"Wow, you sure clean up good!" Jody declared. "If I wasn't a happily married woman, you'd be in trouble."

"Glad you approve, m'lady," he said with a salute.

"But why now? You didn't do this just for today's event did you?"

"Actually . . . yes . . . and no. After you texted me that you were a go, I decided it was time to keep my end of the deal. I emailed Marty Stadler two nights ago with a note and attached a copy of the script for the New York comedy I'm finishing up. I'd just hoped he'd take a look at it at some point. I'd written the lead with myself in mind, but didn't mention that in my email, figuring that might be asking too much, especially considering what happened between Rene' and me on his last film."

"Yeah, that *would* seem a bit nervy."

"You would think. But I was surprised to get a call from him yesterday morning."

"No way!"

"He said he'd been meaning to call me for a while now. Told me I'd actually done him a favor with the Rene' thing 'cause it freed him up to meet Uma."

"*Wow!* So, he has you to thank for those cute little munchkins I saw on that magazine cover at the supermarket check-out line!"

"Yup. Said Uma and the kids are the best things that ever happened to him. Was that ever a relief! Made me think of my grandpa who used to say, 'In business, no matter what you're expecting, expect the unexpected'."

"Wise man," Jody agreed.

"And better yet . . . Marty said he was up half the night reading my screenplay! Described it as fresh, quirky, and hilarious! Said he wants to develop it and even mentioned casting me in the lead! We're meeting on it at his office today at four, so I decided it was time to come out of hiding."

"Hold the phone, Jackson! You're meeting with one of the biggest directors in Hollywood this afternoon, and you still showed up to caddy for me in this silly tournament? That's crazy! Go home and prep for your meeting!"

"Are you kidding? I wouldn't miss today's event for the world. I'm hoping it'll give me some great material for my next script."

"Break a leg today, Jody!" Diane Sharp called out as she walked by the range. "We're rooting for you all the way, girl!"

"Thanks, Diane! Are you playing in this thing? I didn't see your name on the sign-up sheet."

"No way, my pretty," the woman said with a cackle as she rubbed her hands together. "I want to savor every moment of watching you slay the evil dragon." Diane came in closer. "Now the best golf tip I can give you is to keep your guard up this morning." Her eyes darted down the range toward Mandy, who was striking one of her sultry poses for a local newspaper photographer. "Because danger lurks behind every curve of that enhanced physique."

"Thanks for the tip, Diane," Jody said. "But I think I can handle her." She looked over at Mandy and felt a slight chill in the morning air. "At least, I hope I can."

•　　•　　•

At eight a.m., Jody and Jackson were on the 1st tee and ready to rumble. Following protocol, Jackson and Armando would keep both women's scores on the course scorecard that had an illustration of a white trumpet crane flying across the top. Rick Lightfoot stepped up to the tee box to announce the first pairing of the day to the galley of spectators. "Welcome to the 2011 Bellstone Women's Club Championship," he said with the microphone in his hand. "First on the tee, competing for her tenth consecutive title, the defending nine-time Bellstone Woman Club Champion, Amanda 'Mandy' Manville!"

Cheers and wild applause erupted from most of the gallery, though a noticeable few stood in silence as Mandy waved and smiled for the KTLA camera that was filming the start of the competition. When Armando handed his player her pink Big Bertha driver, the crowd fell silent. Mandy walked to the tee box, teed up her pink ball, took a practice swing, and held her finish for three seconds. She then hit her signature 180-yard drive down the middle and halfway up the hill of the first fairway. Applause erupted once more while Mandy grabbed the hem of her hot pink skort and gave a royal curtsy to her fans.

"Next on the tee," Rick continued, "Princeton University's Most Valuable Woman Golfer of 2002, Jody Benson!" The few members who had refused to applaud for Mandy gave Jody a big hand as she teed up her ball. Then, cheers turned to oohs and ahhs as she swung hard and fast and sent her ball screaming past Mandy's and high over the hill of the 1st fairway. Wearing a short red skirt and red polo embroidered with the Bellstone logo, she pointed two thumbs up toward Jackson, who got his share of catcalls from the women in the crowd.

"Hey, isn't that caddy the guy from *The Spinx*?" one of the women spectators asked Diane Sharp.

"It sure looks like him," Diane said.

"If I had that hunk carrying my bag, I'd be out on the course day and night," the woman told her with a sigh.

The players began their walk down the fairway, followed by the news crew and a parade of spectators. Mandy hit her second shot. Though the ball went straight, it was short of the green.

"Good strike, Mandy," Jody called out to the sound of cheers. Mandy waved to her fans and continued her march down the fairway.

"Her form is good," Jackson said after watching Mandy's shot. "But she needs better body rotation to get distance." He spotted a bulge in the rear pocket of Jody's skirt. "Hey, I hope that's not a cell phone back there."

"I set it on vibrate. There's way too much going on at the office to be without it. And don't worry, I told them texts only. No calls."

"Yeah, yeah—give it here," Jackson said as he held out his hand. "I'll let you know if anything that appears remotely important pops up. You just focus on winning this thing."

"Will do, coach." She handed him the phone. "Oh boy," Jody felt a flutter in her stomach. "I haven't played in a real competition in years. I'm a bit nervous."

"Just take a deep breath and stay calm," the caddy said. "And above all, stay focused on your game."

"Stay focused. Stay focused. Stay focused. Got it."

"And Jody . . ."

"Yes?"

"Above all else, I want you to have fun this morning. This is your moment to enjoy the game you learned from your grandfather. Do it for him. And for yourself."

"I sure will. Good words to play by."

Jackson put his hands on her shoulders and gazed deep into her eyes where he noticed topaz flecks that were sprinkled through her light green irises. "You have all the shots, so trust your swing. It's time for these folks to see how a real club champion wins her match."

"Hey, you make it sound fun. I'll give it my best! But Jackson?"

"Yes?"

"You left out Derrick. That I should enjoy the game for him too. I understand you guys had some sort of a problem out on the course a while back?"

"We can talk about that later," Jackson said as he handed her a fairway wood. Jody took a deep breath, lined up for the shot, looked at the pin, and then down at the ball. She made a full, smooth swing and finished with her chest pointed square at the target. The ball soared high in the air, hit the pin with a bang, and bounced fifteen feet from the hole. Her fans erupted in a roar of cheers as the news crew followed the players to film them putting out on the 1st hole.

When the players and caddies reached the green, Mandy was lying three shots to Jody's two. Her ball was farther from the hole, so it was her turn to putt. She knocked it close and tapped in for a bogie. Jody's fifteen-foot putt was for birdie. She'd be satisfied with a two-putt for par, as she knew that the odds of making a putt that long were against her.

"No break there, just straight into the hole," Jackson instructed. While competing in her younger years, Jody enjoyed playing for a crowd. But on that day, knowing all eyes and a camera were on her, she feared that she'd either three-putt by leaving the ball way too short or blast it past the hole. As she took her stance over the ball with her putter, her heart began to pound, and her body tensed up.

"Breathe," Jackson whispered, as he inhaled deeply to encourage her to do the same.

While the air filled her lungs, her eyes traveled in the direction of tournament rock. In the distance, she spotted the giant oak that rose above it. A wonderful feeling of calm came over her as a voice rang out in her head. It was the voice of her grandfather saying, "Always remember to trust your instincts." It was the last piece of advice he'd ever given her.

She looked at the hole and visualized the ball rolling into the center of the cup. She stroked the ball and it traveled toward the hole with a glow around it, as if it were saying that her grandpa's words were golden. It dropped into the cup for a birdie on the first hole of the match.

"Hallelujah! Judgement Day is upon us!" Diane Sharp called out from the crowd.

Jody waved to her applauding fans while a ray of sunshine broke through the Los Angeles morning clouds. Certain that Forrest was smiling down on her, she looked over at Jackson, and knew that the caddy understood what she was feeling.

Over the next eight holes, Jody put on a show like nothing the Bellstone members had ever seen during a women's club championship. She was having the time of her life playing the game the way her grandfather had taught her to play it.

"Mandy logged a forty-one on the front. Pretty darned good," Jackson told her as he totaled up the player's scores after they'd completed the front nine. "But it was no match for your thirty-three. Could be one of the best nine-hole scores ever played by a woman on this course. I'd say you've done your grandfather mighty proud, young lady."

"Playing in this tournament has brought me close to Forrest in a way that's hard to express. And it's all thanks to you for encouraging me to play, Jackson."

"The pleasure is all mine. Just keep up the good work."

•   •   •

When the players began their walk to the back nine, the merriment displayed by Mandy's supporters on the first tee had vanished. Aware that the current champion trailed Jody by eight strokes with nine holes left to play, the TV crew had packed up their gear and moved on to another local story. The club members who had been excited about traveling to Scotland to cheer Mandy on had cell phones glued to their ears while they attempted to cancel their airline tickets and hotel reservations.

"She's losing her shirt to that new girl," a woman cell-yelled into her phone within earshot of Mandy. "Should we fly into Edinburgh anyway, and do some sightseeing?"

Mandy's fans began to drift away to get a bite in the clubhouse or enjoy the pool. Diane Sharp and other victims of the player's tactics over the past decade were happy to stick around and enjoy the slaughter.

On her way to the 10th hole with only Armando by her side, Mandy was certain that she'd lost her one chance to achieve the glory she'd spent her life trying to attain. She felt as she had long ago as a child in Bayonne while walking with her siblings to the public pool in the summer heat as the town's wealthy kids were shuttled past her in their parent's Range Rovers and Volvos to their swimming, tennis, and golf lessons. Her eyes filled with tears as the most haunting memory of all came rushing back. The agony of waiting for the invitation to her friend Randy Sharp's birthday party to be held at Bayonne Country Club—the invitation that never did arrive. Now, her invitation to play in the Scottish Pro-Am would never arrive either. Instead, she'd be stuck at home watching the event on television with her broke loser of a husband and embarrassed beyond belief to have been pummeled by this new girl in a tournament that she was supposed to win in a breeze.

"You go, girl! It's high time we had a real club champion!" Diane Sharp called out to Jody. "I'll be waiting for you in the clubhouse with a bottle of bubbly!"

But as Jody looked over and saw Mandy hunched forward, with downcast eyes, she felt a twinge of sadness for the woman. And though she was playing some of the best golf of her life, it was hard for her to enjoy herself with her opponent looking so miserable.

"Hi, hon! I hear you're kicking butt!" Derrick said as he ran up and gave his wife a hug.

"Hey, Der! What're you doing here?" Jody asked him.

"I just came by to meet a client for coffee in the clubhouse. Then I'm back to the office. But I'll be here again for my three o'clock Gambler's game. And by then, you'll have been crowned the 2011 Bellstone Woman Club Champion. We'll celebrate your new title tonight, so keep hitting 'em straight!" Derrick kissed his wife and headed toward the clubhouse.

Mandy watched the exchange from the other side of the 10th tee. "That asshole," she said to Armando. "He was supposed to keep her out of this thing, now he's cheering for her to beat my ass. And after all I did for the little shit." Aware that it was unacceptable for a caddy to be privy to a member's grievances against another member, Armando hung his head to the ground. "Well, fuck him," Mandy continued. "And, what a hypocrite by kissing her like that in front of everyone! They all know that the guy can't keep his fly zipped!" Like most country clubs, Bellstone was a hotbed of gossip, and the rumor about Derrick impregnating a stripper had circulated through the Gambler's group and made its way to Mandy. "You wait here, Armando," she told her caddy while she took a deep breath and marched toward her opponent.

"Psssst! Got a moment, sugah?" She called out to Jody as she motioned for the other woman to join her under a nearby tree.

"What could possibly be so important that she has to interrupt you now?" Jackson asked his player.

Jody waved to Mandy. "It's okay. She knows the party's over. I'm just glad she wants to show good sportsmanship and congratulate me for playing well." She walked over to Mandy and smiled.

"First of all, I'd like to say that it's been a pleasure playing with you too, Mandy." Jody said. "You played some good golf out there. Now let's enjoy the rest of our round."

"I wish I could, but it's hard for me to concentrate 'cause of my concern for you and your hubby," Mandy said with a sad-looking face.

"Concern for Derrick and me? About what? What do you mean?"

Mandy lowered her voice to a whisper. "Concern about what y'all had decided to do about that child."

"Child? What child?"

"Derrick's child. His love child," Mandy said, keeping her voice low. "Does that stripper plan to keep the baby, or might y'all raise it as your own?"

"I'm sorry, what?" Jody, thinking that her ears must be playing tricks on her, stared at the woman with eyebrows knitted in confusion.

"I'm curious, is all. But whatevah you decide, I think you're a saint for fahgivin' Derrick for his li'l dalliance. I do declah, most women would'a thrown the man out on his eah."

Jody shook her head, disgusted by the other woman's ploy. "Okay. I get what you're trying to do. But do you really think you can rattle me with some crazy and vicious lie about Derrick? Are you that desperate to win this thing?"

"Not at all," Mandy answered in her most helpful tone. "Everyone knew about the gal he'd been bedding at that Dancin' Bare club over on Sepulveda. Then we heard that after he got her pregnant, Norm O'Malley stepped in to try to get the poor girl into a convent."

"You are absolutely *crazy,* lady!" Jody cried out. "Now I get what they were talking about!" She turned her back on Mandy and walked over to Jackson, who was holding her driver.

"That woman is a psychopath! The stories I heard didn't begin to do her justice." She took the club and prepared to tee off. But as hard as she tried to ignore Mandy's words, she felt an uneasy twinge in her gut as she swung the club. The ball went flying over the fence and out into the street that ran along the right side of the fairway.

"FORE!" Jackson called out. The sound of the ball bouncing on asphalt could be heard in the distance. "That one's gone. Better hit another one." The caddy caught Mandy's Cheshire Cat grin from the corner of his eye.

Jody's second ball also sliced right and landed on the road. She tried again, and this time her ball stayed in bounds. Mandy followed by hitting her standard 180-yard drive down the middle of the fairway. When Jody had finally managed to complete the hole, she'd racked up a big fat score of eight against Mandy's par four.

"You just gave up four strokes!" Jackson said as they walked off the 11th green. "What the bejesus did she say to you?"

"Just some ridiculous story she concocted about my husband."

Though the caddy knew that Mandy's story might well have some truth to it, he had to keep his player in the game at all costs. "Jody, whatever it was, this is her M.O.! Don't listen to anything that comes out of her mouth. That woman will do whatever it takes to get in your head."

"I know. I just should have been ready for it."

"No matter what she told you . . . you have to realize she's a master at messing with her opponent's minds. Just stay focused and don't let her get to you."

"You're right," Jody answered with resolve. "I'll be okay. I'll put it out of my head. The woman does have a wild imagination, though. Gotta give her credit for that." She shook her head in disbelief. "Thanks, Jackson! I'm good to go." She marched with head held high toward the next tee box.

On the 11th hole, a long par five, Mandy hit her usual serviceable drive, while Jody's bomb roared two hundred seventy yards down the middle of the fairway. Still four strokes down with eight holes to play, Mandy had to act fast.

"Hey, Jody!" Mandy called out as two women walked to their balls. "I heard Newt Sizemore was planning to round up those baby trumpet cranes that just hatched down at the lake."

Jody turned around and looked at her opponent. "What kind of a head game are you playing now, Mandy?"

"No head game, suga. Just givin' the facts," Mandy said with a giggle. "That new wine cellar is costin' *way* more than folks were told, so Newt and the board need to get a good chunk of cash fast to pay it off. Lucky for Newt, he's found a company in Brazil that will pay good money for those little creatures."

Without giving Mandy the satisfaction of a reply, Jody marched forward, took her club from Jackson and hit her next shot. "Where does she come up with this stuff?" she asked the caddy. "Isn't there some sort of penalty for intentionally trying to distract your opponent during a golf match?"

"I believe there is," Jackson said. "If you want to call her on it, we can take it up with the rules official right now."

"No, that's okay. Let's just ignore her and finish this. I'm actually beginning to pity the poor woman." Jody focused on her second shot and hit it near the pin.

"You're about to close her out anyhow," Jackson said. "She just hit her ball in the sand trap."

Armando handed Mandy her sand wedge as she climbed into the bunker. She hit through the sand, but the tension of the tournament kept her from finishing her swing. The ball popped up in the air, but never left the sand. She tried again with the same result. Jody walked over to the bunker.

"I know you're stressed Mandy, but you have to finish your swing. Try to relax your arms and hit through the sand with your club pointed at the target." Mandy tried again and hit the shot as Jody had instructed. The ball landed a foot from the hole and rolled into the cup for a bogie.

"It went in the hole!" Jody called out. "Nice work, Mandy!"

"Wow . . . um . . . gee . . . thank you! Thank you, Jody!" Mandy said, stunned by the other woman's kindness. She stared at Jody for a moment before speaking. "Ya know, when you helped me like that, you reminded me of a friend I had long ago. *But why?* Why would you help me? I'm your opponent."

"Helping players is a trait I inherited from my grandfather. I want everyone to enjoy this great sport. Not be frustrated by it."

Jody walked to the green and putted out for another birdie. She now had a six-stroke lead in the match. On the 12th tee box, she hit another booming drive.

Jackson glanced at Jody's cell. "Hey, Jody . . . I hate to interrupt you, but you've been getting a flurry of texts from a Rob Trotter. Do you want to take a look now, or can you wait 'til you've aced this thing?"

"Better let me see them. He's my tech guy at work. Wouldn't disturb me unless he had to."

She looked at the screen and shook her head. "Oh boy! Another distraction!" she told the caddy. "My team at work installed some gear on the trumpet crane chicks down at the lake here to test out a new satellite tracking system. We hope it can help us catch those damn poachers."

"Yeah?" Jackson nodded. "And?"

"Rob says the satellite is picking up all kinds of movement by the chicks. He thinks it's just a glitch, but after what Mandy told us on eleven, I'd better go check things out down there."

"I'll handle it." Jackson handed Jody's golf bag to Armando, who slung it over his shoulder. "You guys keep going. I'll make sure the little guys are safe and sound in their nests. You've got about 105 yards to the pin with a green that slopes right to left." Jackson took off toward the Wheeler Garden and Jody studied her next shot.

Confident that the satellite readings were just a technical snafu, Jody stayed calm and hit her shot close to the pin. She sank her putt for another birdie as Mandy carded a par. Though there were still six holes left to play, Mandy knew the match was over. She also knew that she had crossed all lines of acceptable behavior in her desperate fight to win. While the two walked off the 12th green, she turned to her opponent.

"That was a great birdie, Jody."

"Thank you, Mandy. Nice par on your end."

A tear rolled down Mandy's cheek. "Jody . . ."

"Yes?" Jody looked over at the other woman. "Mandy, what's wrong? Is this another attempt to distract me? Because if it is—"

"No, no, it's not." Mandy stopped walking as the tears kept coming. "I'm so sorry for what I've done, and I'm so ashamed of myself. Especially after you helped me get out of that bunker. You did that out of pure kindness. No other female has been that genuinely nice to me in years."

Jody reached in her pocket, pulled out a tissue, and handed it to the other woman. "I told you I'd do that for any player. And I'm still not convinced this is genuine."

Mandy grabbed the tissue and dabbed at her eyes. "It is. Because you've helped me to see who I really am—a nasty, self-centered phony. And it's time to come clean," she said as she blew her nose with the now damp tissue. "I'm not a nice person, I wasn't born with a pretty face or good body, and I'm not from the South. I'm just a plain girl from New Jersey."

"Well, you had me fooled. For a while, that is," Jody said with a wry smile. Still wondering if Mandy had another trick up her sleeve, she looked toward Armando who was marching ahead of the two women with both bags on his shoulders. "Now let's keep going and finish the round."

Mandy walked along with Jody and tucked the soggy tissue in the pocket of her skort. "I wanted to be the ten-time champion so badly, and travel to Scotland to play in that Pro-Am," she said. "And I'd have done or said anything for that chance."

"I noticed," Jody said.

"I grew up poor, and plain looking. My grandparents all died before I was born, and my parents never had any time or money for us kids. I only got to visit a country club once, and that was for a help-the-poor-day where the rich kids teased me." Mandy pulled out the tissue and blew her nose again. "I was desperate to show them that I was somebody after all."

LINDA SHEEHAN

Jody pulled out a fresh tissue and handed it to Mandy. "Well, you are—"

"No, I'm not. I'm not really very good at anything, not even golf," Mandy continued. "You've always been kind and rich and beautiful, and you hit the ball like a pro."

Jody stared at the distraught woman. "Now I get it. You're nothing more than an insecure little girl, who's trying to make up for what she never had." She took a long look at the scenic grounds of the club. "And you're right." She slowly nodded her head in agreement. "I *have* been handed a life of privilege. Plus, I love my job and I love my husband. I guess no real damage has been done by your behavior."

"Oh, but it has. . ." Mandy said. "I've done some very bad things and I'm sorry—"

"You did it out of your desperation to win. It was pathetic and cruel. But—"

"No, it wasn't just the stories. It was what I did to try to get you to drop out of—"

"Jody!" Jackson yelled out as he ran toward the two women from the Wheeler Garden. "Call 911, or whoever you need to call. The baby cranes are gone. Two guys in a gray van took 'em. They were heading for the maintenance exit."

"Oh, my God!" screamed Jody while she turned to Mandy. "You *weren't* lying about the birds!" She pulled her phone from her pocket and punched a number. "It's me, Rob. The chicks were taken! You're tracking them, yes? Good. Relay the coordinates to security, *now!* Then, alert the LAPD for back-up. The thieves were spotted in a gray van minutes ago. They couldn't have gotten far!"

She turned to Jackson. "Tell me exactly what happened."

The caddy was still short of breath. "I went down to check things out and saw two guys. I couldn't see their faces. They were loading crates packed with screaming chicks into the van. The adult birds were going ballistic and circling the truck. I ran and tried to stop them from driving away, but they tore off past me."

Jody turned on Mandy. "You knew about this and didn't tell anyone? You could go to jail for being an accomplice to a federal offense!"

"No, I didn't know! I promise!" Mandy was trembling and heaving with sobs. "I actually did consider having the chicks stolen to raise some cash. That's true. When I told Newt about my idea, he said that destroying the offspring of the trumpet cranes would be a sacrilege to the spirit of Bellstone. The only reason I made up the story about Newt stealing them was to throw your game off. I promise!"

"What's going on here?" Rick asked the group. He and the rules official had driven up in a golf cart to see what the commotion was about. "Ma'am," Jody called out to the woman. "I'm an agent with the U.S. Department of Fish and Wildlife. A crime has been committed on this property that requires my immediate attention."

Rick conferred with the official and informed the group of her decision. "Mrs. Wright has declared the match between the two of you suspended until the situation is resolved."

$$\bullet \quad \bullet \quad \bullet$$

"Yes, Emilio. The merchandise is en route as we speak." Newt Sizemore was talking into his Cadillac's Bluetooth system as he drove north on the 405 Freeway that linked the West Side of Los Angeles to the San Fernando Valley. "Yes, alive and well, of course. Got a good man at the wheel who works for me over at the club. He and another fella'll hook up with their contact in San Diego who'll make the final run to Tijuana. Should be crossing the border in four hours, depending on traffic. So, I can expect a wire by three o'clock, give or take? One thousand per head, like we said? And that hot little secretary of yours has my account number? *Si? Buenos dias* to you too, *senor!*"

Newt clicked off his Bluetooth and accelerated his Cadillac with the mere touch of his toe while the flesh of his face contorted into a satisfied smirk. Thanks to the deal he'd orchestrated with Emilio Fuentes, the wine cellar would be paid for in full, the population of those flying pests would be thinned out, and Newt would be well compensated for his efforts. In just a few hours, the white trumpet crane chicks would be arriving at the lab in Tijuana, and he'd receive a wire transfer for upwards of $200,000 to his bank account in the Cayman Islands that afternoon. The funds would cover the $150,000 he needed to pay his portion of the overages on the cellar. Monty and Bradley were kicking in $75,000 apiece, which would leave Newt with a nice commission of $50,000.

Guiding his sedan down the freeway with just an index finger hooked over the car's steering wheel, he thought about how proud his daddy would be of him now. Born in the back woods of Beaumont, Texas, Newt was raised on the wild hogs and squirrels his daddy bagged and the okra and turnips his mama grew in the yard of the three room shack he grew up in. He chuckled to himself knowing that he could now dine on filet mignon and drink high-priced French wines for breakfast, lunch, and dinner if he so desired.

His thoughts turned to the women's club championship luncheon that he planned to attend that afternoon. In his role as club president, he would once again present the tournament's perpetual trophy to Mandy, with yet another brass plate engraved with her name. A long baritone belch rumbled up from his belly and he grimaced at the thought of facing a roomful of cackling women, especially since he was feeling a bit queasy from hanging out at the club bar and downing six double Daniels the night before. Though he prided himself on possessing an exceptional palate, he knew his diet of rich food and drink was beginning to take a physical toll. The gout attacks he'd been experiencing over the past several years were becoming more and more frequent. He was also becoming more and more bloated, which made the buttons on his dress shirts harder to close with each passing day. He was further irritated by the traffic, which had slowed to a crawl as the northbound drivers were pausing to look at the cluster of police cars on the shoulder of the southbound lanes.

"Move it assholes! I don't have all day!" he called out and leaned on his horn. The driver of the car in front of him—a huge Mexican fellow who was equally angry, turned around and gave Newt the finger. "Fuck you and your fat mother too, buddy!" the president hollered. He was fortunate that the Cadillac's powerful air conditioning system and sealed smoke glass windows prevented the other driver from hearing the tirade.

When his car inched forward, Newt saw that the police cars were surrounding a gray van with the back doors open. Armed officers in green uniforms were removing crates from the van and loading them into a truck marked Animal Control. Two Latino men with their hands cuffed behind their backs were standing against a police car. One of the men looked very much like Jorge, the bag boy at the club. When Newt's Bluetooth buzzed and the name Mike Armstrong, Bellstone Club Manager, appeared on the screen, a familiar wave of nausea rose in his gut.

•   •   •

"You can take a break, Armando," Mandy told her caddy. "I'll have Eddie call you up when I'm ready to hit the range before we tee off." Mandy remained on the 13th tee box as Armando headed back to the caddy yard with her bag on his shoulder. The few spectators who had been watching the match had now gathered near the Wheeler Garden where Jody was conferring with Fish and Wildlife officials. A news helicopter hovered above the lake. Lisa Langheart and the KTLA news crew had shifted the focus of that day's story from the championship to the theft of the birds and were waiting for someone in authority to grant them an interview. From where Mandy stood, she could see Jackson assist Jody in her dealings with the officers, and she couldn't help but notice that the pair made a beautiful couple.

The nine-time club champion had assumed that by this time today she'd be the center of attention. Now, she was the last thing on anyone's mind. She sat down on a bench and hummed the melody of a song she heard long ago on a summer night when she stood outside the gates of Bayonne Country Club.

Twenty-two

Sunday, July 6th 1992
18 years before the Bellstone Woman's Club Championship

"But don't tell my heart
My achy breaky heart
I just don't think he'd understand.
And if you tell my heart
My achy breaky heart
He might blow up and kill this man."

The lyrics of Billy Ray Cyrus' hit song flowed down the parking lot and through the wrought iron gates of Bayonne Country Club where a fourteen-year-old girl stood. "No one wants me. No one wants me," the girl said over and over as she stared at the rambling stone clubhouse in the distance. The club's security guard walked up from inside the gates as she listened to the music and the laughter of her schoolmates coming from the terrace of the mansion.

"What're you doing out here, young lady?" the man asked. "Why aren't you having fun at the party with the other kids? Sounds like they're having a great time!"

"Because I wasn't invited. It's my friend Randi's fifteenth birthday party," a tearful Angie replied. "I don't know why she didn't invite me. She taught me some golf shots. Then, I helped her every day after school with her biology homework. I even showed her how to dissect a fetal pig. She got an 'A' on our final exam. I was so proud. When I heard she was having her birthday party here, I waited every day for her invitation. But it never arrived."

"Oh gee, I'm sorry about that honey." The guard looked down at the sad little girl and thought about his own young daughter. "Why don't you go home now? You'll be invited to lots of other parties. I promise."

Twenty-three

Wednesday, July 6th 2011
The afternoon of the Bellstone Women's Club Championship

Newt pulled into the Bellstone parking lot to see a cluster of police cars gathered near the clubhouse. Once again, he spotted Lieutenant Rocco Valentine questioning Mike Armstrong. Suddenly short of breath, the president tugged at his shirt collar as he approached the two men. The cop turned to him with an amused expression on his face.

"Well, well, we meet again, Mr. Sizemore," Valentine said. "I've been telling your manager that you've all had a tough couple of months here. First, the club's valuable wine is stolen, and now some federally protected birds have been poached!"

"I'm aware of that, Lieutenant. Mike called me in the car. Informed me that the birds were banded with some type of radar. Thank the good Lord for that!"

"Those white trumpet cranes are the club mascots, aren't they?" asked the cop. "I don't know about you, but I see a lot of irony in this situation."

"I'm glad someone finds humor in this outrage, Lieutenant," Newt said as he struggled to stop his arms and legs from shaking. "But the amount of crime in this city is no laughing matter. And I hope you've got some solid leads on this one."

"Oh, we've got more than leads, Mr. Sizemore. We've got the birds, and we've taken the club's bag boy and another fellow into custody. They had quite a lot to say about who was behind this crime. We've also got some strong intel on the wine theft."

The president's face changed from purple to ashen in a matter of seconds, and a leg began to spasm. "Well, that's . . . that is great news, Lieutenant. Hey, could ya just give me a sec here to make a quick call? I'll be right with you," he said as he stepped away. With fingers trembling, he hit Norm O'Malley's number on his cell.

"O'Malley, we got problems."

"What's going on, Newt?" The priest was lunching in the Men's Grill. "I hope you're not involved with the bird fiasco that's going on here."

"I may be up shit's creek, Norm. The operation I had in place seemed a no-brainer. Unfortunately, it appears the birds were banded with some type of tracking devices. Now, that nosy cop Valentine is back. And he's still got a hard-on for the wine theft. Could spell big trouble for me, so I need your help."

"Sorry Newt, bad timing. The big guys are all at the Vatican this week. No cell phones allowed. But hey . . . if I were you, I'd dangle a Courtesy Membership in front of that civil servant. He's a golfer. A good one too. Might very well jump at it."

"Hmmm, don't know. The guy seems pretty much on the straight and narrow."

"They all seem pretty much on the straight and narrow. But they all have their price."

"I'll give it a shot," Newt said. He clicked off his phone, walked back to the cop, and spoke from one side of his mouth with head held low to share a confidence. "Lieutenant Valentine . . ."

"Yes, Mr. Sizemore?"

"I'm sure you can understand that my job here isn't an easy one."

"I didn't think it was, Mr. Sizemore."

"And there are a lot of tough decisions one has to make when trying to run an operation like this."

"I hear ya, sir." Valentine cocked his head to see where this was going.

"And we often need the support of local community officials like yourself . . . to help us meet the challenges we face."

The cop put his hands on his hips. "That's why we're here, Mr. Sizemore. Our slogan is still 'To Protect and Serve'."

"That is a comfort," Newt nodded his head. "And that's why I'm wondering if you'd be open to finding a resolution to this situation that results in a win-win for all."

"I'm not sure I understand what you're asking, sir. The removal of protected wildlife from their nests is a federal crime. The LAPD is here to assist Fish and Wildlife. We'll make arrests where warranted, and chances are that the boys we've got in custody will help us do that."

"I certainly hope so." Newt shook his head in agreement.

"After that, there will be an investigation by the U.S. Attorney's office, which should result in heavy fines and possible jail time for those involved with the crime."

"I'm in total support of your efforts, Lieutenant. I'm even prepared to make you an offer that I see as an opportunity to enhance communications between our two entities, and to have good men like yourself on our team here at Bellstone."

"Just what are you getting at Mr. Sizemore?" Valentine crossed his muscular arms over his expansive chest.

"Rumor has it, Lieutenant, that you're quite a golfer. It just so happens that Bellstone has a Courtesy Membership available right now for a local official such as yourself. It provides for unlimited use of our golf course and all of the other amenities of the club."

"Go on, Mr. Sizemore, I'm listening."

"In return, we would simply request that you help squire us through difficult times like this one and assist in ironing out various obstacles that we may encounter in our dealings with the city."

"I appreciate the thought, but I'm afraid I can't accept your offer." The cop paused to look around at the scene before him. He took in the sight of the rolling fairways, the picture-perfect greens marked by crisp flags waving in the breeze, and the well-heeled members, who all seemed so relaxed and happy to be enjoying what was indeed one of the country's premier golf courses.

Reading Valentine's body language, Newt was able to recognize temptation when he saw it. "Before you give me an answer, Lieutenant, I've asked Father Norm O'Malley, the beloved priest of the All Saints Church in Encino, to join us to share his experiences as a courtesy member with you." Newt labored to finesse the muscles of his bloated face into a smile. "But first, please feel free to stroll around and check out our grounds. I think this club would be a great fit for you, Rocco."

The cop looked over at the driving range where he saw Mandy strike one of her eye-catching poses as she finished her swing. "Well, I guess I should be doing that anyhow, as a part of my investigation," he told Newt. "Might as well take a look at the place." He headed across the parking lot toward the range.

•   •   •

Following a full morning of client meetings at his office in near-by Pasadena, Monty Manville was en route to Bellstone to play the proud husband as Mandy secured her tenth club championship win. Though their relationship had sunk to a new low point since their argument about their financial woes, he didn't want to raise eyebrows by not giving his wife a victory kiss in the winner's circle. As he entered the club's guard gate in his Lexus, he waved to Bob in the booth.

"Have you heard about the goings-on around here today, Mr. Manville?" the guard called out to him. The accountant stopped his car and cocked his head at the question.

"Heard about the goings-on?" Monty asked. "No, why? Was there a problem?"

"Sure was, and it was a doozy! Those baby trumpet cranes down at the lake were poached during the ladies match," Bob said. "The thieves must'a thought there'd be too much hoo-ha happenin' with the media and spectators to be noticed. I've been scanning my tapes to see if their truck came through here when I was on my break, but they must'a come through the back. Now I'm expectin' I'll be turnin' all the video from the past couple of months over to the law enforcement folks. But first, there's somethin' you might better take a look at, Mr. Manville."

"Oh boy, what now, Bob?" Monty shut off his engine, climbed out of the car, and entered the booth. "I've had a tough morning, already," he told the guard. "This club used to be my escape. Now it's just one problem after another."

"I know what ya mean, Mr. Manville. And I feel sort'a awkward bringing this to your attention. But I'm stumped on how else to handle it." The guard was shuttling through footage on the monitor labeled "bag room" mounted on the booth's wall. When he slowed the picture down, Monty could make out the darkened bag room. The date on the screen was April 30th, and the time was eight forty-five p.m. Monty remembered April 30th as the night of the White Trumpet Crane Spring Fling Dinner-Dance. He saw the shelves holding the bags rocking back and forth before the camera panned over to reveal Mandy sitting on a shelf with her bare legs straddled around Jorge's waist. Monty felt his stomach turn over as he recalled Mandy disappearing from the dining table in the clubhouse that night, and on many other nights to "grab something" from the bag room.

"Erase the footage, Bob," he told the guard. "No one should have to look at that filth."

•　　•　　•

The security vehicle carrying the recovered chicks arrived at the Wheeler Garden by noon. After getting a quick check-up from Jody, each bird was placed in a nest by Fish and Wildlife officials.

"We're lucky that the poachers must have received instructions to deliver the chicks alive and well to the lab," Jody told Jackson as the two of them watched the adult cranes return to the nests and begin to feed their young. "None of them seem any worse from the journey. We're also lucky that the poachers either didn't notice or didn't bother to tamper with the transmitters that were on some of the chick's legs."

"There's no way to put the little guys back in the same nests they were hatched in, right?" Jackson asked. "So how do the parents know which babies are theirs?"

"The adult birds aren't as focused on their nests as they are on their offspring. They seek out their own young by instinct."

"Nature's pretty darn amazing, isn't it?"

"It sure is," Jody agreed. "It's just a shame that our species has such little respect for it," she said with a deep sigh. "I've been informed that the LAPD has Jorge and his cousin in custody. They'll be questioned, so we should have some answers today on who else was behind this. The cousin has already given up the contact in San Diego where the chicks were being dropped, which is a big help to us. Hopefully, the San Diego police can make an arrest there and get the info on that Mexican lab. Meanwhile, if we have to put a twenty-four hour a day guard on these little fellas to keep them safe, we will." Jody looked over at the statue of Forrest Wheeler as if assuring her grandfather that her promise would be kept.

Jackson's cell dinged with a text. "That's Rick," he told Jody. "The match resumes on the 13th hole in twenty minutes. Do you want to hit the range for a quick warm-up?"

"No, I'm good." She paused for thought. "Hey, Jackson, do you think Mandy knew the chicks would be stolen? Or was it really just a coincidence, like she claimed?"

"Hmmm . . . I think she was genuinely surprised that the whole thing happened for real. As an actor, I can tell you that her declaration of ignorance could have earned her an Academy Award if she was in on the theft all along."

"So, she lied about the bird napping and about my husband. All in the time it took to play two holes."

"As you said," Jackson reminded her. "You have to pity the poor woman."

• • •

Mandy was making a desperate last-minute attempt to improve her ball striking at the driving range before the tournament would resume. But no matter how hard she tried to increase her distance off the tee, she was no match for a golfer with a swing as powerful as Jody's.

"Muy bueno, Senora Manville," Armando told his player after each strike of the ball.

"It's no use, Armando," Mandy said. "It's time for us both to admit it. I'm no match for that girl."

"Angie, it *is* you, isn't it?" asked a woman with dark blonde hair wearing a gray linen pantsuit who had walked up behind Mandy.

"Ahhh . . . um . . . who are you?" Mandy wondered how it was possible for anyone in Los Angeles to know her real name.

"It's me, Randi . . . Randi King! You remember? From Bayonne Junior High? Randi?"

Mandy, stunned, managed to stammer out two words. "You're Randi?"

"It's me all right! I saw you on the local news in my hotel room. You've changed your name, and you sound and look a lot different, but I knew it was you, Angie. So, I just had to come by. That nice guard at the gate let me drive through. Said I'd probably find you out here. Did you know he's from Newark? Anyway, I think about you so often, Angie. I'm a professor at Rutgers back in New Jersey now. Head of the Department of Animal Sciences. I'm out here to give a seminar at the local college."

"You're Randi King!" Mandy was still reeling at the sight of her childhood idol.

"I sure am. And I bet you never knew that you were the one who sparked my interest in animal sciences in the first place! When you helped me dissect that fetal pig . . . we were what? Fourteen years old? Something just clicked, and biology became my passion. I've always wanted to thank you for what you did for me, but I never got a chance after getting shipped off to boarding school. Of course, I'd have never even gotten into Miss Porters if you'd hadn't helped me get that 'A'. You did hurt my feelings, though."

"*I* hurt *your* feelings?" Mandy asked without a trace of a Southern accent.

"You sure did! By not coming to that birthday party of mine, way back when."

"What? You sent me an invitation to your party at the country club?"

"I sure did! But your mother returned it with a note. It said that you both agreed it'd be best if you didn't attend. You mom mentioned something about the fact that the class difference between us had made you ashamed of your family."

"What? I had no idea she did that!"

"And it broke my heart. I thought you were so funny and hip and smart. My mom and dad were so appreciative of how you helped me ace that final that they planned to present you with a series of golf lessons at our club as a thank you! I had no idea what your mother meant by her note. I thought she was just making an excuse for you not to come. So, I finally just told myself that you didn't show up because you had much cooler friends to hang with than a southern hick like me."

"That wasn't true, Randi. It wasn't true at all. And I did show up. I stood outside of the gates of that country club in tears because I thought I wasn't invited. And I never got over it."

"Oh Angie!" Randi exclaimed. "If I'd known you were there, I'd have run out to get you."

Mandy stood for a moment, shaking her head in disbelief. "After all these years . . . just knowing you did invite me changes everything."

"But tell me, Angie, what have you been doing with your life, besides winning golf tournaments?"

"I've been trying to do whatever it takes to be invited to the party."

Randi held out her arms. "Give your old friend a hug." The two teary-eyed women embraced. "Here's my card. Email me with your contact info and let's never lose touch again. Love you, Angie! And best of luck in the tournament!"

"Love you too, Randi!" Mandy held the card close and kept her eyes on her childhood friend until she reached the parking lot. Armando teed up another ball for her to hit.

"You have time for another few balls Senora Manville. Then we go."

"Thanks, Armando. And hey, let's just enjoy the rest of the tournament. No matter who wins or loses."

The caddy gave her a nod and Mandy hit another one of her serviceable, but not very powerful drives. She heard a man's voice behind her.

"You need a bigger shoulder turn to get more distance."

She ignored the voice and hit several more drives. After completing her warm-up, she turned and saw Lieutenant Valentine with his LAPD badge on his hip and the muscles on his arms and chest rippling under his shirt.

"C'mon, Jersey girl . . . try one more with the driver." His piercing dark eyes gave her an order she couldn't refuse. "Keep your eye on the ball and turn your left shoulder back 'til it passes beneath your chin."

"Thanks, officer, but I don't need your help. Our head pro is my coach."

"Fahget about him for now, Annika. Give this Jersey boy a thrill and try it my way." He gave Mandy a wink, handed her the driver, and teed up a ball for her.

"Well . . ." Mandy said as she spotted Jody and Jackson chatting with several members near Tournament Rock. "I guess it can't hurt." She took a practice swing.

"Take another practice swing, but this time turn that shoulder under your chin." Mandy followed his instructions. "That's right," said the cop. "Now swing for real and imagine that you're gonna hit a home run into the grandstands." Mandy stood tall, turned her shoulders, and hit through the ball. Her shot soared 220 yards down the range.

"Bingo!" Valentine called out. "I knew you had it in ya."

Rick and the rules official pulled up in the cart. "Five-minute call, Mrs. Manville," the pro told Mandy.

"Got it, Rick! We'll be there!" When Rick drove off, she turned to Valentine.

"Thanks for the tip, officer."

"No problem. Just try to remember to make that big turn when you're out there on the course."

Mandy and Armando arrived at the 13th tee box where they were joined by Jody and Jackson. A group of spectators were milling around discussing the theft of the birds and the arrest of Jorge. Before the golfers teed off, Rick announced that Jody was seven strokes up with six holes left to play. Jody stepped up and executed another powerful drive that soared down the center of the fairway.

"That'll work," Jackson called out to his player.

"Wow, I'm toast," Mandy said to her caddy as he handed her the driver. "But ya know what, Armando? I'm okay with that." She hit her standard drive. It was straight but far shorter than Jody's shot.

When Mandy reached her ball, Valentine was watching her from the edge of the fairway. He called out to her again. "Shoulder turn! C'mon, Annika, do it for me! Get those shoulders behind the ball and let er rip!"

Armando handed his player a fairway wood. Mandy stood tall over the ball, took a deep breath, and relaxed her muscles. Keeping her eye glued to the ball, she forced her shoulders to rotate around her spine, paused for a moment, and then untwisted to swing through with a force that surprised even her. The ball shot off the clubface like a rocket.

"Wow! Fantastic strike, Mandy!" Jody called out as the ball hissed down the fairway and didn't stop until it reached the 13th green. "I love that power! Keep it up!"

Jody then hit her own stunning shot and watched the ball drop near the pin. When the players reached the green, it was Mandy's turn to putt. "Okay, Mandy," Jody said. "Knock it in the hole." Mandy's putt stopped just short of the cup. She tapped it in for par.

It was Jody's turn to putt. "You can do it, Jody," Mandy called out. It struck her that this was the first time in years that she'd rooted for an opponent on the course. "Yes! Great putt!" Mandy heard herself cry out as Jody's ball dropped into the hole for another birdie. Armando looked over at his player with saucer-shaped eyes.

"You feeling okay, Senora Manville?"

"Yes, I'm just fine Armando. I think that visit from my old friend has changed my attitude about golf, and about myself."

On the 14th hole, a long par five, Jody hit another bomb. As Mandy teed up her ball, she spotted Valentine at the front of the gallery. He waved, and then made a swinging motion with his arms, rotating his shoulders under his chin, and pretending to hit through a ball. Mandy smiled at him and nodded. Following his advice, she blasted a drive 210 yards down the fairway. Valentine held two thumbs way up in the air.

"You're a player, Mandy," Jody called out.

"She's starting to hit some powerful shots," Jackson said to Jody. "It's way too late in the game for her to have a chance at catching you, but I have to say I'm impressed."

"And she seems to be enjoying herself, which I like even better," Jody said.

Both women followed up their drives with excellent shots to the green. Mandy made a long and somewhat lucky putt for birdie, and

Jody two-putted for a par. It was the first hole that Mandy had won on skill alone. But that small victory gave her the sweetest feeling of accomplishment that she'd experienced in years.

Her victory was short-lived, though, as Jody won the 15th hole with a par four to Mandy's triple bogey seven. On the 16th hole, a one hundred thirty-yard par three over water, Jody used a nine iron that flew the ball toward the pin.

"It's in the hole! It's in the hole!" Mandy heard herself calling out. Jody's ball landed six feet from the pin. Now it was Mandy's turn to hit. After teeing up her ball, she took a huge shoulder turn as Valentine had instructed. Her shot rose high in the air. Those in the galley "oohed" and "aahed", before erupting in cheers as the ball landed close to the pin and trickled into the cup. Mandy had the first hole-in-one of her golfing career.

"Whoa! Yay!" Jody cried out to the sounds of the cheering crowd. Mandy was stunned. She turned to give Valentine a victory sign.

When the two women and their caddies began their walk down the 18th fairway, they spotted a sea of spectators along with the KTLA news crew that had set their cameras up around the green for the finale of the tournament.

"Wow!" Jody said to Jackson.

"Look at the crowd! There must be five hundred people out there! Now I know how my grandpa felt when he played his final rounds of the U.S. Open on this same spot."

"News of Mandy's hole-in-one must have traveled fast," Jackson told her. "People are wondering if she still has a chance to win this thing."

A large leaderboard stood next to the 18th green with hole-by-hole scores of the players. With one hole remaining, Mandy had logged a total of 77 strokes to Jody's 67. When the players arrived at the final green, Mandy's ball was a good twenty feet from the hole. It was her turn to putt. She made a good effort and missed by less than a foot. She tapped in for another par and a final score of eighty-one. The gallery applauded the nine-time club champion for her efforts. She turned and gave them a smile.

Jody had a mere three-footer for birdie, which would give her an eleven-stroke victory over Mandy, and a two under par score of 70. Before setting up to putt, she looked up at the majestic oak that towered above the green. A white trumpet crane was busy pecking at what looked to be gold-spotted oak borers from the bark of the tree. Her eyes traveled across the green at the soon-to-be-beaten Mandy, the very disappointed head pro, and the hushed members of the gallery, many of whom were still wearing their kilts, and tam o'shanter caps. The bagpipers had been instructed to begin their tunes when Rick gave them the signal that proclaimed Mandy as the winner. Now, they would be walking away without playing a note.

Jody looked at Jackson. The caddy gave her an encouraging nod. She paused to take a long panoramic look at the club her grandfather had founded, and whispered to herself, "I'm doing what's best for Bellstone."

She took her putter back and stroked the ball hard enough to make it roll past the cup, down a slope off the green, and into a bunker. Groans rose from the gallery.

"Oh darn," she said, as she grabbed a sand wedge from her bag. Jackson stood and stared at his player.

She climbed down into the bunker. She pretended to look at the hole while she hit her next shot into another bunker across the green. More groans sounded from the gallery.

"How silly of me!" she said, as she walked past the stunned Jackson.

"What's going on?" he asked.

"Just rake the bunker please."

She stepped into the second bunker, where she waited for Jackson to rake her footprints from the first bunker. Looking at the green once more, she hit the ball into the first bunker again, well-aware that a player who hits a shot into a bunker for a second time, after the trap has been raked, must incur a two-stroke penalty. She had now hit seven shots. Climbing into the first bunker for the second time, she paused to count the five strokes she had added since landing on the green in two. She then took seven more shots, hitting only sand onto the green while her ball stayed in the bunker. Next, she carefully dug her feet in the sand, looked at the flag, sliced the club through the sand, and finished her swing with the club pointed toward the flag. The ball flew high into the air and landed in the center of the cup. There was a gasp from the crowd.

For a good ten seconds, no one said a word. Mandy began to count each of Jody's strokes on the hole and concurred with Armando and Rick that the total was fifteen, for a final score of eighty-two. Mandy won the match by a single stroke.

The pro signaled for the bagpipers to fire into *Scotland the Brave.* Mandy's supporters gathered around her and offered their congratulations. Many were on their phones, trying to reinstate their flights and hotel reservations. For the past nine years, Rick had presented Mandy with a bouquet of red roses for her championship victory. For her tenth win, he had a special bouquet made-up that was so large, it required a small truck to haul it out. Reporter Lisa Langheart and her crew pushed their way through the crowd to reach the winner.

"You've won this tournament for the tenth time, Mandy!" Lisa shouted while she held the microphone near the winner's face. "How are you feeling at this very magical moment?"

Jody and Jackson walked off the green. The caddy turned to his player. "That final act was outrageous and impetuous. But I think I understand your motivation. And as a screenwriter, I loved that changeup you threw at your audience."

"Glad you approved of my rewrite, Mr. Lyons. Ya know, when I spotted that trumpet crane keeping the oak healthy by eating the gold-spotted oak borers, I realized that I'm doing something that would make my grandpa very proud. He always wanted what was best for Bellstone. And when it comes down to it, so do I. I'm pretty sure he'd agree that shooting a fifteen on the 18th hole today was a good thing for the club he loved."

Jody's cell buzzed with a text message from Derrick.

Derrick: *Congrats to the new club champ of 2011*
Jody: *I lost*
Derrick: *Say what?*

Jody: *Couldn't let her lose/ meant ( ) to her but () to me . . . crazy day*

Derrick: *Want 2 to hear all about it. On way 2 lunch then game w/ Gamblers @ 3*

Won't be home for dinner / we'll have consolation dinner tomorrow night / luv U

"It looks like tonight's dinner with Derrick will have to wait. My husband is quite the busy bee," Jody said when she looked up from the screen.

"I'm sure he is," Jackson said.

"But he does have time for his afternoon game with the Gamblers," she said with a slight tone of annoyance before brightening. "And you've got your big meeting! You going straight from here?"

"Yup. Just gonna make some notes on casting, locations and so on, and I'll be off."

"Pretty darn cool, Mr. Lyons. Good luck to you. Can you let me know how things go? Shoot me a text?"

Jackson hesitated for a moment, before speaking. "Sure, but . . . Jody, there's something I've been needing to say to you for a while now."

"Whoa! You're scaring me, Jackson."

"It's just that . . . I've caddied for a few of those Gambler games. And I've heard—"

"Hey Jody, I'll save you seat inside!" It was Diane Sharp who was on her way to the clubhouse. "We've gotta talk, girl!"

"Ehhh . . . sure thing Diane." She turned to Jackson. "Now I'm in for it! Anyway, you've got my curiosity going. But I can't be late for the luncheon, so it'll have to wait. How about if I meet you by Eddie's booth after the luncheon? Say two thirty-ish? That work?"

"Yup. See you then, Jody."

•　　•　　•

After her TV interview wrapped, Mandy was making her victory walk to the clubhouse for the championship luncheon. For the very first time, it really did feel like a victory walk—but for a different reason than she would ever have imagined.

"I inspired Randi King! I set her on a path that changed her life!" she whispered to herself. "And now she's doing something that matters! Randi liked me because I was smart. She liked me for who I was!" When Mandy walked by the clubhouse, she caught her reflection in the window. But she barely recognized the woman staring back at her. "Angelina Teresa Fatabina! Whatever *has* become of you?" she asked her reflection. "You've cheated on your husband, tried to poach endangered birds, and lied through your teeth to win golf tournaments. Just what would Randi think of you now?"

• • •

On his way to deliver his speech, Newt called out to Lieutenant Valentine on the golf course. "Well, here he is! I trust you've liked what you've seen so far . . . Rocco."

"What's not to like . . . Newt?"

"Then it sounds like you're seriously considering our offer?"

"I gotta admit—it's very tempting."

"Glad to hear it!" Newt clapped his hands together and gave two thumbs up. "Now, if you'll just give me a few to get something out of the way, I'll meet you at the bar and we can discuss details. Father Norm's waiting for you there now. He plans to open a bottle of bubbly to toast our newest courtesy member."

The cop looked at his watch. "I shouldn't drink while I'm on duty. But I won't tell if you won't."

Newt entered the clubhouse dining room where servers were carrying out bowls of asparagus soup to start off the championship luncheon. Poached salmon and a dessert of coconut layer cake would follow. The bagpipers were playing *Scotland the Brave* as they marched throughout the room. The president spotted Mandy seated with Rick at a table near the podium, which confirmed his assumption that she had secured her tenth club championship victory. He readied himself for his speech, anxious to get back to his real priority—wooing that damn cop.

Jody and Diane Sharp were seated at one of the lunch tables. The attorney eyed the other woman with disbelief. "Whatever ploy did she you use to make you throw the match like that?" she asked. "Was it a threat, a bribe, or hypnosis?"

"I'll be honest with you, Diane. She did pull some pretty darn nasty stunts out there, just like you said she would. But then, she changed. It was after I helped her get out of the sand. She seemed to have some sort of epiphany. Said I reminded her of an old friend."

"Oh, come on! Don't you understand, girl? It was a ruse! That's what she does! That's how she wins! Whatever it takes, she does it. Are you always this trusting of folks? That's gotta come back to bite you in the ass every so often."

"I do tend to look for the best in people," Jody agreed.

"Well, like I told you before, this club is a haven for liars. And criminals! Like that President up there. First, he strong-armed the other board members to build that wine cellar the club can't afford. Then, lo and behold, right before I could schedule an appraisal of our wine collection, some of the most valuable bottles were stolen. I met with the officer investigating the case and told him I'm sure Sizemore and the priest are the crooks behind that fiasco. Then today, the poor birds were pilfered. You can bet that our President is behind that too. And now, what do I see? Instead of arresting these crooks, the cop is having drinks in the bar with the priest and strolling around here like he's about to own the joint! No doubt they've bribed him with one of those Courtesy Memberships! This place is a snake pit. Pardon me for saying so honey, but your grandfather must be turning over in his grave."

Before Jody could respond to Diane's tirade, the feedback from the microphone jolted the room. The bagpipers halted their play, and those at the tables fell silent.

"Good afternoon ladies!" Newt began. The president looked at the seated women and labored to form a smile on his bloated face. He opened his crumpled piece of paper and scanned a speech he'd downloaded online from a site that offered congratulatory speeches for sporting events. Unfortunately, the closest speech that he could find for female athletes was for the winners of a woman's Varsity basketball tournament. "We have a champion among us," he announced as he surveyed his audience. "A woman who has met every type of challenge the game of basket—oops, I mean, the game of golf, has to offer. On my way to see you all today, I asked myself, 'with so many fine lady players at this great college . . . oops . . . club, why has one woman remained numero uno'? The answer lies in the words of the great coach John Wooden, who said, 'Ability may get you to the top, but it takes character to keep you there.'"

"I think I'm gonna be sick," Diane said while she waved her cloth napkin to fan her face.

"So, let's give a big hand to the undisputed winner of this year's Bellstone Women's Club Championship, Mandy Manville! Please join me at the podium, Mandy."

The sound of applause filled the room, as the bagpipers began the regimental tune *Ye Banks and Braes* and continued their march around the room. Newt walked to a nearby table and picked up the perpetual trophy that would be engraved for the tenth time with Mandy's name and the year of her win. Standing three feet tall, it featured a lady golfer swinging a club with a white trumpet crane on the player's shoulder. He tried to hand the trophy to Mandy, who was now standing beside him, but she gestured for him put it down. She then took the microphone, and signaled for the bagpipers to halt their play.

"My fellow ladies of Bellstone," she began in a voice absent of her familiar Southern drawl. "For many months now, I expected this day to be a life-changing event for me. And believe me when I say that it was." Mandy's fans began to clap their hands, but she motioned for them to hold their applause. "It was life changing because of the lessons I learned from two women. I encountered one woman during the break in the tournament—a woman I knew and even idolized when I was just a girl. I hadn't seen her in more years than I'd like to admit, and though we only chatted for a few minutes, they may have been the most important minutes of my life. Because today, she helped me to understand that people don't love you because you're rich or beautiful, or a great athlete. They love you for who you are, and because you're their friend." The women could have heard a pin drop in the room as

Mandy paused to wipe a tear from her eye. "I also learned a valuable lesson today from Jody Benson, who's a shining example of how the game of golf should be played." Mandy's voice was trembling, her lips quivering. "Besides being a stunning golfer, Jody was nothing but encouraging and gracious throughout our match. She was even willing to hand me this victory out of sheer kindness. And though she tried to make me a champion, what I am, is ashamed." A swell of chatter permeated the room as the stunned ladies wondered if they'd heard right. "For too many years now, I've been trying to make myself appear better than I am. No . . . actually . . . I've been a total impostor." Wiping away more tears, she looked into the eyes of the rapt faces in her audience. "My name is not really Mandy or even Amanda, and I'm not really from the South. And I'm most definitely not your woman club champion." The room erupted with shouts of "huh?" and "what?" from the ladies. Mandy blew her nose and waited for the group to quiet down. "I'm dis . . . dis . . . disqualifying myself from today's tournament for breaking a rule of golf several times during the round. I admit to intentionally trying to distract my opponent . . . no . . . to destroy my opponent during play to obtain an advantage." Struggling to suppress her sobs, Mandy continued. "Your real club champion is Jo . . . Jo . . . Jody Benson. Congratulations to you, Jody. And I'd like to offer you, and the other ladies here today my sincere apologies for bending the rules . . . no . . . for cheating at the game we're so blessed to be able to play on this wonderful golf course."

Mandy hobbled from the podium, heaving with sobs. Her chest, once thrust forward with pride, was now hunched. Her breasts, once bouncy and buoyant, hung toward the floor. The chatter throughout the room continued as the ladies tried to absorb the incredible turn of events. Some of them wondered if there was such a rule about distracting one's opponent during the game and if it was even possible to change the outcome of the tournament at this point.

"Well, what do ya know? There is a God after all!" Diane Sharp yelled over the chatter.

Rick and the rules official took Jody aside to question her about the events surrounding Mandy's confession. The official then had a quick meet with the Bellstone women's group rules committee before giving her decision to Rick. The pro returned to the microphone.

"Ladies!" Rick announced as he wiped the sweat from his brow with a handkerchief. "This is a first for me, and for all of you too, I'm sure. According to the United States Golf Association rule 33-7, the tournament committee may disqualify a competitor for committing a serious breach of etiquette while the match is underway. Previous rulings have included intentionally distracting an opponent in this category. And while Mrs. Benson has confirmed that she believes Mrs. Manville did intentionally try to distract her, she insists that her opponent's behavior was not a factor in the outcome of the tournament. After considering this, your committee has decided not to disqualify Mrs. Manville from the championship."

Newt sat at the long table next to the stage, his foot tapping from nerves, and his head craned forward to keep an eye on Father Norm and Lieutenant Valentine, who were seated at the bar. He stretched his buttoned shirt collar to relieve the pressure on his neck and kept his thick fingers crossed that the cop would accept that Courtesy Membership.

When Rick finished his speech, he signaled Newt, who grabbed the microphone from the pro's hand. "Ladies of Bellstone," the president began. "I'm proud to once again present your 2011 Woman Club Champion, Ms. Mandy Manville!" His words received a smattering of applause and a rising swell of chatter from the women. Mandy returned to the podium, her face distorted from weeping, to take the trophy from Newt. The bagpipers resumed their serenade while waiters passed out slices of the cake and filled glasses with champagne to toast the winner.

It was nearly time for Jody to meet Jackson. She made her way over to Mandy's table and extended her hand to the champion. "Well done, Mandy," she said. "You were truly a winner today. In more ways than one."

Mandy took her hand and smiled. "Thank you, Jody. Thank you for everything. I can't begin to tell you how sorry I am for my behavior out there. And I can only hope you can one day find it in your heart to forgive me."

"And I hope that you'll continue on your new path. Now, take that powerful new swing and that great new attitude over to Scotland, and make us all proud! I know you'll be a wonderful representative of Bellstone."

•   •   •

Jody walked out of the clubhouse, still reeling from the highs and lows of her rollercoaster ride of a day. Mandy seemed to transform from a monster to a caring person, all in one round of golf. The theft of the trumpet cranes was terrifying and stressful. But the outcome indicated that the new technology would be a breakthrough in the fight against poachers. Jackson seemed to be on the path to getting his writing, and maybe even his acting career, back where they belonged. And though she'd intentionally lost the tournament, she was once again loving the game of golf.

When Jody arrived at Eddie's booth, she saw the old man inside and waved up at him. He held up his arms, gesturing "what happened?" She made a stretching motion with her arms to signify "long" and held her hands in the shape of an open book to convey the word "story". She then turned and saw a strange girl, who happened to be Amber holding little Derrick who was wrapped in a blue blanket with a blue cap on his head.

"What a beautiful new baby you have there!" Jody told Amber. "What's your son's name?"

Amber turned the infant toward Jody. "Derrick, ma'am," Amber said, while she smiled at her sleeping son. Jody gazed at the tiny boy's face with a dimple in the middle of his chin, and had a feeling that she'd seen that face a million times before.

"I'm looking for his daddy who golfs here," Amber said. "A Mr. Derrick Benson. Do you know that fella?"

Jody froze for a good ten seconds, before taking a step backward. She put her hands to her head in horror. "Oh, my God!" she cried out. "She wasn't lying! Mandy was telling the truth! She was telling the truth! My husband has fathered another woman's child!"

Jackson came around the corner of Eddie's booth. Hearing Jody's words and seeing Amber with the baby explained it all. He went to Jody and took the distraught woman in his arms.

"Jody, I'm so sorry. I was going to tell you that your husband had been cheating on you. But I had no idea about the child."

Eddie stepped out of his booth. "I hope this isn't what it looks like from in there!"

Amber gave Jody a sympathetic smile. "You're the wife, aren't you? I'm sorry ma'am. I know you weren't expectin' nothin' like this. I reckon that as soon as my Derrick sees his own kin, he'll want to git hitched to me fer sure. But I hope you make out okay with the devorce and all. And maybe if ya do git married agin—you'll have learned to treat your man with the kindness he deserves."

The roar of a BMW640i engine, with its sound system pulsating and tires screeching, exploded from the parking lot. The sounds of LMFAO could be heard all the way to the Wheeler Garden.

"Party rock is in the house tonight. Everybody just have a good time, yeah. And we gonna make you lose your mind whoa. Everybody just have a good time."

"I'm gonna kill him. I'm gonna kill that fucker!" Jackson said as he ran toward the car.

"I sure didn't mean ta create any ruckus by coming here," Amber told Jody. "I been textin' and textin' my honey, but never hear back no more. Did he change his number or somethin'?"

When Derrick handed his keys to Bernardo, he was met with a hard shove from Jackson that slammed him into the side of the BMW. The force triggered the car's alarm and the pulsating noise flowed across the golf course while Amber, Jody, and Eddie ran to the porte-cochére to see what had caused the commotion. The ferocious sound ripped through the walls of the clubhouse sending Mandy and the ladies still lingering at the luncheon, Monty, who was working on the club's financials, along with Newt, Father Norm, Lieutenant Valentine, and those in the bar running out to the parking lot to witness Jackson throw a punch to the stomach of the stunned Derrick. The lieutenant grabbed a pair of handcuffs from his belt and pinned the caddy against the car.

"You're going to jail, dude," the cop said as he turned Jackson around to face the car, pulled his arms behind his back, and snapped the cuffs on the caddy's wrists. Though the cop had no idea what the dispute was about, he assumed there could be no possible good reason for a caddy to assault a member of one of the nation's most prestigious golf clubs.

"Un-cuff that man now, Lieutenant!" Eddie demanded. He pointed at Derrick. "That's your perp! Considering the sins he's committed against his fine and trusting wife, he deserves far worse than a pop in the gut."

Father Norm spotted the girl holding the infant and quickly summed up the situation. After his previous attempts to help Derrick with his problem had failed, the courtesy member seized the opportunity to prove his worth.

"Hold on friends," Norm commanded, in his most sincere Sunday sermon tone. "It's true this man may well have sinned. But how many of us here can claim to be free of sin? Jesus said, 'He that is without sin among you let him cast the first stone'. So, if you're that person, feel free to cast your stone." The priest scanned through the faces in the crowd. Wives looked at their husbands, who avoided their stares and shuffled their feet. "No one? I thought not." He pointed to Derrick. "This young man has learned that his infractions have consequences. But God is merciful, and we must be mindful that the innocent child must not be punished for the sins of the father."

"What's goin' on?" a confused Lieutenant Valentine asked the priest. He looked at Amber and the baby, and then at Derrick, and began to make the connection. "Is this the Benson guy who fathered your child, Miss Lane? The golfer dude who impregnated you and allowed you to keep working in that strip club?"

"Yes, officer." Amber told the cop. "I'd like you to meet my baby's daddy, Mr. Derrick Benson."

Ignoring the introduction, the lieutenant began to un-cuff Jackson. "Don't stop what you're doing on our account, pal," he said to the caddy.

"Yeah, give him one for me too," ordered Eddie. "Right on that pretty boy chin."

"Please, y'all!" Amber cried out. "No more roughin' up my honey. Not in front of his boy."

"Well, I'll be hornswoggled!" Newt said to Derrick. "Is that the gal from Dancin' Bare? Just how were you fixin' to explain that to your pretty wife? Looks like you've managed to get yourself tied between two hogs, boy!"

"No need for him to explain anything," Jody said. "It's all crystal clear."

"No Jody, it's not. It's not crystal clear! Don't believe what they're saying!" Derrick cried out, wincing from the punch to his belly. "I've never cheated on you. Not once!"

"Well, that's not quite true, folks," Mandy piped up, causing a murmur to rise up from the crowd as it parted to make room for her to walk forward. "I too have known this man. In the biblical sense, that is." The admission elicited a collective gasp from the crowd. Mandy's friends Noreen Sizemore and Hope Watchtower looked at each other and held their faces in horror while Diane Sharp smiled with satisfaction at the exposure of her enemy's dirty laundry.

"You and Derrick?" asked an incredulous Jody as she stared at her husband in disbelief. "Oh, my God!" She turned back to Mandy. "And just when had you planned to drop that bomb on me? On the 12th hole? Before play was suspended? That would've cost me a stroke or two."

"I tried to tell you," Mandy said, walking up close to Jody. "But it didn't happen. So I'm telling you now, for your own good, that your husband's a louse!"

"Jody, please!" Derrick cried out. "I love you! Things just got out of hand! I'd do anything to take it all back!"

"There's no taking this guy back, Derrick." Jody pointed to the baby. "You be a good father to this beautiful boy."

"But how can I be good to anyone if you leave me? How can I be happy again, without the only woman I've ever really loved?"

Jody stood tall and paused before answering. "Frankly my dear . . . I don't give a damn."

"Just like Clark Gable said to Vivien Leigh in *Gone with the Wind*," Noreen said to Hope. "You go girl!" Diane Sharp called out to Jody.

Father Norm took Derrick by the arm. "Why don't you go wash up in the men's locker room, son? Bernardo can show the girl and her baby to the front lobby where they can wait for you. Then you can all start making plans for the future."

Monty walked up to his wife as the crowd dispersed. "I saw the security camera footage from your bag room grab-fest with Jorge, Mandy. And now, you've surprised me with this little announcement to our fellow club members. You bled me dry and cheated on me for good measure. Tell me why. Tell me why I deserved this."

"You didn't deserve it, Monty." Mandy looked into the sad eyes of her husband. "You didn't deserve it at all. I have no excuse for myself." Her eyes welled up with tears. "The best thing that I can do for you now . . . is to excuse myself from your life."

• • •

Newt and Norm ushered Valentine back to the bar to continue their efforts in persuading the cop to accept the Courtesy Membership. Newt's huge buttocks had barely hit the barstool when he got a call from Bob at the front gate.

"Sorry to interrupt your meeting, President Sizemore," Bob told him. "But two Asian gentlemen have pulled up in a Bentley. They're asking for you. A Mr. Chung and a Mr. Fong. Shall I wave them through to the clubhouse?"

"Chung? Fong?" Newt thought for a moment. "Ju . . . ju . . . ju . . . just give me one second here, Bob," the president sputtered. He put his hand over the mouthpiece of the phone and spoke to Norm in a whisper. "Those Chinese guys that bought the wine from us are at the front gate! What do we do?"

Norm looked up from the plate of cheese canapés he was enjoying. "They're here? At Bellstone?"

"Yes! Here! To see me!" Newt hissed back.

"Holy shit!" The priest shook his head in amazement. "I've been dealing with these guys for years now, but they never showed up in person. What in the name of heaven could they be doing here? You *did* return that money to Li Fong, did you not? I told you he wired it into the account a month ago."

"No, I didn't," Newt said, still whispering. "I needed the funds to cover that fight fiasco Columbo fucked us on."

"Well, that's just great, Newt. Now, they're here to collect. You'd better cut them a check. No doubt they'll want it certified," he said as he popped another canapé into his mouth.

"I can't cut them a check. Because we don't have the money." Newt put his hand on the priest's arm. "Hey Norm, how about if you go and talk to them, to buy me some time? Tell them we promise to get a check out in a few weeks. Maybe they'll be more accommodating to you since you've had dealings with them before—along with being a priest and all."

"They're Buddhists, Newt. This collar won't carry any weight with them. Fong wants his money, so you'd better find a way to pay him now. He's not someone to fool around with."

Newt's neck swelled against his collar, while his right leg and foot began to twitch up and down as if hit by a jolt of electricity. He elbowed the Lieutenant, who was in a heated conversation with Mario the bartender about the promise of the upcoming Rutgers University football season.

"Listen, Valentine, there are a couple of guys trying to cause trouble for the club. We may need you to rough 'em up for us. You ready to earn that Courtesy Membership?"

"Got ya covered, Mr. Prez!" The cop lifted his shirt to reveal the .45 tucked in at his belt.

"No one's roughing anyone up," Norm commanded. "Besides being one of the world's preeminent collectors of French wine, Mr. Fong is one of China's most prominent businessmen."

"What the fuck did you get me into here, O'Malley?" Newt said as he picked up his phone. "Wave the car through, Bob."

•   •   •

Newt, Norm, and Rocco Valentine walked out to the front of the clubhouse to greet the metallic blue Bentley that glistened in the late afternoon sun as it pulled up to the porte-cochere. Bernardo opened the passenger door, then raced around the front of the car to open the driver's door. The two Chinese men wearing dark suits and sunglasses got out of the car, and Newt stepped forward to shake their hands.

"Hello, gentlemen! I'm Newt Sizemore, the president of this country club. How nice of you to pay us a visit today! I'm pleased to introduce Lieutenant Rocco Valentine of the Los Angeles Police Department. I'd also like to present Father Norm O'Malley from the All Saints Church of Encino, whom Mr. Chung has been communicating with via email."

Newt shook the first man's hand, who nodded and said, "很高兴见到你."

"Yes, it's great to finally meet you in person too," Newt answered, though he had no idea what the man had said. "Now, which one of you is Mr. Fong?" he asked as he shook the hand of the driver of the Bentley.

"That is Li Fong," answered the driver, who pointed to the other man. "He speaks very little English. I am Ning Chung, Mr. Fong's wine buyer, and will assist with the discussions. Mr. Fong has come to Los Angeles on business, and we decided that we would take this opportunity to visit you in person to collect the $200,000 you owe him for the wine he did not receive. He will accept cash or a certified check."

Newt bowed to the two men. He turned to Chung. "Please tell Mr. Fong I'm sorry for the confusion over the delivery of his wine, and my delay in sending out the check. Perhaps we could all step into the clubhouse to enjoy a glass of our finest French Burgundy before we work to settle up our debts."

The five men convened in the bar. "Mario, please open a bottle of that '67 Chateau Haut-Brion I've selected for our guests," Newt instructed.

Li Fong's eyes widened, as Mario popped the cork of the premier grand cru that would easily bring in over $800 at auction. He then looked over at the massive glass walls of the wine cellar under construction and said, "对那个酒窖感兴趣," to Chung.

"Mr. Fong is very interested in the design of your new cellar," Chung told Newt. "He is wondering if he could step inside to observe it."

"Of course. We'd be tickled pink to give you fellas the fifty-cent tour!" Newt walked the men through the cellar while pointing out the moving shelves and impressive features of the two-story structure. When the tour had been completed, Chung asked if Fong could also view the club's wine collection. Anxious to keep the relationship cordial, Newt escorted the men down the steps of the basement into the building's original cellar.

Fong spent about twenty minutes examining just a few dozen or so of the thousands of bottles in the collection. He pointed to one bottle and made a request to Chung.

"Mr. Fong has found a very special vintage. He is asking for permission to examine it more closely."

"I have no problem with that." The president's chest puffed up at the collector's interest.

Fong nodded his thanks to Newt and pulled a pair of white cotton gloves from his pocket. After slipping them on, he placed his selection on a small table. He blew a coat of dust off the bottle and studied what he could see of the wine inside. He then produced an eyepiece from a pocket inside of his jacket and proceeded to inspect the glass and the label of the vintage. Fong spoke again to Chung.

"Mr. Fong says that the bottle is from Chateau Laffite, with a vintage date of 1869. There are only of small number of these bottles left in the world. The label is in good condition and the fill remains high. He is asking if you know how long the bottle has been stored in this cellar."

"Let's see . . . hmm . . . probably since before the place was bought in the 1940's," Newt said as he poked an index finger into one of his sagging jowls. "The cellar was most likely put in when the mansion was built in the 1920's by that Hollywood movie studio honcho. They say the guy was a big wine collector."

Chung relayed the information to Fong, and Fong spoke again to Chung. "The fact that the bottle has remained in this cellar under ideal conditions, means the chances are good that the wine is drinkable,"

Chung told Newt. "Mr. Fong would like to make a request to purchase the bottle. This vintage could sell for as much as $230,000 at auction, but you would have to pay a commission on the sale. He would like to offer you $200,000 at this time, which is what you owe him. If you'll allow him to take the bottle now, he will call it, 甚至史蒂文, or in your language, 'even Steven'."

"You've got a deal partner!" Newt cried out. He grabbed Chung's hand and shook it hard, then reached for Fong's hand. In his exuberance, he bumped the precious bottle and set it spinning on its base. He froze in horror as the bottle toppled over, rolled off the edge of the table, and plummeted toward the cement floor.

"Fuck! Not again!" Newt hollered as Lieutenant Valentine dove and caught the bottle before it hit the floor. The president's chest heaved with a sigh of relief. "See, we did need your help, Valentine! You've more than earned that Courtesy Membership already!"

•   •   •

Upstairs, in the clubhouse boardroom, Monty Manville was crunching numbers on his MacBook to account for every dime that he and his cronies owed to the Bellstone treasury. He looked up with tired eyes as the heavy oak door to the room opened. Diane Sharp entered with her laptop.

"Hey, Monty! Why aren't you out in the bar having some bubbly with your wife after her big win?"

"Hi, Diane. Not in a celebratory mood, I guess. Haven't been for a while. What're you up to?"

"Got some work to catch up on. Hey, you look pretty beat. Has all this excitement with Mandy tired you out, my friend?" Monty paused before answering. He and Diane had become good friends while working together on various Bellstone projects.

"You have no idea. I can't handle that woman, Diane. She needs a real rough rider to tame her wild ways. And I'm finally ready to admit, I'm not that kind of cowboy."

"No, you're not that kind of cowboy, Monty." She took a seat next to him at the table and took his hand in hers. "Guess you and I have both managed to screw up our lives with bad choices."

"Was it that obvious to you? That she was a poor choice?"

"From day one, I'm afraid. Seemed like she was looking for something you just couldn't give her. But the good news is . . . we've still got a lotta giddyap left in us. Huh, partner? How 'bout if we go downstairs and have ourselves a drink?"

"Sure, but could we have it in here, Diane? I have some financials to present at the July meeting. Maybe you could give them a first look."

• • •

Newt, Lieutenant Valentine, and Norm stood in the parking lot watching the blue Bentley drive away with Chung and Fong, along with the bottle of Chateau Laffite.

"As you can see, Rocco . . ." Newt said to the cop. "While Norm and I like to live dangerously, somehow, we always win. So, do yourself a favor and take my offer. We could use a good man on our team."

"Tell you what, Newt. Let me sleep on it. I'll give you my answer tomorrow."

"Fair enough," Newt agreed.

The three men shook hands and went to their cars. After Newt and Norm drove out of the parking lot, the lieutenant shut the engine down. He settled back in the seat and made a call on his cell. "How ya doin' Keith? Rocco Valentine here, calling from golf heaven."

"What's up, Rocky? You harassing that good man of the cloth again?"

"This place is sin city, Captain. A visit here is like watching an entire season of *The Sopranos*. Today alone I've seen embezzlement, adultery, the poaching of endangered animals, racketeering, and bribery. Last month was kind'a slow. We only had a burglary, a shooting, and a kidnapping."

"You sound like a babe in the woods, Valentine. This is Los Angeles—the city of angels. But there's nothing 'angelic' about it."

"I hear ya. The top brass here offered me a Courtesy Membership to 'squire them through difficult times'. Gotta tell ya, boss . . . I'm tempted to accept. Would give me a ringside seat to their shenanigans. And we know the chief loves to see rich guys wearing orange."

"You're playing with fire. You know that pal. We go to bat—we could strike out. Especially with the holy man's connections."

"Maybe so. But if we do nothing, and the LA Times gets ahold of the story—we all go down in flames."

"Just be careful. And keep me posted."

"You got it."

"Hey, Rocco . . . one more thing."

"What's that, Captain?"

"See if that Courtesy Membership allows for guests."

"You got it, sir."

When the lieutenant finished the call, he saw Mandy walking in the parking lot. He stepped out of his car to greet her.

"Good evening, Annika! How'd ya do in your match? Did my tip help you?"

Mandy smiled and came over to him. "Did it eva! One of the many things I learned today."

"Hey, you *are* from Jersey! Do I detect traces of Bayonne?"

"Baby B-Town—you got it! How 'bout you?"

"Hackey-sack. My father was state troopa. Yours?"

"Sanitation."

"And here we are in La La Land––go figua! I'm Rocco Valentine, by the way. LAPD. So, what's your real name anyway, Annika?"

"Angie. Angelina Teresa Fatabina. You a new member here, Rocco?"

"No. This place is way too tony for a civil servant like me. Hey, you look like a pretty tough contenda. I'd love to have ya as a partna in one of my LAPD tourns at the publics. Any chance you'd be game?"

"Thanks, Rocco, but I'd be lying to ya if I didn't mention that I'm not a free woman. Fa now, anyway," Mandy said, her voice tinged with regret.

"Ah! Should-a known. But if your situation ever changes, feel free to give me a holla, will ya?"

"Who knows Rocco . . . I just might." She started to walk away, then stopped and looked back at him.

"Hey! Ya know anyone who might wanna buy a Ferrari? I may be sellin' one soon."

"Hmmm, a couple of my buddies are into buying and selling high-ticket Italian sports cars. Here's my card, Angie. Give me a shout if you get serious about partin' with it."

While Mandy walked to her car, the lieutenant saw headlights approaching in the dusk. He walked out to meet the metallic blue Bentley as it returned to the club parking lot. The back door opened, and the cop climbed in.

"Sorry to make you come back, guys. I know you gotta return this rig tonight, but I had to see what we have with my own eyes. I'm going renegade on this, and Keith'll have me strung up by the balls if it doesn't hold up in court."

"No problem, boss," said Li Chung, better known as Detective Sean Lam. "It all looks and sounds pristine. That bug-eyed Texan never looked twice at my ugly tie tack with the mike and camera that was staring him in the face the entire time." Lam handed Valentine an iPad.

The Lieutenant scanned through the footage and audio that was captured in the wine cellar. "Great! Lookin' good. Now get this stuff downloaded and logged. I've got more dirt to get from those clowns, so it may have to sit for a while."

"By the way, what're we doing with this Two-Buck Chuck with the phony label I downloaded? Looks pretty authentic, huh?" Ning Fong, alias Paul Wang, held up the bogus bottle of Chateau Laffite that Lieutenant Valentine had planted in the wine cellar. "I take it you want it inventoried?"

"Please, Paul. And tell those butterfingers at the lab to be careful. We've had enough broken wine bottles for one summer."

Twenty-four

Sunday, July 5ᵗʰ 2014
Three Years After the Bellstone 2011 Women's Club Championship

"Holy shit, Fatha! That's your fifth birdie of the round!" exclaimed avid golfer and Academy Award-winning actor Mark Wahlberg. "Hey, I gotta tell ya . . . it's been a total inspiration playing with ya. Sort-a like going to church, but way more fun!" The actor and Norm O'Malley were on the 18ᵗʰ green at Los Angeles Country Club on a Sunday morning.

In the fall of 2011, Lieutenant Rocco Valentine was able to put together an airtight case that led to the indictment of the priest, as well as Newt Sizemore, Bradley Watchtower, and Monty Manville on various charges that included theft, embezzlement, bribery, and kidnapping. But much to the Lieutenant's frustration, Father O'Malley's pull with the Los Angeles Archdiocese resulted in the city's District Attorney's dismissal of all charges against the four men before the cases could reach trial.

After 2012 Bellstone president Diane Sharp succeeded in having Newt, Bradley, and Norm expelled from the club, she initiated a civil lawsuit against Newt for his various infractions while in office. The ex-president's legal fees and his and Bradley's soiled reputation within the Los Angeles golfing community made it impossible for them to gain admittance to any other private club in the area.

Following his meeting with Diane after the 2011 Women's Club Championship, Monty submitted his resignation from the club to the new board, but it was not accepted. He and Diane are now married and reside in Diane's eight-bedroom, eight-bath home in the Los Angeles town of Brentwood and are looking forward to the birth of their first child.

With the help of Shorty Columbo and his Las Vegas cronies, the priest secured a Courtesy Membership at Los Angeles Country Club in the heart of Beverly Hills. Regarded as one of the premiere private clubs in the nation, the historic facility features two championship golf courses for Norm to enjoy.

"Hey, Fatha, you have time for another game tomorrow?" Wahlberg asked the priest. "Flying back to Boston on Tuesday to start work on my next film, so morning would work betta fa me."

"Hmmm," Norm thought for a moment. "Teeing it up with Clooney at seven a.m. But I'm sure he'd be okay with it if we made it a threesome."

•   •   •

"C'mon, step up the pace, assholes! You hacks are making this a seven hour round!" On that same Sunday morning in July, Newt and Bradley sat in a weathered golf cart on a crowded public course in Encino, California.

"Hey fellas!" the course marshal called out to them. "Watch your language, or I'll bounce you outta here! This isn't one of your fast-moving fancy-ass country clubs. Ya gotta wait your turn to hit like everyone else."

•   •   •

Mandy Manville's invitation to play in the October 2011 Cialis Pro-Amateur Tournament at St Andrews golf course in Scotland arrived in her mailbox that August. Her estrangement from Monty required her to seek the help of her Bellstone playing partners for her airfare, hotels, and entry fees. Tiger Woods never did show up to play, as he claimed to have tweaked his knee in a charity tournament the weekend before the event. Though Mandy's foursome did not do well enough to finish among the top 20 money winners, she did get her five seconds of fame when she appeared on-screen as commentator Johnny Miller made mention of the competition's "well-dressed lassies".

•   •   •

On the same Sunday morning, Angie and Lieutenant Rocco Valentine are playing a not-so-casual game of golf at the public course near their home. "We're still tied, Annika. See if you can pull ahead of me by sinkin' this putt. It breaks about . . . hmmm . . . maybe one ball to the right, I'd say," Rocco tells his wife.

Though Angie makes a good stroke, her ball stays left of the cup and rolls a good five feet past the hole. "Argh! Damnit, Rocky! Ya gave me that lousy read on purpose!" Angie snarls as she bends down and snatches her ball from the green.

"Hey," the cop warns the angry woman as he wags his index finger in her direction, "No more of that sass, Annika, or you're gonna get a good spankin' tonight!"

"Is that a promise, officer?" she asks with a giggle.

•   •   •

Derrick Benson did buy Amber a house, but it was nothing like what she had seen on *Keeping up With the Kardashians* or *The Real Housewives of Beverly Hills*. After his divorce from Jody and the sale of their house in the upscale LA neighborhood of Sherman Oaks, Derrick purchased a two-bedroom home for Amber and their son in the less pricey area of Canoga Park, while he moved into a nearby apartment complex. His obligations as a father have curtailed almost all of his extra-curricular activities, including golf and women.

On that same Sunday morning in July, he received a text from Amber.

Amber: *Halp! My Kemnore is floded over agin! kin u cum earle 2 halp me mop up b 4 takin lil Derrick 2 the zu?*

•   •   •

In a Spanish style home in Malibu with stunning views of the Pacific Ocean, Jody Lyons is packing a bag with diapers, tiny bathing suits, and toys for her family to spend the day at her parent's house in the near-by beach town of Ventura.

"Hey Jo," her husband calls out to her. "The Stud Man just texted. Wants to know if you and I can tee it up Thursday morning with him and McConaughey. Think your mom could watch the kids for us?"

"I bet Grandma would love that. Maybe she'd take them to the club to see Eddie. He's been asking when they're coming for another visit for a while now," Jody answered.

Jackson Lyons' previous screenplay and performance in "Fly-By", costarring Matthew McConaughey and Emily Blunt became the comedy sensation of 2013. He's now working on his next screenplay, a comedy set at a country club in Los Angeles. Jackson is focusing more on his writing than his acting these days, as it allows him to spend more time with his wife, their two-year-old son Forrest, and their one-year-old daughter Belle.

"How's the new script shaping up?" Jody asks her husband. "Are your characters staying true to form?"

"The president is totally consistent. And the priest's motivation remains crystal clear. The Monty fella is a great Casper Milquetoast. Still haven't figured out why the priest hates Mandy, though. I'm not so sure about her character, either. She may be a bit over the top. Don't know if anyone would buy it that a woman could be that obsessed with winning a golf tournament."

"Yeah. Sometimes the truth really *is* stranger than fiction," Jody said. "I hear she's doing hair in Encino now. Married to that nice cop from New Jersey—poor guy!"

"Well, maybe he's got her number. Same as I've got yours." Jackson gave his wife a playful kiss. "I'm still stuck on the title, though, Jo. What do you think about *The Bad Golfers of Bellstone*?"

"Nah, that makes it sound like it's a film about lousy golfers. You can do better than that."

"How about, *The Priest, the Accountant, His Wife and Her Lover?*"

"Ha! Now you're just getting silly."

"Maybe *Fore Play?*" he suggests. "Kind of snappy with a bit of a double entendre?"

"Hmmm . . . that could work," she says. "Let's toss it around on the way to the beach."

The End

About the Author

After working at CBS television in Manhattan, Linda Sheehan moved to Los Angeles where she wrote and produced commercials for movies and spent too much time playing golf on one of Hollywood's most historic and legendary courses. She now lives in Napa, California where she continues to obsess about her not-so-perfect swing. Her first novel, *Decanted*, is also available on Amazon from Black Rose Writing.

Note from the Author

Word-of-mouth is crucial for any author to succeed. If you enjoyed *Fore Play*, please leave a review online—anywhere you are able. Even if it's just a sentence or two. It would make all the difference and would be very much appreciated.

Thanks!
Linda Sheehan

We hope you enjoyed reading this title from:

BLACK ROSE
writing™

Subscribe to our mailing list – *The Rosevine* – and receive **FREE** books, daily deals, and stay current with news about upcoming releases and our hottest authors.
Scan the QR code below to sign up.

Already a subscriber? Please accept a sincere thank you for being a fan of Black Rose Writing authors.

Made in the USA
Las Vegas, NV
01 March 2024

86577186R00142